Pool of Tears

Nights of Alice #2

Melissa Rea

Once again, I dedicate this story to the friends that inspire and support me.

Chapter One

BORN TO BE WILD

There were probably worse things in the world than discovering you are pregnant at forty-nine, but alone in her apartment, Alice Hightower couldn't think of any. She had never been exactly thin. Eating judiciously her entire life, she managed voluptuous. Her work power suits had fit her well for several years. Soon, the entire person growing inside of her would change that and nearly everything else about her life. Were there such things as maternity business suits and if there were, would they be appropriate for her job? Alice doubted anyone at her company, Excellcardia, would say a word if she wore a black trash bag to work, but it wouldn't feel CEO-like to her.

All these trivial notions about what she could or couldn't wear did little to deflect her thoughts from another very real issue in her life. The man she had grown fond of and who'd said he loved her had disappeared from her life. If she closed her eyes here in her apartment, she could still see that look on his face. She shut her eyes tight and tears squeezed out.

Had that doctor's appointment been only a week ago? She could play the scene like some horrible, heartbreaking, movie on the inside of her eyelids with them closed. For some masochistic reason, she just had to do it one more time.

Alice remembered how she and Jonathan had held hands like excited young parents in the doctor's consultation room. She had felt the need to tell Jonathan she was pregnant and didn't expect him to be excited about the news. Children had never fit into Alice's busy career life. Bringing a baby you never dreamed of wanting into this wicked world hardly seemed a good thing. But when Jonathan looked at her with his chocolate-colored eyes that held only love and joy at that prospect, Alice thought it might be okay.

The doctor had looked up from his laptop and smiled a perfect, bleached-white-enough-to-pass-the-tissue-test-white smile at them. Alice found his Justin Bieber haircut more than annoying. How old do you have to be to graduate medical school now Alice wondered? She had been twenty-six and though she had forsaken medicine for business immediately after graduation, she had seemed much older than this kid.

"Great news, Mrs. Hightower. The blood tests indicate that your hormone levels are really high for a woman of your advanced age. How cool is that, right?"

Alice's mouth dropped open. She closed it and said, "How is that possible?"

"Oh, it's possible. You've still got eggs, add sperm and kablam—pregnant."

He leaned back in his chair. "Most of the time, late-life pregnancies are not sustainable for lots of reasons. Your eggs are wicked old. So of course you'll want an amnio. The rate of genetic abnormalities is off the charts. But it seems possible to carry this baby to term, if that's what you want." The doctor had looked quite pleased to share his news.

Alice's mouth fell open again and Jonathan beamed. "I… I…" said Alice.

"We need to know what to do to ensure the health of our

2

child," said Jonathan. He gripped her hand tightly and leaned over to kiss her on the cheek.

"I got those Depo-Provera shots and… I thought I had six months before another one," said Alice.

"The efficacy of that type of birth control is less dependable in the last few months. My best guess based on the size of your uterus…" He looked up in the air like he was working some imaginary calculator "…At least six weeks, more like eight," said Dr. Bieber.

Jonathan's face went blank. Alice knew what the doctor's guess meant, and so did Jonathan. They had only been sleeping together for a month. Several minutes passed before Alice could bear to look at this man who had held her hand until the calculations in his head caused him to drop it like it was hot. She stared at the Betsy Johnson silver spangled pumps she had worn because this was a momentous occasion. Jonathan's Clark Kent good looks were not marred at all by his stricken expression when he realized there was no way this baby was his. Alice had always had a hard time believing anyone that beautiful could ever have loved her.

Without a word, Jonathan had stood up and walked out the door without closing it.

Alice opened her eyes and took in a deep breath, trying to let go of the memory. She grabbed a tissue and dabbed her eyes. She had to keep breathing. Now she was breathing for two.

§♠

Eight weeks! thought Alice as she sat on her immaculate white couch. The doctor's calculation meant not only could Jonathan not be her baby's father, but it might be difficult to discern just exactly who was. How could one tell a child that its father could have been a Roman soldier dead for two thousand years, an eighteenth-century pirate captain, or one of several members of a seventies rock group? As crazy as those suggestions were, there was one other person who believed that her nightly fantasy adventures might be real. Dr. Cynthia Lester, her current therapist, had suggested that she actually could travel in time and did so each night at sunset.

For the better part of a year, clothes had appeared each evening at sunset in her guest room closet. She knew she didn't put them there and that no one else could have. Each outfit was clothing from a different time period and they fit her as if some genius tailor made them for her alone.

The very first one had been an amazing Women's Army Corps uniform from World War II, complete with a name tag that said A. Hightower. Curiosity won, and she tried on the olive drab ensemble that came with vintage stockings, seam down the back of the leg and all. She remembered she'd heard voices from beyond her balcony door as she stood looking at herself in the mirrored closet door. That was impossible when she lived on the eighth floor. No street party was that loud. Impossible seemed to have lost its meaning, and she slid open the balcony's glass door.

The room beyond the door was filled with men in military uniforms. Alice smelled cigarette smoke and as she looked down at the floor, rough wooden planks replaced her balcony's concrete. A handsome man yelled through the door's opening and asked her to dance. She slammed the door.

That first time, she had been certain the incident was the result of a psychotic break. Such occurrences were not uncommon branches on her family tree. But the next night there were more clothes and more desirable men. She began to indulge her every desire night after night, as one would do. Could this person in her belly be absolute proof that Alice's aberrant brain gave her some sort of power over time and space as Dr. Lester suggested? You can't get pregnant all by yourself, fantasizing. Or she could be stark raving bonkers as her genetics suggested. Her mother died after being institutionalized for over a decade with Bipolar depression. There was one other option for paternity that made the impossible nature of the fantasy men as fathers almost preferable. The tears began again.

This workday at Excellcardia hadn't been any tougher than many others, she thought as she kicked off her black patent peep-toe pumps. No one ever said the job of CEO was an easy one. Alice always preferred a challenge, but the industrial espionage that had nearly taken her company down, had stretched her love of a challenge to the breaking point. She could still see Bradley James, her vice president of sales, lying on the floor of the high efficiency freezer surrounded by a pool of blood that had turned to ice around the edges. She had been so certain that Brad, Jonathan and she would die in that freezer as Dr. Petrus, her evil genius of a head researcher, had planned. The three teams of detectives she'd hired had so far failed to locate the "not so good doctor," but Alice would never give up looking for him. No one tries to kill her, steals her company's ground-breaking process, sells it to a competitor, and gets away with it.

"Come on up, sweetest boy," said Alice to a chubby black cat who balanced perfectly on his three legs, looking up at her from the floor. She patted the cushion next to her. The cat did not move but stared at her with round emerald eyes.

"Oh, what the hell? How much of that fur can actually get on the couch in a few minutes?" The cat did not jump up but rubbed against her legs. "Smart boy, I'll get your food." No matter what she said, Otis obviously knew she would not have been happy with even one of his black hairs on her white couch. She reached down and softly rubbed the little nub that had once been his left ear. She'd always wondered how Otis had lost his left ear and front leg. The shelter had no idea. He was still the sweetest of all possible kitties, no matter how he had been injured. His black fur shone in the fading daylight that streamed in through her living room window. "You're the prettiest kitty on the planet." His chainsaw-loud purr answered in agreement.

Alice walked past the solid block of black granite that served as her bar/dining table into the kitchen. She grabbed a can of Kitty Feast out of the pantry, pulled the pull-top and dumped it into a bowl on the floor.

She did not feel the slightest bit hungry and headed across the large, high-ceilinged room that served as her living room, dining room and kitchen. The exposed wooden beams in the twenty-foot ceilings of the classic building made her feel as if she were the Red Queen from Alice's Adventures in Wonderland in her castle.

She walked down the hall feeling sorry for herself and exhausted. She had planned to turn left into her bedroom and turn in early. *Get over yourself, Alice.* She should have known the risks of dating real men instead of fantasy ones. No man from another time could break her heart because they were always gone in the morning.

She turned to her right into the guest room. Whatever she found in there could take a girl's mind off of all of her troubles. Thirty quick minutes on her elliptical and she might open that closet door.

She remembered finding a hot pink mini dress in that closet that once donned, had taken her to a place where she had enjoyed Tweedle Don and Tweedle Dan, twin doctors from the late nineteen sixties who shared absolutely everything. She felt the corners of her lips turn up a bit at the memory. She hadn't peeked into the closet since she had embarked on her experiment to date real men. Big mistake.

Alice had hoped in vain the fact that Brad was her vice president of sales and Jonathan had been her administrative assistant would not complicate matters. The company had no official policy against dating other employees. Why couldn't dating two men have stayed fun and casual?

She stood in front of the closet's mirrored door, reflecting her visibly tired blue-green eyes. She pulled the clip out of her dark blonde hair and it fell limp and lifeless to her shoulders. Real men aren't as good at sharing as fantasy doctors Dan and Don, unfortunately.

She knew it was a minute after sunset, she always knew, and reached over to slide open the closet door. There on the gold hanger she knew she had never purchased hung something pink and fluffy. Some sort of outfit made of silk and netting in several soft shades of pink. On the floor below the hanger sat a pair of silver sandals. They would be exactly her size, they always were.

The something pink turned out to be a short midriff bearing top and a long flowing skirt, kind of "I dream of Jeannie" style. Alice remembered watching reruns with her mother when she was little. The outfit didn't look half bad on her. Being pregnant somehow made her abs look tighter, for now anyway. Taking a deep breath, she slid open the door to her balcony where instead of the street below, she would find this night's Wonderland.

Alice squinted against the bright sunlight and stepped out of the door to a completely different place and time. In front of her, she saw a huge archway covered in tiny cobalt blue and white tiles. It must have been fifty feet at the top. Perhaps the door to a palace, she thought? Alice felt very small in the doorway, heard running water, and smelled jasmine.

"Curiouser and curiouser." Alice giggled and walked through the arch into a garden. Flowering trees grew in pots surrounding a sunken pool. The water bubbled as a little stream splashed from a smaller bowl into the pool. She walked over and looked into the water. The bottom must have been covered in the same deep blue tiles as the path that led to the pool, because the water had the same blue. "At least this pool isn't filled with my tears." Alice was happy right now not to actually be the little Victorian Girl in a pinafore of whom Lewis Carroll wrote. Though she had thought it written for her as a child, her nocturnal adventures were certainly not for seven-year-old girls.

Soft footsteps to her left caused her to turn to see a slender man. He looked like the Genie in Aladdin except he was tanned instead of blue. His neat mustache and closely trimmed beard would have looked appropriate on any self-respecting resident of a wishing lamp. The man wore only white wide legged pants gathered at the ankle. Of course, his head was shaved. She expected Will Smith's voice to come out of him, but he said nothing, bowed and motioned to her to follow him.

On either side of the doorway were smaller versions of the grand entry arch. There were four on each side and Alice followed the genie through one of the arches on the right. He led her into a large courtyard. Sunlight bathed the low chairs and large cushions covering a good deal of the floor. The pillows in many shades of peach, pink and lavender were arranged around low tables. Sitting on most of the chairs and pillows were young women dressed exactly like Alice. "A harem?" said Alice to the genie. "I guess I'm dressed for it." He looked bewildered at her words. Bowing once more, the genie vanished through an archway. *He must have other wishes to grant.*

The young women, who had fallen silent when she walked into the room, now all talked at once in a language she could not understand. Each one's dark hair in various shades hung down their backs. One stood up and the others fell silent.

"The Emir wishes me to welcome you to our home," said the girl. She wore palest baby-pink and had hair and eyes as dark as midnight.

"Great, you speak English," said Alice.

"The Emir enjoys languages and there are many of us who speak several. I am Yasmina and your name, please?"

"Alice. So what exactly is going on here?" Alice usually found pleasure in her nightly travels. She was not attracted to women and certainly wasn't interested in sex with any of these "Harem Girl Barbies."

"My master has arranged a pleasure ceremony." She clapped her hands and through an arched doorway, six men strode into the room.

"Now that's more like it," said Alice. The men all looked similar, tall, muscular and, due to their naked state, she could see they were well endowed and uncircumcised. All six had short dark hair, dark eyes and light brown skin, as if they had just come off a day at the beach, without bothering with swim-suits—no tan lines at all. Every hair had been removed from their beautiful bodies.

The young ladies on the pillows smiled and clapped at their entrance. The men's serious expressions did not change as they stood in a line looking straight ahead.

Yasmina walked in front of the line of men speaking first in a foreign language and then repeating in English for Alice's benefit, "Which of you will be chosen to prepare the Emir's newest wife?" She clapped her hands and two girls led in a figure swathed in gauzy white fabric with only dark, heavily lined eyes visible. *I'll be happy with any of the leftovers.*

"This is Sulia, the Emir's newest wife. She is a virgin, and the Emir wishes that situation to be remedied." The girls leading Sulia unwrapped their gauzy package. She stood naked. Her flesh shone pink and plump against the line of light brown men who responded with cocks quickly at full attention. The naked girl's black eyes scanned the men. She smiled shyly, looked each man up and down and stopped in front of the very last one. She wisely chose the man with the smallest endowment, more suited to one's deflowering.

The girls raised their voices in a cheer. The man hoisted Sulia onto his shoulders and carried her a few feet laying her down gently on a large lavender pillow. Two girls knelt beside the couple and each took turns kissing Sulia's lips and sucking her erect pink nipples. The girl moaned, and the man laughed.

He knelt, parted her legs with his knees and began to stroke between the dark hair surrounding her virgin sex with his fingers, and she moaned louder. Just when she sounded very near a climax, he reached under her, lifting her hips and inserting his cock. She let out a cry that rang with both pleasure and pain. Immediately, the man withdrew his tool and stood up. Evidently, the Emir wanted to plant the seeds himself and must have merely wanted the way paved. A girl in a peach outfit knelt in front of the man, licking him clean as he put his hands on her head and stood, knees locked, and eyes closed.

All around, pretty lips sucked dark nipples as little wisps of tops came off. Dainty hands slipped between soft legs as skirts were raised. Alice felt someone reach around to caress her own nipples through her thin pink top. They now stood at full attention in response to the deflowering spectacle. The man caressing her breasts, turned her around and led her to three pillows. He smiled at her. Yasmina stood beside the man. "The Emir would appreciate the honor of watching the golden-haired one couple with whomever she wishes."

"Fine by me. Where is he? I would love to thank him," asked Alice. The girl motioned toward a window covered by a wooden screen carved of leaves and flowers. Alice waved at the screen and smiled back at the man who now lay below her with a cock hard enough to cut glass. She pulled up her skirt and straddled the man slowly, lowering herself onto his magnificent appendage.

"I am Hassan, golden one," said the man deep inside her. He took her nipples between his fingers and rolled and pulled on them as she slid up and down until she came with a long, loud exclamation. She bent down to kiss his lips.

"Thank you, Hassan. But now it is your turn to come," said Alice as Hassan tried to wiggle out from under her.

Hassan smiled at her and said, "Please, to honor my brother, Husane, with your golden glory."

"Sure, whatever you want." Alice rolled off of Hassan and another of the handsome leftovers straddled her. He stroked her clit with long, smooth fingers and reached up to caress her breasts, kneading them and softly brushing her nipples with his palms. She felt herself climbing up pleasure hill as his fingers stroked. She needed to be full of him and sat up and, taking his muscular ass in her hands, she drove him deep into her. He began a delicious rhythm and soon she came loud enough to scare a dozing gray cat who ran off among the pillows.

"Wow. Are there any more at home like you?" Alice held his shoulders and stroked his arms that seemed carved from brown stone. "Well…yes, there is my little brother Omar," said Husane.

"Oh my," said Alice when a pair of muscular brown legs appeared next to her sporting another delicious hard on.

"I'm sorry, he does not speak English." Husane shook his head.

"Ask him if he minds if I suck that gorgeous cock of his, please."

"No man would mind such an honor," he said. Alice got to her knees and wrapped her lips around little brother Omar's cock. She encircled the delicious appendage with her lips wetting with her saliva every erect inch of him.

"There is nothing little about your brother Omar," said Alice and she slid her mouth over each vein and along the steel encased in silk cylinder that she enjoyed so much. Omar looked young, probably not much more than twenty, and in no time, he gave a long moan and filled her mouth with his pleasure.

She felt strong arms reach around her and she spread her knees as something hard, lovely and masculine, filled her from behind.

"Please to serve you once more." Alice couldn't tell if Hassan or Husane spoke, but he felt perfect. She moaned with each stroke and felt him come inside her a few strokes before she climaxed. He laid his head on her shoulder and tenderly caressed her back, her arms, and her thighs. Leaning back on a stack of pillows, Hassan/Husane pulled her with him.

Alice relished a little time to rest, leaned back and watched the dark-haired beauties at play.

The pretty lips, lovely breasts and perky asses enjoyed each other's company immensely. Touching anything soft, not her own, was not to her taste, but she had to admit she had fun watching the girls moan and writhe.

"To each her own," said Alice, safe in the knowledge she would wake up tomorrow morning in her own bed with her faithful little black furry buddy curled up behind her knees. She closed her eyes for a minute, her head resting on a strong shoulder while a smooth hand caressed the curve of her hip.

Chapter Two

SWEET BABY JAMES

A lice had been glad the traffic moved slowly that morning on the highway—the highway to hell…270 this morning. She had too many thoughts running through her head to concentrate on the traffic. Memories of last night's adventure painted a smile on her lips briefly. So what if fantasy sex was not quite as fulfilling as sex with a man you cared about? The fantasy men never tried to complicate things by telling her they loved her.

Jonathan had walked out the door and disappeared during her doctor's appointment. It felt at the time that she had lost her one true love. Yeah, as corny as it sounded, Jonathan might have been that, for about a minute. The tears she couldn't manage to stop as she drove made it hard to see the road. *Damn hormones.* Work always took her mind off her personal issues as long as she could stay away from certain male co-workers. A world class medical device company didn't stop because its pregnant CEO's lover left her heart bruised. Pacemakers and defibrillators had to be made and sold. The eighty-four employees in her company were capable of working without her, but she hoped they never figured that out.

After answering or forwarding half of her day's one

hundred ninety emails, Alice closed her eyes. How could she be so tired? It wasn't even ten o'clock. Growing babies must take a lot of effort, she thought.

Louise O'Neil, Excellcardia's head engineer, stuck her head in Alice's office door. "I have some apple and kale yogurt smoothy with plenty to share," said the tall, elegant woman in a white silk sheath dress. She could have graced the cover of any fashion magazine even at somewhere past sixty. She stood six feet tall and the chocolate color of her skin contrasted beautifully with the dress. Today she had pulled her dark hair back into a severe bun, held it in place with a large white bow. The fact that her last name started with an O, reinforced her resemblance to JFK's celebrated first lady. On some women, the bow would have looked juvenile. Louise made that bow nothing but chic, as she imagined Jackie Kennedy would have.

Louise set a paper cup on Alice's desk. She gave Alice a questioning look. When Alice gave a nod, Louise filled the cup full of thick, lumpy green liquid from a plastic container. Without a word, Alice picked up the cup and began to drink down the cup's contents.

"Okay, now I know something is wrong besides Jonathan's absence. You never touch the healthy stuff I offer you."

Alice nearly blurted out the fact of her not so delicate condition, but baby hormones that made you weepy and tired should not make you stupid. She wasn't ready to say it out loud to herself, let alone announce it to the entire company as it would be doing if she told Louise.

Louise crossed her legs at the ankle and dropped into the chair in front of Alice's desk with the grace of a ballerina. She set the rest of the smoothie on the desk and grabbed the arms of the white leather chair. "I'm guessing something went wrong between you and Jonathan. He has never missed a day of work in three years and a half years. No one has seen him in days."

"He's gone," said Alice. She looked only at the smoothie and downed the remaining contents in three gulps.

Louise opened her mouth but must have thought better of it and closed it. The expression on Louise's face softened. She waited for Alice to speak.

"He left. He swore I was the love of his life and he just left." Alice looked at the objects on her desk to keep from reliving that scene for the ten-millionth time.

"Oh, Alice, baby girl, what can I do?"

Alice began to laugh. At this moment, she envied that little blonde girl on the front of the first edition of *Alice's Adventures in Wonderland* that sat on the front of her desk. Today, the rich leather-bound treasure merely reminded her how much she was not that little girl.

She laughed until she could see her mirth scared Louise. *Inappropriate laughter, Alice.* Laughing like a crazy person might prove her ex-shrink, Dr. Elliot's theory, that she needed medication for her mood disorder. *Could pregnant women even take that stuff?* She set down the cup. The green goo tasted a lot better than it looked. Babies needed healthy crap, Alice knew. This one deserved only the best, as it had not caused her to gain a pound yet.

"Is it Brad James? Did Jonathan find out that you were seeing both of them?"

"I hadn't seen Brad for weeks. It was only Jonathan until…"

"We really need to talk more about this, but I came to warn you. Some weird juju is going on. The main conference room has been reserved for two days and board members were seen in the building. What's that about?" Louise stood up, put her hands on the desk and gave Alice a very serious look.

"What! How can there be meetings and I do not even get an agenda?"

Louise then picked up the now empty container of smoothy and headed to the door. "I am due at a meeting in two, but I also need to warn you that James is on his way up. I can meet him at the elevator and tell him you're busy?" Louise looked back over her shoulder with a benevolent smile.

"No, I need to talk to him."

"Okay and I promise not to tell anyone that you drank some of my healthy smoothie for the first time in the three and a half years you have been CEO. It's our secret. And I will see what I can find out about these meetings." Louise turned back around, examining Alice with her dark almond-shaped eyes.

"Thank you, Louise," said Alice.

Alice stared at the closed door in anticipation. She knew very well that without Brad James, Excellcardia might never have recovered from Dr. Petrus's industrial theft. She had led the team that, in a mere two months, replaced the millions of dollars lost on research and development for a stolen product they could no longer produce. The patents had been filed under another company's name, thanks to Dr. Henry Petrus. Her personal history with Brad probably had a little to do with the fact that her hands were shaking in anticipation of the meeting.

A quick rap and the door opened. "Hello, Boss Lady." Brad did not sit down immediately, but stood with his hands on her desk, leaning toward her and looking at her with his impossible blue eyes. His silver-haired good looks could have sold Viagra on the pages of a glossy magazine. Today he wore a navy blazer and khaki pants. Alice had a weakness for men in beautiful suits, but the lovely tie the color of his eyes with Excelcardia's logo would do.

"I see Salter is gone," Brad said.

"Yeah."

"I'm sorry."

"Thanks." He didn't sound sorry.

"I was no real fan of his, but…" He settled into the chair in front of her desk, his eyes still trained on her.

She wouldn't let Brad see tears in her eyes and so dug her

fingernails into the palm of her hand to distract her. "I'm okay, really. He will be missed. He was very good at what he did."

"Administrative assistants are not that hard to find." Of course, Brad knew Jonathan was more than her administrative assistant. What was she thinking dating both of them, like that could ever have worked? Jonathan had made a demand for exclusivity and professed his eternal love. Alice gave in and Brad stepped back like a gentleman. Right this minute, looking into Brad's eyes, she knew she had made the wrong choice, though a little nagging suspicion had made her doubt her choice all along. She would not give another man the chance to break her any time soon. She knew Brad's wife had left him fairly recently and not wanting to be his rebound girl had helped her to make the disastrous choice of Jonathan. Alice simply let him talk.

"That's my Boss Lady. Did you get my email summery of the trip to Japan?" asked Brad.

She didn't react, but continued to stare at him. She couldn't read the look on his face. Did he look as if he was hiding something? "Once again, the legendary Bradley James makes the big deal," she said. "I read the schedule and I think we can get the units they need out a little ahead of their requested date. That kind of above and beyond service may encourage a reorder. Do you have any contacts in South Korea? That's a market we need to explore."

"Good thinking." His eyes searched her face. "I know a guy." Brad leaned back in the chair. His expression suddenly grew serious. "How are you? I've been thinking about you. Worrying about you."

"I'm fine." Why would he worry about her?

"Glad to hear it." Brad smiled at her. "You know I'm here, if you need a friend." He nearly burned her with his gaze.

His offer tempted her. Any fantasy man that might wait for her at sunset would be a lot less dangerous to her healing heart. She remembered the hurt in his eyes when he had told her about his wife leaving him for someone else. She couldn't be sure that pain had cooled enough to make him ready for any relationship.

"I do appreciate the offer," she answered. "Thank you. Now go do what you do best."

Brad stood up to go and turned back. "You've gotta eat? Any time you say. You could come to my place. I grill a mean salmon. Barney would love to see you." He looked at her with his eyebrows raised.

She loved salmon, and bringing up the sweet old basset he had adopted from the lab made the deal nearly irresistible. But it might still have been too soon for both of them. The little tyrant inside her had made her randier than a high school boy. Could she give her heart again this soon? I'm not ready for…"

"You would be doing me a favor. I'm so tired of cooking for myself, and Barney says you give much better belly rubs than I do."

She laughed. "I'm sorry…"

"I get it. But you can have a rain check anytime."

She watched him walk out the door. He hadn't said a thing about any meeting with the board. The dread, dark fist of fear clutched at her stomach. The board would naturally want to thank him for his excellent work increasing Excell-cardia's sales nearly enough to erase the loss from the Biocardia project. They probably offered him a bonus, and she knew he deserved it. Somewhere in the pit of her stomach, the icy hand squeezed tight. She was CEO of this company and it had come back from the losses because of her hard work. That board could not forget she had hired Bradley James.

Alice typed five emails to department heads, inquiring as to why she had not been informed of any important meetings. If there were no adequate answers by 9:00 a.m. tomorrow, she would call each one and demand answers. Finally, she would demand an answer from Brad. It would be better to know the answers to any questions she asked him beforehand, as any good cross examiner would insist.

❧

By the time she opened the door to her apartment, she felt as though she had left every molecule of strength she had in the elevator to her home. She could do nothing but sit on the couch with her coat still on. Otis had other ideas. He meowed loudly until she opened her eyes.

"Okay, I will get your food." When she walked into the kitchen, Alice realized she was hungry. Taking a container of Chef Boyardee out of the pantry, she pulled off the metal top, and she placed the plastic bowl into the microwave and hit the two minutes button.

Alice fed Otis and sat down on a white stool at the black granite counter to eat. She loved picking up the steaming bowl and digging in with a spoon, no dishes to wash. It was mini ravioli this time. The containers looked pretty much the same, and she preferred to simply grab one. She was not good at trivial choices. Alice's immaculate kitchen usually contained only microwaveable or frozen delights, though she had augmented her choices lately with some fresh vegetables for salads for the sake of the baby. Tonight, it felt like way too much work to open the refrigerator, let alone chop up stuff and put it in a bowl.

She planned to go straight to bed, but what could it hurt to take a little peek in the closet? The sun had been down for half an hour and she had learned that, though the clothes appeared at precisely sunset, they were still there much later. Her guest room closet was always empty in the morning when she woke up in her own bed.

As had happened many times before, the thought of what might be in the closet and where it might take her gave Alice a burst of energy. She slid open the door. On the hanger was a long blue gingham dress. She found a pair of what could only be called bloomers and a pair of short cordovan leather boots that laced up the front.

"Now that's sexy," she said as she tugged on the bloomers .She smiled at the booties, a little sad they would be gone in the morning. They were adorable. Alice slipped on the dress and struggled to button the buttons down the back of the dress. No bra came with the outfit, but the dress was fitted enough to provide some support. When dressed, she looked in the mirrored door of the closet to see "Ma" from Little House on the Prairie. She and her big brother Sean had watched it when they were little. Suddenly she was not tired at all and wondered where in the world and in what time this pioneer woman garb would be appropriate?

Alice peered into the darkness on the other side of the balcony door. She heard soft music a little ways off and smelled burning wood and pine trees. In the distance, she saw a glow, and she walked toward it on soft grass. After a few steps, she could see it was a campfire, and the music came from a man playing a guitar and singing low and sweet.

"Sweet Betsy from Pike. Crossed the wide prairie with her lover Ike. Two yoke of oxen and big yeller dog…" The man singing stopped when he saw her.

"Don't stop on my account," said Alice.

The man jumped to his feet, pulled off his hat and nodded an acknowledgement. She could see by the light of the fire he was handsome and dressed as any self-respecting cowboy would be complete with chaps. Alice could hear the sound of what she thought must be cattle.

"Are you real, Miss?" asked the cowboy.

"My name is Alice, and I think I am real. Sometimes I am not entirely sure."

"I was dreamin' about having someone to… The cows ain't too interested in my singing, and here you are. I'm James," he said, standing with his hat in his hand.

Alice walked around the fire to stand a few feet from James. She had been wrong when she thought him handsome. He was exquisite. He couldn't have been much older than thirty. The muscles of his arms and chest were clearly visible beneath his shirt worn thin. He had large dark eyes, a strong square jaw and any of the Kardashian sisters would have paid dearly for the filler to recreate such beautiful lips.

"Won't you come sit by the fire, Miss Alice? I ate all my supper but I have a little coffee if you want." James motioned for her to sit next to him on a log he must have pulled up near the fire. Alice saw a blanket spread out a few feet away inside the circle of the firelight.

"No coffee for me, but please don't stop playing."

"Nah, I only play to kill the time. I'm not very good and I only know the one song. But..."

"But what?"

"Every evening I sit and wonder what it might be like to... well... if someday...

"Have you ever had a woman, James?" Alice gave him a smile she thought seductive.

He didn't say a word, but turned and looked into the fire. Alice watched as the fire light bathed the shoulder-length brown hair she longed to touch, to bury her face in. Here sat a beautiful virgin for her to eat up with a big old spoon. She slid a little closer to him on the log and he turned to look at her.

"You're not a woman, you're an angel that walked right outta the dark." His voice cracked a little.

"Oh, I am far from an angel, but you are right, I walked out of the dark...for you." Alice leaned near James and kissed him, soft at first. She teased his lips with her tongue, until with a breath, they parted and her tongue slipped in. He growled low in his throat as her tongue touched his. Alice laughed and reached up to unbutton his shirt and slide her hand beneath it to caress his chest smooth and hard with muscle. She rubbed her thumbs over his nipples and he groaned.

"If you don't stop that, you're gonna kill me." His eyes were half closed.

"Hardly. I'm just beginning." Alice tried to remember every wonderful thing any man had ever done to please her, because this time, she controlled the pleasure. Neither of them has the correct equipment for him to feel her deep inside him, or at least she hoped not. She turned away from him and said, "Unbutton my dress."

"Sure." His hands shook, or maybe this was the first dress he had ever unbuttoned, but he fumbled and it took a while to get the job done. She slid the dress down to her waist and turned back toward him.

"Oh, my God. You are an angel," said James.

Alice smiled, took his hands and put them on her breasts. "Now you do to me what I did to you." He lightly brushed her nipples with his rough thumbs, like Alice loved so much. She moaned and watched him look at her as if she actually had wings and a halo.

"Oh my God, James. You are a natural." Alice slid her hand into his pants to find his branding iron, or at least something almost as hard and nearly as hot.

"I saw a blanket over there…" Alice said.

James stood and took her hand. He stumbled over a rock, but he never took his eyes from hers. She wondered if he imagined that if he looked away, she would disappear. He stopped beside the blanket and watched her as she knelt on it. She happily discovered that the blanket was spread over soft grass and she took his hands and pulled him down to her. Wiggling out of the skirt and bloomers, she watched as he tore off his shirt and removed his pants and leather chaps. She almost asked him to leave on the chaps, but thought better of it. His beautiful erection now inches away, called to her, and she answered by wrapping her fingers around him and pulling him close.

His eyes went wide at her touch and Alice put her hands

on his hard round buttocks and pulled him close. Leaning back and spreading her legs, she said, "Give me your hand." James followed her command. She took one of his fingers and slowly rubbed it against her clit until he took up the motion. Alice writhed and moaned.

"Oh, James, that feels so good. Put your other hand on my breast. Yes, oh yes, James. I'm going to come." Alice did as promised, loud enough to make a horse tied ten feet away rear up. Alice caught her breath and found that James began to improvise and slid three of his fingers into her wet depth. Alice reached up again, grabbing his ass and pulling him down on top of her. She took his cock in her hand, guiding him. Gently, gently, he slid into her. He lay on her, filling her and not daring to move, looking deep into her eyes with what she read as desire mixed with wonder. She moved her hips a bit, and he again followed her lead. Thrusting slowly at first and then as Alice once more disturbed the sleep of some animal with her climax, James roared like a bear, stiffened and lay still on top of her. She kept her arms around him, savoring the feel of his cock inside her, his chest flattening her breasts against her. She closed her eyes and cherished the feel of his semen dripping out of her.

James rolled off of her but kept his arm around her and his eyes locked on hers. He shook his head slowly, as if there were no words he could think of to say.

Alice said softly, "Yeah, that is one of life's greatest pleasures, but I can think of another thing or two when you've had a little rest." He smiled at her and put her hand on his cock once more, hard and now slippery with her satisfaction and his. "Well, ain't that, grand," she said.

She knelt between his legs and took a moment to admire his lovely cock in the firelight. Alice always thought the male sex organ far too magnificent to be labeled with a flaccid word like penis. In front of her, a hard young cock begged her to wrap her lips around it and she did.

This time James moaned with every stroke of her fingers and tongue and his eyes caressed her. She could almost feel his eyes on her as he came hard and filled her mouth.

"You are a fast learner, James. Let's rest a little, and I have a couple of more ideas." Alice fell asleep laying with her head on his chest and her legs still wrapped around him.

Chapter Three

THE FIRST CUT IS THE DEEPEST

This morning, as she looked in her bathroom mirror, Alice couldn't stop smiling and singing. "There was a young cowboy who lives on the range." How could James Taylor have known…? He didn't know. It was her mind that created the fantasies, whether she made them up or actually manipulated time and space. This morning, she managed to pick a few pieces of prairie grass out of her hair. Or at least she thought she did. Her nocturnal adventures were nearly always sexually satisfying, she thought, as she applied concealer beneath her tired eyes. Why did last night feel so magical? She loved a good orgy, in her fantasies anyway, but orgy sex, while fun, was anonymous. Sex with random strangers always felt good. Last night, with the virgin cowboy, she felt such a connection that it made her shiver with pleasure even now. Alice thought sex was like pizza, there was really no bad pizza; sometimes it was good, sometimes great and sometimes gourmet delicious. Last night's was five star yummy.

Alice buckled the straps on her red satin pumps. She felt the need for something special in the shoe department this morning. At four inches, the heels were a little tall, but with a little care, she wouldn't fall flat. Somewhere deep inside, her a little speck of worry that started yesterday squirmed and twisted deep inside her. Had the Board of Directors actually called a meeting without her? A year ago, she would have been certain that fact spelled disaster. Now, she felt confident that her hard work had been appreciated, but she was more than curious about any meeting. She chose a plain black suit this morning, surprised that the skirt still fit. Patting her stomach, she said, "Good boy, or girl, no rush to turn Mama into a barrel." This was an extremely well-behaved little person. It hadn't felt the need to remind her of its presence with any nasty nausea or inconvenient fainting spells yet. Maybe she could keep this her little secret for a while longer. She knew ignoring the fact that she was pregnant wouldn't change a thing, but it worked this morning.

With a little spring in her step, Alice managed to arrive ten minutes earlier than usual to the Emerald City green glass tower that was Excellcardia. She couldn't help feel a twinge of anguish as she walked past Jonathan's empty parking spot. A couple of nights of closet fun couldn't erase the pain of Jonathan's desertion. A nod and a salute to Andy, the security guard, and she took the elevator to the 23rd floor. She still loved the black marble and white leather she had chosen to decorate the entire floor she had claimed for her office. Alice walked past Jonathan's empty desk and through the door in the glass wall separating her desk from the reception area.

"Do I have to switch to decaf?" she asked the coffeemaker as she filled it with water and hit the switch. No one could hear her talking to inanimate objects and judge. It was better than talking to herself, as she had done so often as a child. Alice realized once again how little she really knew about being pregnant. Had she been asleep during that whole section of medical school? She made a mental note to ask the doctor at her next appointment. She could google it later, but this morning she really needed caffeine.

Alice filled her mug, added four sugars, and looked out the

window at the parking lot. She liked to see who came early and who did not. This morning at seven-thirty, there were far more cars than usual already filling the spaces. "What the hell?"

Most of the filled spaces were in the visitor's lot. Alice sat down at her desk and opened her laptop to check for the information she had requested. Her door opened. Bradley James stood looking at her with what she construed as concern on his face. Now she knew something was wrong. He never arrived until after eight.

He stood in front of her desk like he had a thousand times before, but she saw no playful look of seduction on his face this time. Or even the proud of himself grin he had when he came to report of his successes. "Alice, I had to come and tell you myself."

"What? About that board meeting nobody invited me to?"

"Yeah." He dropped into the white leather chair. "The board asked me to become CEO."

"Of course they did." She stared at him.

"Believe me, I tried to…"

"Right. Did you tell them no?" He looked at her with sad eyes and she wanted to punch him in the throat. She had never punched anyone for any reason, but never had someone who took her job stood in front of her pretending to be sad. At that moment, baby Hightower chose to send Alice to the trash can beside her desk to heave up her morning coffee. She wiped her mouth with a Kleenex, picked up her purse, her laptop and her first addition, and walked out the door. She could hear Brad saying words, but she didn't stop to listen.

❦

Alice sat on her couch, unable to remember driving home. It had finally happened; she had lost her job as CEO. Her greatest fear had come true. Such a dismissal, one for cause other than simple restructuring, might make it difficult to get this lofty a position ever again. There would be a settlement meant to cushion the blow financially for her as she had had written into her contract, but to someone who lived for her job, it felt as if her life was over. She had spent nearly every waking moment of sixteen-hour days for months to undo the damage of the industrial espionage. It is true that Brad James's sales talent had been key, but she had chosen most of the targets for his sales. He could sell, but she knew who to sell. She knew what products to push where and when. She had overseen the development and productions of new products as well. It must have been only the sales numbers the board saw seen fit to consider.

Alice had no idea how long she had sat on her couch staring at the wall. Otis had given up on ever getting food—she didn't even hear his cries. She continued to stare at her oak plank floor. The black cat curled up next to her feet and lay purring. Alice could feel the deep dark gathering inside her head. She could feel the heavy strands of sadness and desperation begin to settle into her brain and weigh her down, slow her thoughts, her movements and even her breathing. Dr. Cindy would have called this a depressive episode, but it felt a lot like a death. She had thought she would survive if the board decided against her after the trial period, but now....

Sometime later, Alice fed Otis and moved to her bed, where she did not bother to take off her favorite black suit or put her red shoes in the rack where they belonged. She kicked off the shoes and lay on her side, feeling nothing but dark, heavy and hopeless. Some time passed, and she got up only to pee and feed Otis. The sound of her phone ringing incessantly finally roused her a little, and she managed to get up and fetch it out of her purse. The caller ID said Louise. She pressed the button to answer. "Hello?"

"Alice! What the ever-loving hell? James? They made James CEO?" said Louise.

"Yes."

"What does he know about running a company? Sales isn't all it takes, he can't…."

"There is nothing I can do, goodbye," said Alice. She touched the screen to disconnect and set the phone down next to her on the bed. The tone for texts chimed one after another. Deep in the dark in her brain, something stirred. She sat up. Who would want to talk to an ex CEO? Curious to know exactly who wanted to talk to her, she touched the screen for voicemails. There were twenty-seven; one from Susan, two from Louise, one from Dr. Cindy and 24 from Brad. She chose to listen to one from Dr. Cindy.

"Hello, this is Dr. Cynthia Lester. You missed your appointment and since that's not something you have ever done, I'm concerned. Please call to reschedule as soon as convenient." One question became two in her head and she got out of bed. Standing under the hot water in her shower, Alice knew what she had to do. As soon as she dried off, she would call Dr. Cindy.

Chapter Four

IF IT MAKES YOU HAPPY

This morning, the soft blue colors of Dr. Cindy's office did little to soothe Alice. She didn't even bother to rub the buttons on Scarlet O'Hara's velvet fainting couch the doctor used for clients. This morning, none of her usual devices could calm her.

"It's not a relapse to react to a disastrous situation with sadness," said Dr. Cindy over her black framed reading glasses. "A day in bed does not mean you have Bipolar I Depression like your mother. You know Bipolar II is a mood disorder and this depressive mood might seem warranted under the circumstances."

"I thought because I gave it everything I possibly had, I would be fine. I never thought Brad would…" said Alice.

"Which fact bothers you more, the loss of your position or the fact that Brad replaced you?"

"I don't know." Alice studied the flowers on the carpet. "It seems like everyone I care about betrays me. Jonathan, Brad, the Board of Directors of Excellcardia."

"Do you think that is your fault?"

Alice sat silent for several minutes. When she looked up, she knew. Alice knew, terrible as the betrayals and recent disasters were, none of them were her fault. She had responsibly taken progestin injections, a nearly foolproof form of birth control, still she got pregnant. If Jonathan had really loved her, wouldn't he love her child as a part of her, no matter who fathered it? She had spent every bit of her energy to replace the revenue lost in Dr. Petrus's theft. She had done nothing but help Brad make those impressive sales.

"No, I don't think any of it was my fault," said Alice.

Dr. Cindy smiled like she did anytime Alice said something that must have shown progress, or so Alice thought. "You didn't answer my question. Which betrayal bothers you most?"

"I'm not sure. The board made a financial decision based on what they wrongly thought would be best for the company. I never thought Brad would take my job."

"So it's Brad's betrayal that hurts worse."

"I thought we were at least good friends. He got shot trying to save me from Petrus, for God's sake. I guess you just can't trust men."

"Because some men have hurt you…?"

"Every man I have ever been involved with."

Dr. Cindy set down the yellow legal pad she and every other shrink used to write their clinical notes. "Have you done any time explorations of late?" Dr. Cindy examined Alice over her glasses as she often did, but Alice thought she saw a faint smile on her lips.

"As a matter of fact, I have enjoyed the company of several luscious fantasy gentlemen, and they have left my heart unscathed. My not so delicate condition has left me even more horny than usual."

"You do realize that because there may be a real component to your fantasies, you need to consider the safety of the child when indulging."

"Sex doesn't hurt a baby. I remember that much from medical school."

"It seems the perfect solution for you, then. I think you discovered something important today. Next time, perhaps we might examine exactly why Brad's betrayal hurt you so much. Did we say tomorrow?" Dr. Cindy picked up her tablet. "I have an opening at ten if that would work."

"Sure, I have nowhere else to be."

Chapter Five

BRIDGE OVER TROUBLED WATERS

By the time Alice reached the garage in her apartment building, it was nearly 6:00 p.m. Her rarely wrong internal clock told her sunset was an hour away. She pushed the elevator button to Susan's floor. What good is a best friend if they can't be there when you felt as if your world was ending?

Susan opened the door wide to let Alice into her apartment. "Hey girlie, how's they hangin?"

Alice followed Susan into her apartment without answering.

"I know they are not hanging because you have those double DDs restrained with the best underwires money can buy."

Alice looked at Susan with a look she knew must hide nothing of the way she felt.

"Come on in, tell your bestie all about it." Susan put her arm around Alice and walked her over to a pale pink striped chair with ruffles around the bottom. Alice sank into the cloud of a pink chair as comforting as everything in Susan's home. The beautifully handmade quilts on the walls and overstuffed pastel furniture always made Alice feel at home. She knew she had made the right decision to come here.

"Let me get out of my spit covered scrubs and I will be right there," said Susan, her voice trailing off as she walked down the hall pulling off the ceil blue scrubs. Alice sat and stared.

Susan came back down the hall in a pair of jeans shorts and a Destin Florida DayGlo pink t-shirt. "I'm sorry. It's been one of those days. I had to leave it behind and get out of my work clothes as soon as possible. Some people don't deserve to have teeth, but here I am dentist to the masses doing the impossible for the ungrateful." Susan walked into her impossibly bright colored kitchen, grabbed a bottle of wine out of her stainless-steel refrigerator Alice had thought big enough to hold a dead horse. Susan thought that the stainless cooled down the bright lavender walls with scarlet cabinets.

Susan poured two glasses of wine and headed back to the living room. "Okay, tell me what happened at work," said Susan who sat down crossing her slender tanned legs that usually gave Alice a pang of jealousy. Susan handed Alice a glass of amber colored wine.

"There is no work. The board replaced me with Brad." Alice set the wine glass down on an end table. She knew enough about being pregnant to know it meant no alcohol for nine months.

"What! How could that happen?" Susan knelt in front of the pink chair and put her hand on Alice's shoulder.

"My life is crashing down around me." She still stared straight ahead.

"Well I am sure, Jonathan…"

"Oh yeah, and Jonathan left too while you were on vacation." Tears began to flow down Alice's cheeks.

Susan sat back in her chair and after a big gulp of her wine, she managed, "I never completely trusted Mr. Perfect, but I would have sworn that he did love you. The way he looked at you and would tell anyone who'd listen how amazing you are."

"He disappeared. It says blocked when I try to text or call him."

"Ghosting somehow fits his London hipster style. But Brad surprises me. I liked him that one time he cooked dinner for us. The boy can cook and is a great storyteller." Susan shifted in her chair. "It worried me a little when Jonathan got all lovey dovey so quickly."

"You know, I doubted that anyone that wonderful could love me, too." She dabbed her eyes with the tissue Susan handed her.

"Oh, I'm calling bullshit on that. He is no more wonderful than you. Don't even think that." She took another big gulp of her wine. "I see you're not drinking. No sin to take a sleeping pill or whatever when life gets tough."

"Yeah." If she couldn't tell her best friend she was pregnant, maybe it hadn't been such a good idea to consider keeping this baby. After all, telling Jonathan had not worked out well. She couldn't think of a single person, other than her OB, who would be happy about the news. Was refusing to tell anyone an expression of her real feelings? Feelings were something Alice had never been good at. Both of her marriages had failed. A lifetime of caring for someone might be more than she could handle. This person inside of her deserved someone who could at least admit it existed.

Susan set her now empty wine glass on the end table and leaned toward Alice. "I know your job is your life, David is in Mozooby or some such Godawful place, but he has a friend who is a headhunter."

Alice burst out laughing. "There is no place called Mozooby."

"I am sure if there were, he would go there to do surgery on some kid or another. He seems to be the only pediatric heart surgeon Doctors Without Borders, has." Susan got up and headed to her kitchen. "I already ate my Mean Cuisine but I could make you a peanut butter and jelly. I have home-made grape jelly from Baily's co-op farm?"

"I am sure it's good, but I think Otis is probably hungry."

"Oh no you do not. That freaky three-legged, one eared cat is round as a football. He can wait a little while for his dinner. I will text David for that headhunter's name. I wonder what time it is in Oobadooby?"

This time, Alice stared ahead blankly at Susan's attempt at humor.

"You need a plan, girl." I have known you for more than twenty years and you always have a plan. Susan touched numbers on her phone's screen.

Alice felt the slack muscles in her face tighten slightly and she raised her eyebrows a little. Nobody loved a good plan any more than Alice Hightower. "I do. Excellcardia is not the only company that needs a slightly damaged CEO."

"Oh, bullshit again, my dear. You made that company a metric crap ton of money. Any company would be glad to have you. Have you talked to Brad about this whole deal? I can't believe he sold you out. He didn't seem like the kind of guy who…."

"No."

"No what?"

"No, I couldn't talk to him."

"I get it. Let a few days pass. I'll text you the name and number of the headhunter."

Alice stood up. "Thanks so much. I promise I will work on my plan."

"You haven't asked to see them yet." Susan pulled up her t-shirt, exposing her breasts sans bra. "Go ahead, touch em."

"Wow. That's amazing. They look great, but I am not feeling them."

"They feel pretty numb, and the plastic surgeon says that

won't change. Getting rid of the cancer took most of the sensory nerves too…but David likes how they look."

"I'm glad." Alice stuck her arms out and Susan returned her hug. "I appreciate you being here for me. Thank you."

"Hey, you helped me with my gross drains after the mastectomy and even cleaned up my chemo barf. I owe you. I will be coming by to check on you so…"

❦

Her visit with Susan had lifted her mood just enough for a bit of naughty adventure, balcony style. A long gown hung on the golden hanger this evening, a pair of odd pointy leather shoes lay on the floor beneath. As much as she appreciated fabulous shoes, though these were obviously hand made of soft leather, they were odd looking. The gown was gorgeous. She had thought it velvet by the sheen, but upon closer examination some marvelous, quilted brocade made up the gown. Tiny embroidered pink roses covered a soft rose background. The roses formed triangular patterns, creating quilting on the sleeves and bodice. The skirt had the same roses but without the quilting. Tied to the hanger under the gown, she found a golden cord.

When she picked it up, assuming it was a belt, it felt like real gold, cold and metallic, but was soft enough to easily tie the tasseled ends around her waist. There were no undergarments at all. After her previous historical encounters, she had Googled and discovered that before the late seventeenth century, undergarments were pretty scarce. The dress had no buttons and the sleeves tied on with several tiny rose-colored ribbons. Again, thanks to Google, she knew this meant the gown was made before the thirteenth century. It took a little doing, but once she had the gown on, Alice felt like a queen in strange pointy shoes. The rose-colored gown even smelled like roses.

She thought a queen would wear her hair up and left her dark blonde hair twisted in its usual clip on top of her head.

The light beyond her balcony door was identical to the light she left behind in St. Louis, soft twilight. The awful smell on the other side of her balcony made her wrinkle her nose. She reached up and pinched her nose closed. Alice saw only tall grass in front of her, parted by a narrow dirt path. The smell of everything awful she had ever imagined still assaulted her nose. She smelled urine and feces, of course, but the unmistakable scent of blood and death seemed to get stronger as she took each step. She heard voices, shouting and laughing in the distance, both male and female.

"This doesn't smell like a good time?" she said, though the voices were too far away for anyone to hear.

It turned out that her odd shoes handled the rough ground beautifully. The tall grass thinned out, and the path led her to a clearing between tall trees where heavy draft horses stood tied to a rope line around the trees. Six dirty and ragged little boys bent over scrubbing some objects in a shallow creek. As she walked closer, she could see the boys held metal helmets and breast plates. The boys scrubbed the armor with their little hands and the creek ran red with blood. Alice could see a naked corpse lying in the water a few feet away. She knew he must be dead, as no one could survive that many arrows shot through them. The smell confirmed her conclusion.

Closing her lips tight not to vomit, Alice stepped across the creek on flat stones, heading toward the voices. While she couldn't see much of an opportunity for a royal rogering, this scene was one of the more historically detailed and interesting she had ever imagined or created or whatever.

After a few more paces, the trees thinned and she could see rows of tents. The round tents were red, blue, green and white. Some tents were plain and others decorated to look more like birthday cakes than tents with scalloped trim and colored fringe. Each tent had a flag at the pointed top. The voices and laughter led her in the dimming light into a circle of ground covered with straw. A fire blazed and Alice saw dozens of men sitting around it. She could hear women's laughter and screams that she hoped were of pleasure. The smell seemed better now, and she let go of her nose. Someone grabbed both arms and pulled her backward into a tent.

Alice strained to see in the darkness of the tent when she felt two women take her arms.

"Who have we here? Some fine lady come to steal my business," said a short bent woman holding her right arm. She was the color of night herself with black hair, eyes that seemed to have only pupils and skin a greyish color not normally found in humans. The woman dug her fingers into Alice's arm. "You come to work my camp?" She squinted up at Alice.

"I have no desire to hurt anyone's business. I'm here for a little…fun," said Alice to the woman.

The woman who held Alice's left arm said, "You looks a bit fresh for this sort of fun."

"Men who is come from battle ain't none too gentle." This woman stood nearly as tall as Alice and was round as a barrel. She smiled dimpling her plump pink face. Both women wore dirty white blouses unlaced to expose most of their breasts and their dark skirts were caked with dust and, for all you could tell, might once have been white.

"So that's what's going on here. Are you camp followers?" Alice asked.

"We are the camp's women ain't no following about us." The dark woman said, "We cooks and we cleans the tents and after a battle like today's, we cools the men's blood with our cunnies for coins."

Alice laughed. "I appreciate the simple truth." Alice strained her neck to look out the door of the tent as she heard some noise outside. A small blonde woman stumbled through the door. Her nose was bloodied, and her clothes were in tatters. The woman looked exhausted as well as injured. If that's what comes of cooling a soldier's blood, Alice would have none of that.

She would sneak off somewhere and go to sleep. Tomorrow she would wake up in her own bed.

"How many Elsbeth?" said the dark woman to the poor girl.

"Half a company I'd say." She rubbed the bruises covering her arms and breasts.

"Twenty?" said the round woman. She rubbed her hands together. "You done your duty and the captain owes me a pretty penny, hey, Gert?"

Alice yanked her arms hard, breaking the grips that still held her. "Thank you, ladies, for the warning. I will be going now. Sorry to interrupt your evening."

The large woman stood in front of the door to the tent, squinting at Alice. "If a bit of fun is what you're looking for, the prince don't want no slattern like Elsbeth or my other girls." She turned to her comrade in prostitution. "But maybe I could earn myself a bit of coin by introducing him to this…this…"

"Alice is my name."

"Well, Alice, the prince likes 'em fine and clean like you. None of the rest of the bunch is much better than Elsbeth here."

That's more like it, thought Alice. "I would be happy to meet your prince."

"I will take you around the back way. Them what ain't had a turn with the girls might rip that fine rosy dress right off you." The short woman laughed and dragged Alice through a slit in the back of the tent. They walked past the back of a dozen tents before stopping at one larger than the others and decorated with golden cord. Torches stuck in the ground lit a circle around this tent. A winged lion decorated the flag on top. The woman walked around to the let go of Alice's arm and shoved her into the opening.

Inside smelled like a completely different planet from the rest of the camp, sweet and fresh. In a small pan near the opening, something smoldered that must have been lavender and pine branches. A dozen candles sat on a carved wooden table providing dim smoky light to the inside of the tent. Alice could see a man sitting behind a table, but she couldn't see the man's face.

"What is this, Gert? I have told you I do not want to be bothered," said the man.

"This 'en ain't no bother. Her name is Alice, and she smells as sweet as summer roses."

The man stood and Gert shoved Alice forward just when she was about to get a good look at the Prince. She nearly fell over the table, but strong arms reached out to hold her tight by her waist to keep her from falling into the candles. "Are you unhurt, milady?"

"Thank you, I…" The man holding her let go. He stood just out of the circle of light shed by the candles. He could be ugly as a mud fence, but he wore lavender smelling velvet and had a strong, rich voice. How much passion could a man have to share fresh from battle? Alice wondered. There were two chairs on either side of the table made of some hides stretched over branches.

"My name is William. Do you care to share my supper?"

"Sure. I have never had supper with a prince, though I met another William with a similar accent once," said Alice.

"It will be my pleasure. What a scarce and lovely surprise. So rarely are the women of the camp so…interesting." He leaned forward and the light revealed Prince William. He was no great beauty of a man, his nose large and his chin weak. Short, dark hair covered his head. The look in his light eyes reflecting the candles was arresting. The passion behind those eyes… something to behold. She had seen that look before and it could transform the plainest of men into George Clooney in her eyes. His eyes slowly surveyed her, lingering on her lips and coming to rest on her chest. He clapped his hands.

A young boy in green tights and a matching short jacket ran in, carrying a tray. He set the tray down deftly between the candles. The smell made Alice's mouth water. With a deep bow, the boy ran around to William's side of the desk and began cutting the fragrant meat into bite-sized pieces with a huge knife. The prince held up his hand, and the boy backed away. A slight movement of William's hand sent the boy running out the tent's door. Now that's power, Alice thought.

"Please, help yourself," said William. His smile was warm and in his eyes the look remained.

"Thank you." On the tray sat a slice of bread as big as a plate with an entire small chicken laying on it. The bird dripped with a delicious smelling brown sauce. Several small wooden bowls sat around the big bread plate. One bowl held something green and lumpy that reminded her of barf from her few over-served incidents in college. She saw no flatware but a wooden spoon and the huge knife. "I'm not hungry, thank you," said Alice, having absolutely no idea how to eat without taking utensils from a prince.

The Prince picked up one of the pieces the boy had cut for him and plopped it into his mouth, but his eyes were still on Alice. She smiled at him. He picked up another piece and held it close to Alice's mouth. "This foul is quite good."

Alice opened her mouth and wanted to lick the sauce from his finger, but politely chewed, swallowed and thanked him. She didn't want His Highness to think her easy, though he probably had some idea since the mistress of camp whores had delivered her to him. She watched as he dipped his little finger into a bowl of salt and by waving his finger over a bit of chicken spilling the salt onto the meat. He held the salted piece to her lips this time and she took the piece with her teeth after teasing the tips of his fingers with her tongue.

William stood up, and she saw that his velvet robe hung

open, revealing an erection even more delicious than the chicken. It was a good size but uncircumcised and bent markedly up like it had been broken in the middle.

Though his face was nothing to write home about, his body looked as heavily muscled as an MMA fighter and his weapon stood ready to do battle. William came around the table, took Alice by the hand, and led her to a low bed covered with furs. He did not wait to undress her but pulled up her skirt and entered her. With his weight on his arms, he pounded into her with stroke after powerful stroke, his eyes closed tight. He came growling like a bear. Alice needed a few more strokes to follow his growl with her own exclamation. He collapsed and lay still on top of her. She savored the weight of him and caressed his muscular buttocks and back as he lay motionless.

"I will return to that tight cunny of yours later, but I find I am still hungry for food and my cook is excellent," said William against her ear.

"Sure, I could use a little food myself," said Alice. The Prince offered her some tasty dark beer from a leather mug and sweet wine with spices from a fine crystal glass. Then he spooned some of the green lumpy stuff into her mouth that turned out to be delicious. A meaty pea soup with oatmeal he called pottage. It felt strangely intimate to share dinnerware with the future king of somewhere and after a while the long looks over chicken led to William pulling Alice to the furs once again. He pulled off her sleeves, tearing the little ribbons and tugged the gown over her head.

He rolled her over onto her stomach.

"Doggie style it is Willy," she purred.

William obliged. He slid slowly in and out of her. The bend in his cock hit her in the perfect place to make her come hard and fast.

The Prince laughed. "I have killed men in battle who died more quietly than you crown your pleasure." With a grunt he began to thrust his hips hard, lifting her off the furs with an arch of his back and once again growling like an angry grizzly bear, he nearly knocked Alice off the bed. But hang on she did to at least one more mutual climax. William didn't seem one to cuddle. Perhaps cuddling wasn't a thing in the thirteenth century. They lay on their backs, catching their collective breaths, and Alice closed her eyes.

Chapter Six

POOR, POOR PITIFUL ME

How strange it felt to Alice to be wide awake at 5:45 a.m. with no place to be. Thank God she had an appointment with Brian the Headhunter and one with Dr. Cindy. Both were hours away and lying in her bed relaxing was not something Alice ever did. When her eyes opened, she got up and on her way, always. Her work ethic had helped her through med school, an MBA from Northwestern, and finally and her highest achievement, CEO of Excellcardia. Now looking up at the ceiling of her bedroom, Alice felt the dread weight of failure pressing down on her chest.

She had not managed to become a physician because she could not handle bodily fluids or sick people, but she did graduate second in her class at med school. Her grades at Northwestern were in the top one percent and she became CEO of Excellcardia after three years of hard work. Brad was now CEO, both of her marriages had ended in divorce, and Jonathan had left her. Maybe it was time she accepted that she was becoming very good at failure.

❧

She had worn her most powerful white suit, her conservative nude shoes and the resume she handed the headhunter was stellar. Alice could tell from the look on the guy's face as she sat down in front of his desk, he had nothing good to tell her.

"Finding another CEO position for you would not be easy." He sat round and bald behind his desk with a cocky look on his pale face. She really wished right now she could push him off a wall and wipe that look off his face as he shattered into a million pieces like Humpty Dumpty.

"News of the Biocardia disaster has spread throughout the industry and you would naturally be blamed. You were at the helm when Excellcardia hit the iceberg. We might be able to find you something abroad. I have heard a large company in Turkey is looking," Brian, the Headhunter said. She had no desire to move to Istanbul. Ten years ago she would have moved to the moon for the right job, but now, she had roots here. Though her mother was dead, it still felt like her roots here mattered.

❧

"So, I am a failure at everything," said Alice as she sat on Dr. Lester's couch. "The headhunter I saw today said I would be a challenging client. That unless I wanted to move to London or Turkey or some place, I would have to accept a lesser position at a smaller company."

"Would that really be so terrible? Starting over in a new place could be very challenging," answered Dr. Lester.

"It feels like going backwards to me." Alice looked up from the floor at Dr. Lester. "Can I ask you a question?"

"Sure." Dr. Lester lay down her pad.

"I have never heard you refer to yourself in any way, but as Dr. Cynthia Lester, why does the sign in the waiting room say, 'Dr. Cindy?'"

Dr. Lester stared at Alice for a long moment, unblinking.

"My mother made that sign for me when I received my doctorate. It's counted cross stitch, she always called me Cindy. She died before I set up my practice and the sign makes me feel like she is contributing. But none of this is about me."

Tears rolled down Alice's cheeks. "My…mother…never… knew that I was CEO. She was just too ill…and…"

Dr. Cindy handed Alice the tissues she kept near for the weepier of her clients, Alice always thought. Today she was one of them. She couldn't stop crying and they were not silent tears, but hard, ugly sobbing. After several minutes, Alice accepted the bottle of water Dr. Lester offered, drank half of it, and said, "I'm sorry."

"There is no reason to be sorry. Your mother's death was less than six months ago and maybe it is time you had a good cry about it. Because her Bipolar depression and dementia took her away from you long before she died, doesn't mean you can't grieve her loss. It is normal to feel relief when someone with an incurable condition dies, but she was your mother. Would you like to talk about her?"

"Yeah," Alice blew her nose. "Even though the last years of her life sucked, she was an amazing woman. She could do anything. She could cook and sew, play the piano, paint like a master and even speak Italian, evidently, though I had no idea. And so beautiful. Her hair wasn't dirty blonde like mine, but perfect platinum. Eyes Elizabeth Taylor violet. She was tall like me, but slender and graceful. Even in her seventies she could manage four-inch stilettos." Alice looked down at her black patent pumps with the little bows and four-inch platforms.

"Looks like you are managing those pretty well," said Dr. Cindy. "It is okay to mourn, you know. You will never see your mother again." She offered the tissue box to Alice once again. Taking another tissue, Alice dabbed her eyes. "She did the best she could to raise me. I was a weird kid, always making her life hard." Alice dabbed her eyes again. "I think that's enough. She was wonderful, but she is gone and I have to go on. I was a failure as a daughter, too."

"Feeling sorry for yourself will cost you double. Mourning is one thing, self-pity another. I think you know the difference. Next time, let's talk about accepting setbacks with grace and the value of mourning. Tomorrow same time?"

❧

Alice realized as she dumped food into Otis's bowl, that the big ugly bawling in Dr. Cindy's office had lifted a weight she didn't even know she'd still carried. She had been so relieved when her mother no longer suffered that she had felt only relief, not grief when her mother died.

She opened her shiny black refrigerator's door to see if there were any veggies that weren't black and furry. There were not. A knock at her door distracted her from searching her pantry.

Out the peephole, she saw Brad smiling at her.

"Go away!" She yelled through the door.

"Please let me in. I have to talk to you."

"You've got my job, what more do you want from me?"

"I need to talk to you." He sounded more serious than she had ever heard him.

Alice unlocked the door. Brad looked to her as if he hadn't slept in days. His normally perfect silver hair was rumpled, and he wasn't wearing a tie with his black suit. His jaw muscles clenched tight and his eyebrows knitted into a tight line. She backed up to let him in and hoped she wasn't making a huge mistake.

He stopped two feet from her and put his hands on her shoulders. She took a step back. Those weapons-grade blue eyes would not turn her to jelly this time.

"I don't blame you for being angry, but I need to explain." He backed up and stood looking at her.

Alice sat on one of the tall white stools at her bar/dining table. He couldn't look down on her or sit down next to her. She only had two stools and the other one sat on the other side of the bar. She crossed her arms. "I'm listening."

"The board told me they were starting a search for a new CEO and they planned to remove you. I tried to reason with them. It is ridiculous to blame you for anything." He gestured as he spoke, like she had seen him do when really passionate about a thing.

Alice uncrossed her arms.

"I tried to convince them that it would be a mistake to replace you." He stopped talking for a minute, as if what he had to say next was difficult. "I really think it was because you're a woman. As much as I hate it, they blamed you without good reason. It seemed pretty clear that the nine old guys had decided a woman couldn't do the job and the three women didn't stand up for you. I'm sorry." He now stood with his arms outstretched.

"No big surprise. I remember when they hired me, they acted as though they were doing me some big favor. I agreed at the time. All the good I had done evaporated when Dr. Petrus sold us out." Alice lowered her chin and narrowed her eyes. "You saw an opportunity and you took it."

"It wasn't like that. They were piling on the praise so I offered myself as an easy solution to a sticky problem and they bought it."

"I'm sure they did."

"I know you won't believe this, but it felt like the best thing at the moment."

"Of course it did."

"I think what the company needs most now is one person to head R&D, replacing Petrus and overseeing all the engineers."

It was an excellent idea. She had thought such a position necessary but never got around to creating it when the industrial espionage crap hit the fan. She was pretty sure he would struggle to run Excellcardia, and the right person would be a big help, but what was this to her?

"Exactly what do you expect me to do?"

"I have carte blanche to hire, I made sure of that. I want you to come on board as head of R&D. You found Petrus and without you, his idea would never have become reality. You have a good relationship with the engineers and production people." He unleashed on her that look she could never resist. It had led her to several unwise decisions in the past.

"Give it some thought. I know this position might feel like a demotion and I bet some Fortune 500 company is already chasing after you." He took a couple of steps toward the door. "But don't wait too long. I'll need to make this brilliant hire if Excellcardia is going to prosper again anytime soon. You're the best there is." He closed the door behind him.

In truth, no company chased her at all. Her interview with the headhunter made that clear. Going back to Excellcardia would be comfortable and coming up with another ground-breaking project would be just what the company needed. That kind of challenge is what Alice lived for. Maybe she did have something to prove to the Board of Directors and to herself. But did she dare risk close proximity to any man as dangerous as Bradley James again?

Alice thought as she ate her hearty Chef Boyardee delight, she needed to buy some milk. She knew babies needed calcium. Crap! She had drank alcohol with William, the thirteenth century prince. While she only sipped a little of the dark beer and the spiced wine, no alcohol consumption was safe during pregnancy. Maybe tonight was the perfect night to sleep in her own bed. Tomorrow would come with a whole new set of circumstances she could mess up or maybe figure out.

Chapter Seven

I'M STILL STANDING

D r. Bieber told her most of the things she already knew, after she had Googled them in the waiting room. No alcohol, no caffeine, no pain relievers except Tylenol, no shellfish, blah, blah, blah. She knew these things were important, but it seemed more like nine months of sacrifice rather than the joy of impending motherhood. He told her that she was about to enter her second trimester and if she planned to end the pregnancy it needed to be done ASAP. Her stomach clenched at those words. She had made the decision without another thought. This child, no matter who the father, was part of her.

❧

She heard Susan's signature knock and quickly stashed her prenatal vitamins in the bread box that never held any bread, and opened the door.

"Did I see Brad leaving the building last night?" said Susan.

"Yes, come on in."

Susan sat on Alice's couch in her work scrubs and said, "Okay, spill it."

Alice paced back and forth in front of Susan. "He says he tried to keep the board from firing me. He says he wants me to come on as head of R&D for the good of the company."

"Did you believe him?" Susan's large green eyes narrowed.

Alice stopped pacing. "I don't know. The headhunter said I might have to move somewhere overseas to find a CEO position. I kinda like it here and Brad…"

"Is a stone silver fox and single now."

"Yeah, dating men who will hurt me is my thing. But I'm not sure what I would do without you to…" Alice walked into Susan's arms and Susan hugged her tight.

"There's your answer."

❧

Dr. Cindy agreed with Susan about Alice taking a chance with Excellcardia. After an hour of discussing the ins and outs of being Alice with Dr. Lester, she headed home to check out a few scientific journals online and see what was cooking in the world of cloning and cell growth. It would take a whale of a project to get Excellcardia back on the right track to the top of the medical device industry.

After six hours spent with Cell Proliferation, The Energetics of Mammalian Cell Growth and Cell Biology articles, Alice discovered how much she had missed the research end of her career. Her job before Excellcardia had been Head of R&D for a Biozene a small company where she discovered Henry Petrus. Henry was a thief and an attempted murderer, but he was also a genius at cloning cell lines and human cell growth. Biocardia's brilliant process to produce blood vessels for heart by-pass surgery without having to remove leg veins, had been his baby. Some of the most brilliant work in the last few years, Alice discovered had been in cloning bone and cartilage.

Wouldn't a new joint made of one's own cells be a major step forward in the field of joint replacements? Excellosteo had a nice ring to it as a name for the new division. It would be a completely new area for Excellcardia but maybe it was time for some diversification from plain old pacemakers and implantable defibrillators.

After reading every article she could find on the cloning bone and cartilage, one name turned up time and time again as the principal researcher…Ami Wen. Googling Dr. Wen turned up little except that she lived in Detroit. At least she wouldn't have to entice her into moving to St. Louis from Maui, Manhattan or the French Riviera.

Alice fell asleep with Otis curled up behind her knees, planning her presentation.

§

Her usual two egg breakfast included a tall glass of whole milk this morning. Baby Hightower deserved the best. He or she had still gifted her with very little morning sickness, and her OB said she had lost two pounds. "Thanks, baby," said Alice, patting her flat stomach. Alice went with her red suit for the meeting Brad had so eagerly agreed to on the phone this morning. Brad had once called her his Red Queen at a Christmas party, and perhaps she could remove his doubts about her scheme with the precision of a guillotine before he knew what hit him. Red shoes were too matchy-matchy, and she chose a pair of zebra print Jimmy Choos. She could easily manage the two-inch kitten heels with her level of grace no matter how nervous she felt.

It seemed odd to arrive at Excellcardia with so many cars already filling the lot. She parked in the far corner to avoid seeing Brad's car in her CEO space. She waved at Andy Garcia, the security guard who returned her wave. No need to salute her now. She was no longer captain of the ship, just a woman in a red suit on her way up to see the boss. At least he didn't make her sign in.

When Alice arrived at the twenty-third floor, she was surprised that Brad had not yet changed much in the executive suite's decor. The white leather couch and chairs still sat outside the administrative assistant's desk, now occupied by a twenty-something brunette that looked like she had been runner up in some beauty pageant or another. The prints of scarlet flowers she had chosen still offered the right pop of color to the walls. She noticed both were slightly crooked, but since it was no longer her office, straightening them was not her responsibility.

She stood in front of almost Miss Arizona's desk and planned to say, "Alice Hightower to see Mr. James," when the door in the glass wall to the inner office opened. That was one difference. Mr. James had replaced the clear glass that walled off the CEO's office with frosted glass.

"Alice, so good to see you." Brad wrapped his arms around her in a bear hug and kissed her on the cheek. It had been exactly two days since she had last seen him, but he was a hugger, she remembered, and very good at it. Though this was strictly a business meeting, she couldn't help but shiver a little as she felt her breasts pressed against his chest.

He ushered her in with his hand on the small of her back and she sat in the white leather chair in front of the desk that had once been hers. He wore a dove-gray suit and deep blue tie. Why did men in suits always do this to her? She recrossed her leg, shaking off the completely inappropriate but fleeting thought and began outlining plans for Excellosteo before her mind wandered to what was under that suit.

She opened the meeting and said, "We still have the 3D printers and from what I understand, dogs will serve as an excellent research model for transplantation and that lab is still set up. We will need to use a larger breed, like labs, but the shelters are full of large dogs. I still think it is best to use older dogs that might be in need of new knees after chasing one too many Frisbees—your call." Alice shamelessly lowered her chin and glanced at him through her lashes. There was no lash batting, just the type of slightly deferential expression she knew well he responded to.

"I have done some research into the right person to head the team. She absolutely rocks the cloning of bone and cartilage, Dr. Ami Wen. Not sure if she's available, but those researcher types are usually amenable to significant salary increases depending on the budget."

He sat silent for a minute. "Boss Lady, I would have expected nothing less." He smiled a smile she had never seen. It wasn't his wide, warm smile or his small, self-satisfied grin, but this one puzzled her. What the hell was the man behind those smoking blue eyes thinking?

Brad, now on his feet and with his hands punctuating his words. "I have some experience with titanium prostheses, used to sell them back a million years ago and know a few people still. I understand that market. This is good. The process would be similar to Biocardia only with joints. Could we do hips as well as knees?"

"I don't see why not," said Alice. "I think it might be prudent to stick to knees at first. Once we get the patents and clearances, we can branch out." She couldn't help but smile. Of course, she was no longer his boss, but hearing him call her the name he had whispered in her ear while pounding her deep and hard, did not make her unhappy.

Brad stood up. "We can get started right away. I will work up a budget based roughly on Biocardia and you see if you can get that researcher on board." He came around the desk, wrapped his arms around her again and said, "We make one hell of a team, Alice." There was the smile she knew best, the one full of heat that made her squirm in her chair.

Alice decided to travel to Detroit and try to entice Dr. Ami Wen in person. She had called one of the private security firms who she'd hired to track down Henry Petrus to arm her with the ammunition to snag the brilliant Dr. Wen. She currently worked at Eastern Michigan University in Ypsilanti. Not exactly Harvard. She had no family, owned nothing of value, and was heavily in debt. This seemed a bit too easy.

She tipped the Uber driver with cash as she preferred and appraised the dingy once-white renovated trailer that was Dr. Wen's office. Below the tiny opaque windows sat several empty bowls tucked under the wooden steps leading up to the door. Did she have a fondness for raccoons? Alice wondered.

Alice opened the door and felt as if she was entering someone's bedroom rather than an office. It smelled sweet of perfume or incense and the walls were draped with pieces of fabric of bright pink and orange. A small statue of Buddha sat in front of a desk. Behind the desk sat Dr. Wen.

"Welcome to my lair. Who the hell are you?" said a tiny Asian woman with a blue Mohawk hair do. It wasn't exactly a Mohawk, Alice thought. Her hair, several inches long, hung to one side and was shaved on the sides extremely short. Black rimmed round glasses perched on a smallish nose. A white lab coat over her blue scrubs gave the only indication she was the brilliant researcher Alice sought.

"I'm Alice Hightower. I phoned yesterday for an appointment, left several messages but no one answered any of the numerous times I called."

"Yeah, I don't answer the phone if I'm working. I got your message. You are one tall drink of water." Dr. Wen stood and stuck out her hand.

Alice returned the shake and stood looking at Dr. Wen.

"I will give you ten minutes. I have some itty bity osteoclasts soaking in some growth solution and I need to check their growth rate soon."

"Osteoclasts? Don't those break down bone? I thought you were working on growing bone tissue."

"Yeah, osteoclast are critical to healthy cancellous bone. That's the main reason those bone density meds cause problems…but enough about me and my shit. What are you here for?"

"I am very interested in your shit. I'm," she almost said, CEO, but she corrected herself, "head of R&D for Excell-cardia in St. Louis. We are in the beginning stages of a project to grow bone and cartilage over a printed matrix to produce joints for replacement in humans."

"Huh," Dr. Wen cocked her head to one side and reminded Alice of a parrot she had once seen and nearly laughed.

A fuzzy gray and white cat jumped up on the doctor's lap. Without glancing away, she petted the cat on its head and narrowed her eyes behind her round glasses. "Didn't I read something about somebody doing that for blood vessels?"

Alice was certain she knew about Biocardia. Those in a field of research keep track of others' accomplishments. "Yes, we pioneered that, but…"

"But the process got pirated by some schmuck and is now in human trials for a different outfit. Am I right?" Now Dr. Wen leaned forward, peering at Alice with her lips pursed tight. Alice wondered if the lipstick Dr. Wen wore was actually black or a very dark purple.

"That's pretty much the story." Alice stood clutching her leather briefcase and wondered if she would be offered a place to sit, though she didn't see a chair anywhere. Huge potted palms stood guard on each side of the desk. She could see a shelf covered with plants behind the desk.

"Sorry there is no place to sit," said Dr. Wen. "The extra oxygen the plants make is much more important to my creative process than chairs for people I don't want to talk to."

"I always thought of research as a creative process…"

"Cut the bullshit, Ms. Hightower, and get to why you are here."

"We would like to hire you to head up our project. We are willing to help with moving costs to relocate to St. Louis and…"

"How much?"

"We are prepared to double you current salary."

"Yeah, state schools don't pay much and my major grant is about to run out. If you are planning to grow joints, ain't another person on this planet that knows more about it than me. And I have needs."

Alice set her briefcase on the floor, opened it and removed an envelope. Holding it out toward Dr. Wen, Alice said, "Here's a check for 127, 000 dollars. All I need is your signature on this contract, after appropriate consideration, of course, and it is yours." The private dick couldn't manage to find Henry Petrus, but he had informed Alice the exact amount of Dr. Wen's debts. The laugh that resulted caused Alice to take a step back and the cat sitting on Dr. Wen's lap to jump off.

"I like you, Alice. You can call me Ami, pronounced Ahme, like my French speaking Cambodian Grandma insisted. I will look this over and I can be there in a week, but I bet that don't surprise you one teensy tinsy bit." She peered at Alice.

Alice put the envelope in Ami's hand. It held a cashier's check dated a week from the date and payment could be stopped if she didn't return the contract by the date on it. Alice was pretty certain she wouldn't have to do that. Ami Wen was different, but exactly the genius required.

Chapter Eight

IT'S GOOD TO BE KING

S he chose her serious blue suit but grabbed her navy pumps with the crimson heels for her update to Brad of her recruiting success. A touch of red for luck might be what she needed when dealing with the Red Knight. She figured he probably thought of himself as the White Knight, though. Her new project and genius hire insured she stood at the power position on this chessboard.

"I would like to take over the space behind the security desk on the ground floor," said Alice, taking advantage of the fact that Brad's admin was not at her desk and walking right into his office. "It's never been used for community education or whatever. It has big windows, overlooks the park, has its own bathroom and separate entrance and I want it."

"It's yours." There was that smile again that she couldn't fathom.

"I won't need staff for a while, and I won't need a decorator. I'll have Office Max deliver what I need. If you don't mind, I would like the paintings of scarlet flowers in the reception area of my old…your office."

"They're yours." he still smiled.

"By the time Dr. Wen gets here, I should be up and running. I have a few personal things to attend to, but until there is a budget..."

"It will be in your inbox by end of the week." Now she saw the cocky, self-satisfied grin that made her want to punch him or fuck him half to death, and she was never sure which. Few people in any business could get a budget together for a project of this size in ten days.

"Great, Boss Man." He winced at her words and she walked out his door.

After ordering the furniture for her new office and arranging meetings with Production and Engineering, Alice headed home to her apartment. She had picked up some green things from the grocery store's salad section and as she munched, one single question kept running through her mind. *What and who could be behind her guestroom closet door tonight?* Alice had left her work clothes in her bedroom closet and stood naked and curious in front of it.

The answer was both fascinating and disappointing. The hanger held a piece of rectangular cloth with a bright red flower pattern covering it. On closer inspection, the piece of cloth was long enough to be wrapped around her body, but there were no shoes and no undies. A tall and fascinating hat sat on the floor of the closet. A band of flat seashells covered a leather circle that looked like it would fit her head. Alice picked it up and the long strips of dry grass that hung from each side rustled softly and tickled her bare shoulders as she set it on her head. Three huge black iridescent feathers stuck out of the top.

"Wow," Alice said to her image. "I look like the queen of some island or another."

She wrapped the cloth around her body tight. With no way provided to secure this thing, she decided to tuck the corner in above her breasts and opened the balcony door.

Alice squinted into bright sunshine and stepped out on warm sand. She could smell the ocean and hear waves crashing. Ahead of her stood a line of tall palm trees. Turning, she looked into the surf. The warm sun on her shoulders almost made her forget the main reason she opened that closet door, but perhaps a walk along this lovely beach was what she actually needed. Maybe she would just sit on the soft sand and watch the waves roll in.

Behind her, Alice heard the laughter of women. She turned her head to see four women wearing sarongs a lot like the one she wore. They laughed again and ran toward her. Two of the women reached down to take Alice's hands and pull her to her feet. They were tan beauties with long black hair and each looked no older than twenty. They said nothing but led her through a break in the palm trees down a path made of smooth black stones. The scent led her forward and made her shiver…men. Not sour old sweat, but the musky essence of men fresh and hot. A few more steps and she saw a line of ten magnificent, tanned men standing in front of a huge structure woven of grass. Each man had to be nearly seven feet tall. They wore short sarongs wrapped around their waists and tucked into the front. Alice's nearly reached her ankles. The men's shorter version revealed muscular thighs that made Alice smile. Each man had jet black hair hanging to his shoulders. Each man wore a heavy necklace made of shells and something that looked like claws or teeth. Below each man's knees, he wore a band with grass attached. Who knew Ugg boots made a grass version?

As the women led Alice closer, the men began to stamp their feet in unison, making a rustling that again caused a shiver down her entire spine at the flexing of all those lovely, muscled thighs. They seemed to be standing guard on either side of the opening to the enormous, round hall. *Ten might be a few too many, but she would do her best.*

Eyes as dark as night swept over her. She could almost feel the touch of those eyes on her face, her shoulders, and her breasts. Alice felt her nipples stand at attention under those invisible touches. Beads of sweat dripped down muscled chests. Alice followed one bead down one particularly beautiful muscular man's body and watched it disappear into his shorty sarong. He smiled at her and the stamping grew faster. How much fun would it be to untuck the smiling man's sarong? Suddenly, a drum sounded from deep inside the hall and the men stood still. In the opening stood the man who must be their king.

He stood nearly half a foot taller than the others and wore a head dress similar to hers, but with two rows of shells and large tufts of feathers of black and white. His body as muscled as any body builder, Alice sighed. Covering his right arm and chest were intricate tattoos. Alice longed to run her fingers over those designs, and as if he read her mind, he reached out and took her hand. His dark eyes surveyed her, and his nostrils flared. He must have liked the smell of her because he bent over and threw her over his massive shoulders as if she weighed nothing at all.

The king sat her down once inside the hall, on what was obviously a bed. A low pedestal covered in fresh soft ferns and flowers of lavender, pink and red, looked more than inviting to Alice, whose body raged with the hormones of early pregnancy. He stepped back a few feet and looked at her. "I am Manawatu," boomed a voice that would have made James Earl Jones sound squeaky.

"I am Alice." Her voice cracked.

"The missionaries taught me these words and I am glad you speak them." His fierce look softened and his full lips turned up into a smile, revealing strong even teeth she could have sworn were bleached. He took a step toward Alice and spread his arms wide. "It was foretold that a light-haired pale woman would appear and would bring me great pleasure. Is this your wish?"

"Yes, I am all in for great pleasure," said Alice.

Quick as a cat, Manawatu scooped Alice up and wrapped her legs around his waist. Her sarong pushed aside, he reached down and tugged off the cloth covering a magnificent royal erection. Before she had time to exclaim her delight, he filled her. Standing with legs slightly bent and holding her buttocks in his huge hands, he pumped into her.

She had seen people in movies have sex standing up, but never expected to encounter a man as physically strong and capable as Manawatu. Alice was no tiny woman. She locked her legs around him and pulled him deeper into her. Just as she was about to come loud and hard, she felt his massive arms pull her tight and he let out a long loud cry that drowned out her pitiful little scream. He held her in his iron grip for a few seconds, took a couple of steps and gently deposited her on the soft, fragrant bed.

"Well, that was some pleasure," said Alice as he sat down beside her.

Manawatu smiled and looked over his shoulder. He motioned to someone. Two of the women who had met her on the beach removed their hats with down-cast eyes. *Yeah, you know you're watching your king get laid.* A small table made of sticks with woven grass top appeared carried by another woman, who looked up and giggled. They quickly set the table with platters of fragrant meat and fruit. Alice now noticed that the four women who first welcomed her and the ten guards stood at attention against the far wall. *Never let it be said that Alice Hightower didn't appreciate an audience.*

"You must eat. The night is long," said Manawatu.

"I hope that's a promise," answered Alice and she shivered at that promise. He looked into her eyes and again with amazing speed, tore off her sarong and crushed her breasts in his large hands. The pleasure and pain made her squeal as he slipped into her. She reached around to grab those tan granite boulders of his ass. Caressing his buttocks as they clenched, driving him into her, Alice sank deep into the pleasure of his hard cock. Again, it took a few strokes for him to shout his war cry of coming, and she followed shortly behind.

"We will eat now." He sat up.

"Whatever you say." Alice had barely caught her breath when Manawatu plopped a bit of meat into her mouth.

"Wild boar, as juicy as Alice." A wide smile nearly blinded her.

"Thank you. Delicious." Alice watched as Manuwatu reached into a large bowl filled with fruit she had never seen. He picked up a luscious red globe and peeled it with his teeth as she watched. When no skin remained, revealing its scarlet interior, the king reached over and cupped Alice's breast gingerly.

"I like my fruit ripe." Manawatu slathered both her nipples with the cool red juice. She closed her eyes and moaned. She opened them to see him licking the fruity delight off of her, finishing the last drop off by sucking vigorously on each of Alice's erect nipples as she writhed and made little animal noises deep in her throat.

"Two can play at this Manny," said Alice as she searched the fruit bowl for just the right…berries? She grabbed a handful of what looked like a cross between, blueberries and raspberries. Crushing them between her fingers, she applied them to his half erect cock. His eyes widened. She began licking and sucking at the crushed berries, which tasted more like cherries, off of him. He moaned loud and low. Alice continued. When the berries were gone, Alice took the lovely, dark, nearly purple cock in her mouth. Manawatu growled with passion and pushed Alice back onto the bed. This time, he lifted her legs as if they weighed nothing and put them on his shoulders. His thrusts were hard and deep. Alice came first and let out a war cry of her own, followed by Manawatu.

As they lay catching their breath, Alice wondered if Baby Hightower liked the ride Manawatu had given it. Though it was no bigger than a bean, it must have felt something as each deep thrust slammed into her cervix. It felt perfect to her. He pulled her onto his chest, and she closed her eyes.

Chapter Nine

I'M STILL STANDING

The following morning, Alice paced as she planned her day. She had six impossible things to get done. She needed to order several million things for her office, and it was time she visited the Hillhouse Institute again. Very soon her days would be completely consumed with Excellosteo.

An institute of Alternative Psychology was undoubtedly a strange place, but Alice gave up long ago describing what happened to her at sunset as normal. If they could help her explain her nocturnal fantasies, it would be worth a little oddity. The appointment secretary said Dr. Hoffman would be available this afternoon.

With everything ordered and assurance it would be delivered tomorrow, Alice headed off to the imposing red brick building in the Central West End that housed the Hillhouse Institute. Months ago, she had come here at the suggestion of Dr. Cindy, to examine the outrageous idea that her fantasies might be real. She had often found evidence of her time travels still visible in the morning. The tiny bruise on her breast or chaffing on her face left by a handsome man's beard. Her therapist had told her that The Hillhouse institute investigated theories that some people had abilities far outside the normal because of the unique structure of their brains. She also told Alice that these unique individuals often exhibited pathology like bipolar disorder or even schizophrenia.

Could her brain actually cause some type of time distortion and manipulate matter to create the clothes she found in her closet? It was a fascinating question and if the answer could be found in this odd building, what had she to lose?

A young woman stood in front of her nearly as soon as she hit the bell beside the mammoth wooden door. This short, shapely girl, smiled a wide smile and looked at her through black eyes. Her dark hair cut straight across, and the black-framed glasses she wore reminded Alice of Velma from Scooby Doo, but she kept that to herself. The young woman wore snow white scrubs and carried a clip board.

"Good afternoon Ms. Hightower. I'm Megan Bringer, Dr. Hoffman's assistant, and I'll be showing you to Dr. Hoffman's lab." She walked toward the stainless-steel elevator door at the end of the foyer. The door opened as a door does that is motion activated and Megan typed a number in to the keypad. Unlike normal, non-alternative elevators that had numbers, the floor number typed in rather than chosen out of an existing list of floors.

"He's a strange trip, Dr. Hoffman. It can't be easy working for a man who reads your every thought," said Alice as the elevator dropped. She hadn't been close enough to see the number, but she thought it had two digits. Alice remembered at her last visit, her guide punched in 8 for the floor. Alice had also remembered thinking it odd that a building built in 1900 and appeared to have three stories at the most, had an elevator to floor 8. But when the elevator dropped rather than rose, she realized The Hillhouse Institute must have one hell of a basement. This time it took a long time to reach whatever floor Meagan had punched. The doors opened into a space dark and cavernous. A golf cart sat in a circle of light from an overhead spot.

"Dr. Hoffman's lab is a little remote. He doesn't want us to waste time walking. Her bright smile Alice first thought cheery, was beginning to get on her nerves." Her smile never wavered and Alice thought it now looked pasted on like the grin on a mannequin. She got in the driver's side and Alice sat beside her. Megan headed toward a spot of light and then another until Alice saw a path created out of spotlights about twenty feet apart.

"He is brilliant and you learn to be very honest in your thoughts," said the girl behind the wheel.

Alice peered ahead into the dark, straining to see anything resembling a lab. Megan stopped the cart, got out at a door, invisible until it whooshed open. Alice followed Megan into a brightly lit space full of computer servers. They walked past the servers and another door opened. This one had a desk and a chair. Behind the desk sat Carl Hoffman.

"So happy to see you again, Alice." The last time she had visited, the supremely strange, mind-reading Dr. Hoffman, had told her that her brain scan looked far from typical. Maybe she was some sort of time travelling savant. This did seem worth further investigation, and so here she was. He stood and motioned for her to sit in the chair. The door opened once more as Megan left without a word. Undoubtedly she had thought something Dr. Hoffman's way. "I'm sorry I can't give you an entire day, but we can get some preliminary experiments out of the way. I assure you, none of this will endanger the life of your unborn child."

"Well, that's a relief." His mind reading did save time not having to explain things to him. The little pointed beard he had last time she had visited the institute had been replaced by a bushier one. Still dressed all in black, he now looked like a negative of Sigmund Freud rather than of Colonel Sanders like last time. He no longer wore glasses.

He smiled his creepy half smile she remembered from before and said to her, "Freud was actually the first Alternative

Psychologist. Though traditional psychology would never accept him being labeled as one."

He walked to a door she hadn't noticed before and opened it. "Let's get started, shall we? It is important for our sensitive equipment to be shielded from any electro-magnetic interference so we are twenty stories underground," said Dr. Hoffman answering a question she hadn't consciously asked.

"We shall," she said. It felt better to Alice to say the words rather than think them at him. The room beyond the door contained a beige recliner, a chair with a computer monitor on a desk, and a wall of dials and blinking lights beyond. Attached to the recliner was the same old time beauty shop hair dryer looking thing with wires coming out of it as last time. She knew the points leading from the wires that would touch her head were not sharp.

She expected him to offer an explanation of the objects in the room, but he merely sat in the chair in front of the monitor and motioned toward the recliner. The chair leather felt soft as butter. As she sank into it and wiggled around a little, metal straps closed around her wrists.

"Hey this isn't…"

"Relax Alice. I'm not going to hurt you. It is important that you stay still and the restraints can easily be removed by tugging on them twice."

She tried it. The restraints fell away. Still, her heart beat a mile a minute.

"Close your eyes and relax. I am going to have you respond to my simple instructions and we will see if your talent at manipulating time and space live up to your impressive 3D scan." She woke up, still listening to the sound of his voice.

"You may sit up now, Alice."

Her heart pounded and her ears rang. "What did you do to me?"

"I gave you a series of instructions and my computer read your reactions."

"I don't remember any instructions."

"There is no need to panic. You were not hurt in any way."

Alice sat on the edge of the recliner and felt like bolting out the door.

"I'm sorry you are upset. We tested your ability to alter both time and space. You must have fallen asleep after the last test. I can show you the tape...."

"Yeah, I want to see it." He turned the screen around and typed a few commands on the keyboard. Alice saw herself lying on the chair peacefully. She could see the doctor typing, but she seemed to be asleep.

"Looks like I am sleeping."

"Isn't that when your time travel manifests?"

"Yeah. But it doesn't look like anything is happening."

"I assure you, we were having quite a conversation. You can watch as long as you like, though it is all pretty much like this." Alice felt a shiver down her spine. She had to know what he found.

"I would like to discuss your results as it will take a while for Megan to get here with the cart."

Alice sat back down on the edge of the recliner.

Dr. Hoffman typed on the keyboard. "While you do have the ability to manipulate time. I could, however, find no evidence at all that you can affect the structure of matter."

"So, what does that mean?"

"It does not rule out the fact that your fantastic nightly fantasies might be actual occurrences, but it is doubtful that you could achieve these feats on your own."

"What? Who the hell helps me?"

"If you don't know, how could I?" Carl Hoffman's expression made her skin crawl. How could she have ever thought him hot, and she did not give a rat's ass that he read that thought?

He looked at her with the look one might give a naughty child. "I am sorry I could not determine definitively about your ability to time travel. Your ability to affect our equipment measuring time was impressive. Perhaps if you could give me a full twenty-four hours as your episodes seem to be tied to sunset."

Alice tried not to think of any rebuttal to his opinion. She didn't want any more discussion; she wanted to get out of there. This afternoon had gone way past the time she wanted to spend with Dr. Creepy.

"I'll think about it. Kinda busy right now." Alice stood up.

Fine. He must have thought, as his lips didn't move.

The door opened, and Megan stood smiling and said, "Ready to go."

Her watch said eight-thirty. Had she really been laying there like a corpse, mind-talking to Dr. Hoffman for six hours?

❧

That evening, she told Dr. Cindy of her strange encounter and her discomfort about the whole place.

"I don't really know Dr. Hoffman. I got involved in a conversation at a party and he told me about the institute. He said that if I ran across any clients that seemed to have unusual abilities, we might collaborate. It sounded interesting, and it seemed a real possibility that your fantasies were real."

"I don't blame you. I went there willingly. I wasn't hurt."

"How do you feel about going for further tests?"

"Like it would be a waste of time. Maybe I didn't even go. Maybe there is no Institute of Alternative Psychology. Maybe it's just another large brick building with a bottomless basement and a guy who reads minds. Who is to say a person crazy enough to make up fantasies like I do? I couldn't have made that whole thing up, too." Alice put her hand on the door handle. "I say," said Dr. Lester. She stopped and reached for Alice's arm. "You are not psychotic. You know real from fantasy. I know. That's what I do."

"Do you think I could actually travel in time?"

"What I think doesn't matter."

Perfect shrink talk. "You know, it doesn't matter to me either. I open my closet door and go where it takes me. I always come back and it's amazing fun. I'll call your office tomorrow for an appointment." Alice walked to her car, still thinking about her nightly fantasies. "They sure are fun," she said to her steering wheel.

Exhausted, she expected to fall asleep as soon as her head hit the pillow. That didn't happen. She lay there, eyes wide, until she drifted off about 4:00 a.m.. As usual, she opened her eyes as soon as it was light. There were a few hundred thousand things to get done today, and none of them were impossible.

The delivery men from Office Max didn't arrive at 8:00 a.m. as promised. When she called to check, the dispatcher told her it would be noon at the earliest before they delivered anything. Alice had arrived at Excellcardia at 7:25 a.m. like always and after some paperwork for HR she sat on the floor of her new office reading emails on her laptop. It surprised her that the head of R&D averaged only seventy emails per day rather than the one hundred eighty she had received each day as CEO. She didn't know whether to be relieved or disappointed.

When all emails had been answered or properly forwarded, Alice stood up and began to pace. She found it more and more difficult to stay still as the day went on. She had nearly worn a path in the blue industrial length carpet when the door opened.

"Ms. Hightower?" said a voice.

Alice saw a young man in a security blue uniform looking at her. Skeletally thin, he must have had his uniform tailored for him. She didn't really like the "Skinny Pants" look on men.

His shaved head set off a Duck Dynasty beard that couldn't have been trimmed much this decade.

"Yes," she answered, and stopped her pacing.

"There is a problem on the tenth floor and Mr. James said I should come get you to handle it."

"What exactly is the problem?"

"There's a cat loose in the dog pen's and…"

"A cat. What the hell? Thank you, Austin." She had read his name tag but took delight in knowing all co-worker's names but reading name tags was definitely cheating. "Tell Mr. James that it's already handled."

It surprised Alice that the retinal security scanner still recognized her and let her into what had once been the most secure and important research lab in the building. The air smelled stale with a hint of sweetness, of course, formaldehyde. Research subjects had to be preserved.

Down the long hall dogs barked and growled as they would do if a cat were allowed anywhere near the cages. She hadn't realized that any research subject dogs remained after it became impossible to continue the Biocardia project. She had given orders to find all the remaining dogs homes and Jonathan always—but he was no longer her administrative assistant or her lover. He was gone.

A grey and white streak ran between her legs and someone ran out of Dr. Petrus's office straight into Alice, nearly knocking her down.

"Sorry, stretch. Pookie isn't digging the doggie vibe around here," said Dr. Ami Wen. Her mohawk had been combed over, hiding the shaved portion on one side. Still it was an amazing shade of iridescent blue.

"Dr. Wen. What a wonderful surprise. I didn't expect you…"

"The check cleared yesterday and here I am." She beamed at Alice. Her two front teeth were significantly larger than the rest of her smile, and it reminded Alice of Bugs Bunny. But just like Bugs, it was charming rather than goofy.

"The cat?" asked Alice.

"Oh, Pookie and I are a package deal. She helps me with my best ideas, but man, she don't like dogs."

"You knew the intended subjects would be dogs."

"Yeah, she'll get over it. She learned to like howler monkeys and those little shitheads will bite your finger off without even a 'howdy do.'"

Alice burst out laughing.

"Glad you have a sense of humor. Some 'stick up her ass' chic stopped by earlier. She looked like her face would crack if she laughed. She wore shoes that cost more than my last home and when Pookie made herself to home sitting on them, I thought she'd faint. Said her name was Louise something."

"Louise O'Neil is our head engineer. She's great at what she does, and a nice person, but she doesn't like change." Alice began walking toward the dog pens where the frenzied barking started again. The bright summer sunshine caused her to shade her eyes against the brightness streaming in through the wall of glass in the dog's area. Alice was relieved to find that all the dogs but two had found homes. The gray cat sat down in front of one of the cages and the dog inside stopped barking, sniffed the cat and lay down.

"Man, these dogs have the life. Their cages are bigger than my apartment in Romulus, and they have all this grass to run on." Dr. Wen pointed at the turf area thirty feet long and twenty feet wide between the cages. "I have never seen a more humane housing for research subjects."

"I think it's important to treat them well if we are going to use them for our profit," said Alice. "Please see that these last two dogs find homes. We will need larger ones to use for Excellosteo, Dr Wen."

Dr. Wen stopped and turned toward Alice. "I like that about you stretch. Call me Ami."

It was two o'clock before the delivery guys showed up and Alice talked them into assembling everything rather than face her wrath. Her new office was not as plush as her old one on the twenty-third floor. The veneered black fiberboard, fake marble top and black pleather chair didn't feel faux to her at all.

Alice could definitely call this day "high energy." Dr. Cindy had another name for this convenient burst of energy produced by her mood disorder. She had put everything in the office where it belonged, working around the delivery men who seemed to work in slow motion. She had planned to be done by sunset, but beat that deadline by two hours.

With everything in its final place, Alice took her First Edition of Alice's Adventures in Wonderland out of the heavy wooden box made to protect her treasure. Flipping through the pages, she smiled at the original illustrations. She was definitely not that little girl and probably never was. Closing the box, she placed it in the perfect place on her new desk, the right-hand corner.

"There," said Alice.

"Where?" answered Bradley James. He stood in her doorway wearing a blue suit with a faint windowpane pattern, a snow-white shirt and a tie the exact color of his eyes. Alice squirmed in her chair. Nobody wore a suit much better than Brad. He walked to her desk and stood in front of it. She hadn't thought it necessary to buy a chair to go in front of her desk, as the head of R&D hardly had as many meetings as the CEO. Instead, she had chosen a long black couch to go against the back wall a few feet from her desk. From the couch, one could see a wonderful view of the little park next to the building out a window unusually large for what had become a huge storage closet before she commandeered it.

"You know, I like this office better than the one up there."

Brad pointed with his thumb to the ceiling. "And this view..." He plopped down on the couch and propped his feet on the little fake wood table in front.

Alice walked over and stood looking out the window. "Yeah, when I discovered this gem, I was sorry I had redone the twenty-third floor." She realized how close she stood to Brad. She could reach out and touch him and there was the couch. He stood up and took a step toward her. She could hear the blood rushing in her ears.

"Alice, it's so good to have you back."

She opened her mouth to remind him that he was the reason she had left, but he stood so near. He reached up and, placing his hands on either side of her face, kissed her. His thumbs softly caressed her cheeks. She kissed him back. His tongue teased her lips, and she opened to him. Brad stopped and looked at her as if waiting for permission. The small smile she returned gave him what he needed, and he unbuttoned her blouse and unhooked her bra.

"Oh, God, I have missed these." Sliding Alice's bra down, he took one in one hand and with his other hand held the other, licking the nipple while she watched his tongue stroking her, sending waves of pleasure through her.

Alice moaned. Brad had his tie and jacket off and his pants unzipped in the time it took to draw a breath. Alice took a step back, dropping onto the couch. He pulled off her jacket, blouse, and bra in one motion. Grabbing her hands, he held them up over her head and kissed her again. She moaned again. Brad pulled up her skirt, tugged her panties off, and knelt in front of her.

"There's that wet pussy I've missed so much." His fingers slid into her. "I'm going to finger you 'til you scream, baby."

He did, and she did.

She hoped the door was soundproof enough, but she knew most of the employees were home and Andy had left an hour ago and that the outside window was a one-way mirror. "Fuck me, Brad, hard and deep," she breathed hard against his ear. His pants were off and as she leaned back, he slid her skirt off. He leaned into her, kissing her and filling her as he looked into her eyes.

"Yes, baby." He slid into her one of the most gorgeous cocks she had ever seen or felt. It was not excessively long, but deliciously thick and hard for her. The lovely large head of his cock hit her in exactly the right place inside her to make her come again after a few strokes. Brad knew this well.

After he came with a groan, Brad lay down the length of the couch and pulled her into his arms on top of him. She had determined not to say anything mushy to him. This was probably another mistake born of a bipolar hyper episode's poor judgement, not true love.

"I've missed you," said Brad, his breath soft against her ear. "Things don't have to change because I am your boss. I never reported you for harassment when it was the other way around"

"We are physically compatible." Alice settled down with her head on his chest. She actually dozed off while lying in his arms with the warmth of his body against her. She jerked awake. Brad laughed.

"I guess we broke in this place." He kissed her shoulder and his strong, rough hand caressed her hip and slid down her leg.

"Yeah." She had no idea what to say. This wasn't a date or an attempt at a relationship. They had just had sex on her new office couch. She knew in a hyper state her judgement could be impaired and that getting naked and riding him to tuna town proved that to be true.

"This was amazing. You are amazing," said Brad.

"Yeah," was all she could manage.

Brad sat up, taking Alice with him. "I gotta get home. Barney isn't good at holding his pee all day." He gave her a quick peck on the lips and began to dress. He finished and stood looking at her. "Thank you," he said and walked out the door.

Alice sat on the couch looking out the window with her clothes in a pile on the floor. Thank God she had made sure the office window was mirrored on the outside except for a little corner where the coating had been peeled back. Nobody would be looking in at this time of day. What the hell was she doing? Brad was now her boss. What business had she of naked dancing with him on the work premises? Hadn't she decided against irresponsible behavior? Not that they hadn't done that before when the positions had been reversed and he had made her scream on the couch in his old office, weeks ago, before Jonathan had insisted that he loved her and she needed to see only him. Exactly how many weeks ago?

Chapter Ten

MY KINDA LOVER

Alice sat behind her new desk the next morning, staring at her fake leather couch and smiling. No thirteenth century prince or Samoan king knew how to make her come like Brad. Jonathan had been extremely skilled in bed, but he never looked deep into her soul with those blue eyes and called her Baby. She had way too much to do to sit thinking about Brad James.

Just because his wife left him single, didn't mean a relationship with him would be a good idea. His beauty pageant contestant administrative assistant probably kept him satisfied. Anyway, he said, "Thank you" and left. Checking her phone every half an hour had not made him text her either. The closet men were a lot less trouble, and she never had to see any one of them again.

A quick rap on her door and Louise O'Neil walked into Alice's office. "Thank all the powers that be, Brad James hasn't managed to drive this place into the ground yet."

"We need to give him a chance."

"Uh huh. At least he was smart enough to create a new position we have needed for a long while and talk you into taking it." Louise walked to the couch and smoothing the skirt of her palest pink linen dress, sat down.

"So you've met Dr. Wen?" asked Alice.

"Yes, I have. Her skills are what we need if we are going to expand into orthopedic implants. I hired some brilliant engineers away from Stryker and Zimmer like you suggested. My people are great at designing pacemakers and cardiac implantables, but we need help making the jump to designing any kind of orthopedic prosthesis." Louise's black eyes were staring out the window. Louise turned back toward Alice. "There are plenty big challenges with this Excellosteo, but I think it is undeniably brilliant. It utilizes so much of the setup and materials we already have and everyone agrees we need something big to pull us back up where we belong." Louise leaned forward to the edge of the couch. "I wanted to give you a heads up about the new hires before our meeting next week. I emailed you the info about them."

Alice pulled up the email on her laptop. "Yeshia Douglas. Looks like your usual engineer wonder kid. Whooo hoo, look at those awards. I bet she didn't come cheap."

"It is pronounced Y like the letter, plus eshia. She came to us within the range you gave me," said Louise with a wry smile.

"Vincent Torresi, hmmm. With this much experience, he can't be a kid."

"No, mid-fifties is my guess. He was worth the little bit I went over budget. He's worked on knees for Stryker over the last decade and that is exactly what we need. Knows how to work within a budget. Happens to be single and pretty hot for a white guy."

Alice rolled her eyes. "Not sure I need any more employees to fraternize with."

"Yeah, well, James is your boss now, and has that newly single horn dog thing going on." Louise leaned even farther forward on the couch. "Marsha from accounting saw him doing the pick-up boogie at Bar Napoli in Clayton. She said he left with someone young enough to be his daughter."

"None of my business, said Alice without raising her eyes from her screen." Alice hoped Louise hadn't noticed she no longer looked at anything but her hands.

"You alright?" asked Louise.

She closed her laptop and looked squarely at Louise. "I'm tired. Burning some mid-night oil getting Dr. Wen on board."

"She may be brilliant, but she is an odd one. There's something about her…" Louise stood up and headed toward the door.

"All geniuses are odd. I like her. Thank you for your heads up." Louise knew well that Alice did not like to be blindsided at a meeting any more than she did.

§⚭

It amazed Alice how much she could get done without all the interruptions that a CEO would have during their day. She actually found she didn't need an administrative assistant at all. No one could adequately replace Jonathan, in the office anyway.

It felt a little odd to get home so early, but she was no longer responsible for the entire company's functioning. Baby Hightower made her very tired this evening and after eating a little dinner, she settled on the couch with her laptop to solve the wardrobe problem this baby was creating. None of her skirts or blouses would button. It seemed to happen overnight. Yesterday her suit fit perfectly and today none of them would button. Switching to dress pants with elastic waists, a stretchy top and a long lab coat might do the trick for a while. Perhaps everyone at work would accept the change as part of her new position. She had ordered everything she needed and decided to treat herself to a good night's sleep with her favorite tripod feline.

❧

"Are you afraid of a relationship with this man?" asked Dr. Cindy a week later.

"A little," said Alice as she sat on Dr. Lester's velvet couch. "He is freshly divorced and I'm not sure he is…"

"It may be wise to take this slow, but he is not asking you to spend the rest of your life with him. Spending time with a real man could be a very good thing."

Alice opened her mouth to reply, and it felt as though someone kicked her in her abdomen. She bent over. "Wow. Something…" It happened again. "This really hurts." She wrapped her arms tight around herself. "Do you think it could be Braxton-Hix contractions?"

"I had them with all three of my children, but not until the last trimester. You need to call your OB. We can talk about your love life next time."

❧

Alice looked up at the ceiling with her feet in the stirrups as Dr. Thompson completed her pelvic exam. She tried to remember that his name wasn't Justin Bieber just because he looked like it should be. It had been only two minutes by the clock on the wall, but it seemed like an hour until he spoke.

"Pain and spotting is pretty common in pregnancies in women of…"

"My age," answered Alice. "You sure it's okay?"

"Heart sounds strong. You've only gained six pounds. Sweet! These kinds of pregnancies do have a high rate of spontaneous abortion or even becoming nonviable, but no need to freak."

"I'm not freaking, this is my child and I don't…" Tears ran down her cheeks.

"I get it. You are understandably worried, but don't be.

Everything is normal at this point. The only risk is your age. The pains have stopped and I will see you soon for the ultrasound. But you need to stay off your feet for a while. At least until there is no more spotting." He flashed his blinding white teeth at her and left the room. Alice took the rest of the afternoon off.

§

Wrapped in a quilt Susan had made her, she sat on her couch reading everything she could find online about geriatric pregnancies. That is what they called it if you were pregnant after forty. Alice would turn fifty by the time the child arrived. *What to Expect When You are Expecting*, would arrive tomorrow, her eBay app told her. She needed to do everything she could to make certain her child arrived healthy.

Susan knocked on the door, and Alice let her in. "I saw your car," said Susan. "What's wrong? You're never sick and if you are, you still go to work." She sat down next to Alice. "Now I know something is wrong. You didn't even wince as I sat on your snow-white couch in my nasty scrubs."

"It's nothing. I was feeling a little tired and decided to spend the afternoon working from home."

Susan leaned close to Alice, examining her face. "You look great. Your skin is…" Susan stopped talking and Alice could see the little wheels in Susan's head turning? She looked down at Alice's belly bulging out of her unbuttoned skirt.

"You're pregnant! That's why you wouldn't drink my wine and you have the skin of a fifteen-year-old."

Alice didn't say a word, but it was no use. Susan knew her too well. Keeping the secret couldn't go on forever and it felt good that someone else knew. "Yeah."

"Wow." Susan got up, walked into Alice's kitchen, and opened the refrigerator door. "Good girl. Milk, salad and yogurt. I thought I would have to drag your ass to the grocery store. Babies can't grow on the crap you usually eat. When are you do?" She took the milk out of the fridge, checked the expiration date and found a glass to fill.

"Middle of December, the doctor's best guess. Aren't you going to ask who the father is?"

"No. Can't be Jonathan's or no way would he have ghosted. That's probably why he left, so there is really only one other possibility. Have you told Brad?" She handed Alice the milk.

"No." Alice concentrated on the screen of her laptop. She knew Susan was right, and she had to tell him, but she couldn't bear the thought that he might reject her too once he found out.

"Don't you think he has the right to know?"

"I have time, and I'm afraid he won't…"

"Auntie Susan will be here no matter. They'll call you Grandma at Kinder Swim, but I think you can handle that. You look younger than you did five years ago. Being preggers works for you."

Chapter Eleven

PEOPLE ARE STRANGE

"So happy to have this incredible team on board," said Alice to the four people seated across from her at the long table in the conference room. Yeshia Douglas looked at her unblinking. Her huge red framed glasses befitted a brilliant engineer nerd. Her hair was shaved close and would have looked masculine if her face hadn't been so lovely. Large brown eyes surveyed Alice as she spoke. Her bright red lipstick made Yeshia look more like an exotic African super-model than a celebrated engineer. It was Vincent Torresi that made Alice falter from the script on her screen.

He sat directly across from her and wore a golf shirt with the Excellcardia logo. The form fitting shirt displayed the muscles in his arms much better than the suits that she loved so much. His face had the ruddy look of someone who spent a lot of time outdoors. His mouth formed a hard line as he looked at her with a pair of amazing eyes. Their color, hard to discern as it seemed to reflect several colors at once. Lush, dark lashes framed his eyes. Above them, thick brows gathered like storm clouds. The closely trimmed beard and mustache made Alice want to stroke his face. What would it feel like to run her fingers through his dark brown hair a little on the long side for an engineer and tied back in a neat ponytail? *Snap out of it, Alice.*

Louise explained in detail the progress so far and Alice tried not to stare at Mr. Torresi. Alice had all the information in front of her. This meeting, mostly a formality for the head of R and D to meet the new engineers on her team, left her well pleased.

❧

"What the hell happened here?" said Alice two hours later as she stepped over the files scattered on the floor of Dr. Wen's office. Everything that had been on the desk was now on the floor. The bright pink cloth she had hung on the wall lay torn in two on the floor and Ami knelt, picking up pieces of the Buddha that had been next to her desk.

"Nothing for you to worry about. A little disagreement," said Ami Wen looking up at Alice.

"With whom," said Alice.

Ami laughed. "So proper, 'With whom.'" She continued to pick up the pieces.

"I need an answer."

"An acquaintance…has a temper. No real harm done." She stood up and Alice could see the skin under her left eye turning purple beneath her crooked glasses.

"Are you all right? I'm calling security." Alice reached into her lab coat pocket for her phone.

"No!"

The force of Ami's voice nearly made Alice drop her phone.

"There is really no serious harm done. They won't be back. I can clean this up later. I want to show you the progress we've made growing doggie bones." Ami smiled at Alice.

Returning to her office, Alice still felt uneasy about what had happened in Ami's office.

She called Security and learned that two Asian men had been let into the lab by Dr. Wen about an hour before Alice. Whatever the problem, Ami seemed to have no intention of sharing any more detail than she already had. She thought about instructing Bill, the new head of security, to keep an eye on anyone entering the tenth-floor lab, but then she remembered, security no longer answered to her. Still, she could not risk anything happening to their star researcher.

Alice stood smiling at her reflection in the one-way glass window to security five minutes later. "Do you think you could pull up some surveillance footage for me?" said Alice, pouring on all the sweetness she could muster to the new head of security. He stood arrow straight, and his blue Dickey work uniform was ironed with sharp creases at every opportunity. Colonel Bill must have been retired military. Bill's eyes narrowed. "I'll need an okay from Mr. James."

"Call him, now." She reminded herself that she would have insisted on approving such a request when she was CEO and stood patiently or made an attempt. She knew Brad would okay it since the tenth floor was her responsibility.

She stood watching the screen two minutes later. Alice watched as Ami let the men into the lab. The look on her face was not fearful or friendly, but blank. The men were well dressed and looked like sales types. Undoubtedly, the Excellosteo would involve substantial purchases resulting in a company sending salesman to close the deal in person, but why would they wreck her office if all they wanted was to sell her stuff? The men appeared going into her office, but there had been no reason to set up cameras to watch Excellcarda's new resident genius. Ami must have called down to Andy to okay their coming up the elevator as no one could simply walk into Excellcardia.

Could one of the men in skinny dark suits have been an old boyfriend? Bill pulled the image in closer. One of the two wore his short dark hair moussed straight up. His features were sharp and attractive, looking somewhat familiar, and he filled out his black skinny suit well at the shoulders. The other looked younger, with a softer, but still handsome face and wore his dark hair in a man bun. He obviously worked out by the way the fabric of the suit jacket hugged his biceps. She doubted Ami could have been romantically involved with either of these two violent hotties. A man who would come to your job and wreck your office was better off gone. Ami's explanation proved far from adequate. Alice would remember their faces.

With her very last email of the day sent, Alice hung her lab coat on the back of her chair.

"Heading home?" said a voice that made Alice jump. Ami Wen stood inside her door, holding a plastic storage box. She walked to Alice's desk and set down the box. She had applied makeup to her bruise and her round glasses were again straight.

"I was planning to, but what can I do for you?"

Ami walked to the door that led to the patch of trees behind the building in one direction and the parking lot in the other. She opened the door, looked around and let it slam close. "Yep. They're out there."

"Who?"

"The ferals."

"The what?"

"Feral cats. There's the dumpster where food is discarded and a large patch of trees, that's all they need. I saw a black one from the window in the Dog Lab dragging garbage to the woods. They are never loners." Ami took two stainless steel bowls out of the storage box and headed to the door again. Alice followed. Ami emptied a bottle of water into one and filled the other with dry cat food. She set the bowls down in a patch of dirt near the door and made a kissing sound. A skinny grey cat ran to the food bowl and began gulping down the dry food.

"Poor little guy," said Alice.

"I don't feel sorry for them. I just don't want them to be hungry. They are free to live their lives as they choose." She shut the door. "I will keep the bowls full, if that's alright with you?"

"Sure. I don't want any cats to starve."

"Tomorrow's gonna be an exciting day up on ten. I'm going to try overlaying some osteoblasts over the sample matrix engineering sent me. I have to run simultaneous tests on both doggie and human cells. Dog bone is pretty similar to human but can't take no chances if we plan human trials. That Torresi seems to have given me what I need. Big Stuff."

"Can't wait," said Alice.

෴

Alice's evening would be spent with *What to Expect When You are Expecting*. It mostly told her things she already knew, but it also calmed her fears. "Most women that have spotting and cramps deliver perfectly healthy babies," said the book. She really didn't want to buy all new bras, but her large breasts seemed to be getting huge and very tender, as the book said. If her tops were big enough, no one would notice her bras weren't quite doing their job. It was all she could do to stay awake during work let alone go anywhere for an historic boff this evening. Tomorrow she would see her child for the first time, and she did not want to be uninformed.

Alice woke up two hours later to the sound of her phone. Dr. Wen said the caller ID.

"Hello Ami."

"Hey, Alice. Sorry to bother you at home, but I wonder if you could loan me some money? I'm good for it. I'll pay you in a week."

"How much are we talking about?"

"Ten large. I had some unexpected moving expenses."

Ten thousand dollars was a lot of money, but Alice knew that Ami's salary was sufficient to allow her to pay it back. Still, she did not want to become a bank for any friend or colleague. Nothing sours a relationship like a money issue and a good relationship with Dr. Wen would make things so much smoother and insure the success of Excellosteo.

"I'm sorry, Ami, I can't…"

"Alice Please? It's for my sister, and I can't explain, but it is a matter of life or death," Ami's voice cracked. "You are my only hope."

Alice had a little more than that in her emergency fund. Something in Ami's voice made Alice believe her. "I can get it tomorrow." Might not be a bad idea to have her head researcher in her debt.

"It won't happen again and I will pay in full next Thursday. Believe me, this is a good thing you do and I won't forget it." She disconnected with a beep.

Alice could only hope she had done the right thing.

❧

"The baby is right on track for nine weeks," said her OB with one hand on her abdomen and the other somewhere inside of her.

"We might be able to tell you the sex if you want today?"

She didn't want to spoil the wonderful surprise that would come as a reward for the grueling labor the book had described to her. "No, thank you."

"Okay. I'll tell the tech. She'll grease up your bump and bounce some waves off the kid. I'll be back to go over everything."

Keesha, the ultrasound tech, seemed almost as excited as Alice. "Don't let anybody tell you that you're anything but beautiful," said the young woman who reminded Alice of the actress who played Lysterine in Booty Call. Coolly beautiful, but the expression on her face indicated that, like Vivica A. Fox in the movie, she was not taking any crap from anyone. Alice and her ex-husband had both loved that movie, and she had to admit it was one thing they shared. The sound of a rapid heart-beat that sounded more like a whoosh than a beat, made Alice's heart race and Kesha's eyes go wide. That was the sound of her child. She looked at the screen as the tech moved the probe around her belly.

"That's your baby."

Alice could not believe that it was real. "Dr. Bieb… Thompson said it's perfect for nine weeks."

"He's been out of residency about a minute, but he is a star at delivery." She gave Alice a wide grin.

"Well, that's what matters." Alice sat up to get closer to the screen, eager to see everything.

"There's the head and the spine."

Alice thought that those both looked normal. Suddenly, the little grey speckled blob reached out an arm and Alice felt a flutter. She laughed. This was the first movement she had felt, and she was lucky enough to see as well as feel it. "Wow," she said.

"That's the first you've felt movement? A lot more where that came from. A little early, though. I will have Dr. Thompson come in and go over everything."

Alice had spent the rest of the evening reading about pregnancy and smiling like an idiot every time she glanced at the grainy picture of the odd aquatic creature that would soon be her baby. Did it really look a little like Brad? Of course not. It looked like a gray blob. She was pretty sure he would not want a baby messing with the "horn dog" mojo that Louise had described.

Chapter Twelve

ROCKETMAN

The cell growth experiments had been wildly successful and were proceeding ahead of schedule. Ami had paid her back exactly like she said she would. Alice made Vincent head engineer on the project, with Ami's approval. Almost everything in her work world was good, except that she had seen nothing of the father of her child since they christened her office couch. Must have been too busy giving fuck lessons to the young women he picked up in bars.

Nearly time to go home, Alice wanted to make sure the feral cats had their dinner. She opened the door and six sets of hungry eyes looked at her. She filled the bowls. There were now three, and she watched as the cats munched. It amazed her how they calmly shared the food, two to a bowl. Ami told her they may all be related as is often the case in a feral colony. Tonight, two black ones, two grey tabbies, a little orange one, and the original large gray male devoured the brown chunks. Ami called the big one Elvis, and he was indeed blue suede. Alice heard someone behind her and turned to see Louise.

"What's going on out there? A cat convention?" Louise said, looking out the door.

"It's our feral cat colony. I'm feeding them their dinner."

"Those things can be dangerous. They kill birds, you know."

"Less if you feed them." Alice closed the door and walked toward her desk. Ami usually fed them in the morning, but Alice didn't mind seeing to their supper.

"I guess. I wanted to let you know, the new engineers have a prototype of the femoral head and will be delivering it to Dr. Wen for testing next week. I emailed you the specs and a diagram, but I wanted to brag a little bit in person. Have you seen your boss lately?"

"Who?"

"James."

"He is your boss, too. But, as a matter of fact, and I have not." Alice started to take off her lab coat, but hesitated. Would Louise notice that her pants were not buttoned and Baby Hightower was stretching her blouse's buttons? They would have to know someday, but not today.

"Uh huh. Well, he looks terrible. He has so many meetings, I'm not sure he has time to use the restroom let alone eat anything. He looks like he hasn't had a good night's sleep in weeks."

Alice hid the flash of anger at the mention of Brad James's nights. Alice knew communication was key to being a good leader, but there was such a thing as too many meetings. For the first time since she lost her CEO gig, she did not envy Brad. She remembered how she had struggled in the beginning. She had been an outsider. They all knew Brad, but in a completely different capacity. Alice had no idea which was more of a challenge.

Alice sat back down in the chair behind her desk. "Don't tell me you are feeling for our new CEO. Smarmy, wasn't that what you called him? And aren't you the one that told me of his current social situation? What he does when not at work means nothing to me."

"Glad to hear that. He's still smarmy, but he's working like a dog and not doing the worst job." Louise headed to the door. She smiled and disappeared out the door.

§&

Alice finished her dinner of salad with chicken and yogurt for dessert. She had cooked the chicken breast in the microwave as the packaged kind had way too many preservatives. "Imagine me caring about preservatives," she said to her belly. Rinsing the dishes, she smiled at the fluttering in her abdomen. "You are a busy baby tonight, and you are making me as horny as a goat." She hadn't even peeked into the closet for a couple of weeks. Tonight, what she needed, might well be in there. She needed to be careful, but she could protect the baby and still enjoy the company of some fantasy guy. Besides, Dr. Hoffman had said she had no remarkable ability to affect matter, so what would a little erotic imagination hurt?

A long light blue garment hung on the hanger and booties for her feet sat on the floor.

The garment was a sort of jumpsuit with a zipper down the front made of a sleek, clingy material. Where on earth would one wear a light blue onesey? It had patches sewn on the front. One had a picture of a rocket circling the Earth and some writing she couldn't read. It looked like the Cyrillic alphabet, which looked Russian, maybe? Alice zipped up the front of the suit, which felt snug, as if the material had somehow adapted to her. *Cool.* Even pregnant ladies needed a little style, she thought. The booties were also much more than they seemed. The material she first thought was paper felt warm and shaped to her feet like it was alive after she slipped them on. The whole outfit looked like something a crew member on Star Trek, the Next Generation would wear.

"Oh, please let me have the whole crew tonight." She felt as if she could take on Captain Jean Luc Picard, his first officer, Will Riker, and have libido left over for the anatomically correct android, Data. If she made stuff up, why couldn't that stuff be from her favorite television series in college? She decided to leave her hair clipped up. The look is definitely professional on the Enterprise.

"Whenever, here I come." She slid the balcony door open.

The bright artificial light hurt her eyes as she stepped into what looked like a large artificial tunnel. She smelled nothing. The air felt cool and had no smell at all. Alice felt the world spin and realized her feet were not touching anything. She felt weightless and held her lips together tight to keep from vomiting. The nausea passed. Moving her arms sent her body careening across the tube she now found herself in. It was not a room at all but a long white tube, twenty feet in diameter with metal fixtures and various shaped projections covering the walls of the tube. Holding on to a line of square outcroppings, she made her way down the tube to a small round glass circle. When she pulled up, even with it, she discovered it was a window. Out the window, she saw darkness and stars. At the top, she saw a blue half circle. There were white swirls and large brown blotches on the half circle. One looked like North America. "Wow!" She was in a spacecraft orbiting the earth.

"Hey, where did you come from?" asked a voice from behind her. She tried to turn around and slammed into the wall. An arm reached over and held her still. The arm belonged to a man wearing a dark blue jumpsuit with a patch that read NASA on his right shoulder and several other patches sewn onto his left. He sported a short dark brush cut and startlingly light gray eyes. He held her at arms-length and his eyes swept over her like a man who hadn't seen a woman in months. Alice smiled.

"I thought the Ruskies were sending over a repair guy from Soyuz, not the answer to my every wet dream. Are you real, beautiful?" He smiled back at her.

"I think I'm real. And you are not so bad yourself. I don't know how to fix a damn thing, but I think the company is much better here. Can you think of anything we can do for fun?" Alice reached up and stroked his face. He pulled her toward him and kissed her lips roughly. They crashed into the side of the padded tube. She laughed and reached out to him, putting her hand on his chest, which felt hard with muscles beneath his blue jumpsuit.

"If you're up for a good time, we could head to the fueling bay. The walls are padded and it's narrow enough to keep us from slamming into the walls?" He smiled with one eyebrow raised.

"Oh, padded walls, sounds amazing. I'm Alice, by the way. I'm new up here and haven't adjusted to the weightless thing."

"I'm Jim. I had no idea the Russians had anyone who spoke English, let alone any hot babes. It's just you and me. The next crew doesn't arrive for a week. I'm pretty sure I've lost my mind, but give me your hand. Go stiff and I'll pull you." He towed her as if she were a barge floating on a river of air pushing off of the walls here and there to propel them. Her stomach had settled down and Alice enjoyed the feeling of weightlessness. He opened a hatch and pulled her into another padded section as promised. It felt a little cramped, with only a foot of space on either side of them. Jim gave her another big grin and pulled him to her. He held her head so she didn't move and kissed her. His tongue slid between her lips and his hand reached out, coming to rest on her left breast.

"God knows if I'm going to dream up a woman to end my perpetual case of blue balls, it's going to be a gorgeous blonde with big hooters. May I see them?"

Alice rested her butt against the soft white material of this tube's wall, bent her knees to stabilize her body against the opposite wall, and Jim unzipped her jumpsuit all the way to her waist. Her breasts floated. Jim managed to stabilize himself and reached over to place his hands on her breasts. "If I'm dying of hypoxia, these are exactly the tits I would dream of on my way outta this world."

Alice closed her eyes and moaned. "Make me come, Jim."

He rubbed her nipples, and she moaned louder. Alice reached over and pulled her suit down, freeing herself of the suit by kicking her legs. It floated off.

Jim followed her lead and kicked off his suit and the tightey-whiteys he wore underneath.

Jim's body was covered in fine dark hair culminating in a large dark patch between his legs, thick as an old growth forest. His gravity defying erection called her name, and she worked her way down his body, holding on to his arms and then his hips until she was eye to eye with his lovely cock. She stuck out her tongue and slid it down the long length of him. She reached around to hold on to his ass to steady herself and took him deep into her mouth. His muscular butt felt as furry as the rest of him and she giggled.

"Oh yeah. If this is what hypoxia feels like, I don't want no oxygen. Suck it, Alice. Oh God." His hips bucked, slamming her into the padding on the opposite wall, and she felt him come in her mouth. He tasted sweet, like maple syrup and basil. She pulled away and a drop of semen escaped from her mouth and formed a tiny glistening ball hanging in front of her face. She swallowed and stuck out her tongue, catching the little globe and pulling it in to her mouth.

"I haven't touched a woman in nearly a year. Give me a few minutes and I will be stiff as a board. I know me. Beating myself off every night to sleep. Want me to eat you while we are waiting?"

"Use your fingers," said Alice, taking his hand and placing it between her legs. Two fingers slid into her and began the motion that would make her scream in short order. "Suck my nipples," said Alice with her eyes closed. She climaxed.

"I bet the Russians can hear that even across ten miles of vacuum. Damn girl, spread those legs. I'm hard as hell."

Alice obliged with a smile on her face and moaned again, her butt bouncing off the wall as Jim pumped into her, over and over. He was indeed hard as hell, and the sensation of him sliding into her over and over and never quite touching her drove her off the edge of Fuckville to a place she had only imagined. She looked down to watch his considerable cock disappear again and again inside her. She made not a single sound as she felt him fill her and she saw stars in constellations.

Laughing, Jim pulled a little hose from out of a silver fitting and began hoovering up the little pearl spheres of semen now swirling around them.

"For fuel spills, but works on my spooze lickity split." Jim laughed again and his cock bobbed with the motion. "Bring those gorgeous tits over here. If a meteor hit this tin can, I want to my last breath to be sucking those."

He pushed off and managed to grab Alice around her waist, and true to his word, began sucking on her left nipple. She moaned loudly.

"You're one of those broads who can almost come from nipple sucking, huh."

"Yeah," was all she could say as she felt his tongue circling her nipple. She felt his fingers slip inside her and once again, she was nice and slippery. The fingers rubbed her clit to a properly loud orgasm.

"Damn girl, you come easier than apple pie. Let's rest a little and I will send you back into orbit." He wrapped his arms around her and they floated, locked together in a weight-less cuddle. She closed her eyes and rested her head on his furry shoulder.

❦

Alice must have managed to get some rest after her delicious space sex last night. She felt especially rested and peppy. Her stomach felt a little queasy this morning, maybe the aftereffects of low gravity sex or more likely morning sickness.

Running her emails in record time, she glanced up to see Brad standing in front of her desk, giving her that smile she could not read.

"I want you to know how proud I am of you," said Brad.

"Why?" She thought he looked tense and tired, but no less handsome standing in front of her cheap desk in his very good navy suit.

"You created Excellosteo and you are making it happen."

"I have some pretty amazing help." She smiled at him over her keyboard.

"No doubt, but this will be just what the company needs and I couldn't be prouder of all you have done."

That strange smile was pride, Alice realized. He was proud of her. She had seen him smile when he wanted her; smile when he felt sorry for her; and even smile when she she gave him orders in the past. This was different, this expression of pride. So what if he was into younger women? They could still be friends and amazing coworkers, thought Alice. "Want to make me some dinner to show me how proud you are?"

This time he gave her his very familiar hungry look she had seen so often. "Anytime you say." He smiled widely.

"I will check my schedule and let you know." She pretended to type. If she didn't do something to encourage him to leave, she might drag him over to the couch and....

"Soon?" he asked.

"Soon," she assured him. It would take some thought and courage to tell him about a baby he hadn't thought possible. She knew he had two grown daughters, and she could not imagine the look on his face when she told him he might have another child by Christmas.

❧

Alice sat on the edge of Dr. Cindy's velvet fainting couch that evening. "I am a little anxious about telling the father he is going to be one."

"That is quite natural. Does he have other children?"

"Yes, two daughters, one married and one in college. I can remember him saying how happy he was not to have little children anymore." Alice rubbed the soft tufting of the couch.

"That doesn't mean he doesn't want anymore. Some men enjoy the challenge to feel young again by having a child when their others are grown." Dr. Cindy looked up from her yellow pad at Alice. "Are you prepared to raise the child on your own?"

Alice sat in silence for a long moment. "Yes. It would be ideal if he would be around for the kid, but I will do whatever it takes." Alice patted her belly.

"Well then, his reaction could be emotionally upsetting, but will not directly affect your life or the life of your child. It is amazing how the mothering instinct kicks in when you have never felt it before. Same time next week?"

⚜

Unlocking her apartment door after a long work week that felt successful, Alice realized she couldn't remember that last time she felt the baby move. How could she have been so involved with work and life that she didn't even notice such a thing? Her heart pounded, and she took the elevator down to Susan's.

"I haven't felt the baby since…I don't know when. Something's wrong," Alice said to Susan the second she opened the door.

"Come on, I'll drive you." Susan wrapped her arm around Alice for a brief and reassuring hug and they headed down to the garage in a serious hurry.

The fact that Dr. Thompson wasn't on call caused a hard knot in Alice's stomach as soon as she heard. She lay on the exam table, gripping Susan's hand tight and staring at the ceiling. The OB on duty looked old enough to be Alice's grandfather. He looked at her over the sheet as Susan held her hand. "I'm sorry. There is no heartbeat."

Alice closed her eyes and squeezed out tears. It felt like her own heart had stopped.

"Listen to me, Methuselah, get somebody in here that knows what the hell they are doing. My friend has a picture of a baby in an ultrasound!"

The doctor pulled off his gloves, took his stethoscope from around his neck, and listened to Alice's belly again.

"There's no heartbeat and her uterus isn't overly large for a woman of this age."

Alice heard the words, and she knew he was correct. Her pants had felt looser for the last few days. It must have died. Her baby had died.

"Oh, Alice, I'm so sorry." She hugged her friend tight against her. Alice stared ahead, and the tears stopped.

"I didn't even know when… What kind of mother doesn't even know when her child dies?"

"These late in life pregnancies are often not sustainable. There's not anything you could've done. I recommend making an appointment for a D&C as soon as possible. Your uterus needs to be cleaned out to avoid infection. I can have the nurse schedule for you."

The old doctor stood looking at her as if he wanted to say something more but did not. This was probably where he usually told the woman she could have another, but Alice knew this conception had been some freak miracle that could not be repeated. He turned and walked out of the room.

Alice sat up, her face still blank. "Can you hand me my clothes?" She could feel the lead gather. Heavy metal strands of sadness wrapped her brain, shutting off the world and shutting her down. She wouldn't be devastated, she would be nothing at all.

"You're coming home with me tonight, no argument," said Susan. Alice was in no condition to argue with anyone about anything. She put on her clothes and followed Susan in silence.

The next morning, Susan drove Alice to the outpatient surgery center to have the D&C. Alice said nothing as Susan dropped her off and someone in a pair of blue scrubs wheeled her in to have the procedure.

Alice could only think that when she woke up, any remnant of her child would have been scraped out of her.

Opening her eyes as the anesthesia wore off, she asked the masked person who stood over her, "Was it a boy or a girl?"

"It was simply a mass of tissue, Ms. Hightower, no way to know. I could have run some genetic tests if you had told me beforehand." The voice was Dr. Thompson's and, with his hair covered by a surgical cap, he almost looked like a grownup. He reached over and squeezed her hand. "You should be up and around in a day or two. You may have some spotting for a few days. The cramping will stop in a couple of hours."

Alice didn't want it to stop. It was the last reminder that her baby had ever existed.

Chapter Thirteen

STRAY CAT STRUT

L ying in bed for two days with Otis curled up behind her knees, changed nothing. Alice shook her head as if she could shake off the thick metal fog wrapping her brain and insulating her against the anguish that threatened to burst out of her like lightning. Bless Susan for scouring the apartment for baby stuff and removing it all. Even the milk in the refrigerator was gone.

Alice hadn't purchased any baby furniture or nursery decorations for her guest room yet, but she had a few catalogs and the "What to Expect" book...all gone.

Susan had fed Otis and filled the fridge with plastic containers of soup. Though she still felt the grip of her loss tight inside her, on Monday morning, Alice went to work. A hole opened in the middle of her chest where her heart had once been, but her project was at a critical stage and the team needed their leader. There was no way having this baby had been a good idea, and things do happen for a reason. That is what she told herself when the tears welled up and ran down her cheeks and the sadness threatened to tear her into pieces.

She wiped her eyes and looked up from her laptop to see a

huge bag of Meow Mix moving toward her. Ami's face peaked around the side of the bag, smiling her Bugs Bunny smile.

"Hey Alice. I got this on sale and I thought the gang might appreciate some of the brand name stuff." She set the bag down and dragged it to the door. Opening the door, Ami made the kissing sound that the cats knew was their signal for chow.

"Wow, so now there are seven of them," said Alice, watching Ami fill the bowls.

"I think there may be a lot more if we don't start doing some TNR."

"What exactly is TNR?"

"It stands for trap, neuter and release. That's how you get a stable and healthy colony." Ami beamed. "I've got traps at home, but I can't do it by myself. You know Elvis the big blue one, his Priscilla is the little gray tabby." She pointed to the cats. "The two fuzzy black ones are Milli and Vanilli, Can't tell if they are males or females, their butts are too furry."

"Very musical."

"Yeah, and then the big black one is Wolfgang, the orange one wearing the white boots is Nancy…

"Sinatra no doubt." Alice realized she was smiling as she watched the cats.

"Yeah, and last but not least, the beautiful calico girl is Donna Summer. Ain't she something?" Ami stood up and Elvis rubbed against her leg. "What kind of car do you have?"

"A Porche."

"Well, that can't hall traps." Ami closed the door.

"My friend has a Cadillac Escalade," said Alice to Ami and took her seat behind her desk. Smiling felt a bit easier. She knew Susan wouldn't mind swapping cars for a few hours.

"Now we're talkin'. We could fit a butt load of traps in that metal monster." Ami dropped onto the couch and propped her feet up on the table in front of it. "I came here mainly to tell you that we have bone growing like weeds all over the new matrix. It took them a couple of tries but this stuff seems to be perfect."

"Great. Any luck on the cartilage matrix for the joint surfaces?"

"Nah. The last stuff was too slippery. My teensy tinsy cells need something they can grab on to...more surface area for attachment. I have been reading about joint designs. It might work to replace the head of the trochanter with our bone and use some of the patient's stem cells to regenerate the cartilage. They are doing that kind of regeneration as a therapy. Would cut down on the design time and the clearance time too. Easier for the surgeon, too. I gave engineering the results and the new specs."

"Sounds like another genius idea. I am pleased with the progress so far. We should have a trochanter head to show the board of directors in a few weeks?"

"Thanks, but I kind of stole the idea from titanium joint designs and I'll give it my best. Now let's talk about trappin' cats. Can you meet me here on Saturday? There's a vet doing a special TNR event and we can get as many as we can catch for forty bucks each."

"Sure, I don't have any plans." That was true and Dr. Cindy had recommended staying busy as a remedy for the scalpel of grief that hid in the corners of her mind and sprang on her out of nowhere cutting deep as she tried to go about her life. Keeping busy didn't make her feel any less sad, but it helped fill the time that might otherwise be wasted in bed or crying on her couch. Maybe helping kitties was what she needed.

§

"I'm taking your advice, busy, busy, busy," said Alice, staring at the ceiling in Dr. Cindy Lester's office. "It doesn't make it hurt any less, but it keeps me out of bed. Work is really crazy, new project. I have become fairy godmother to a feral cat colony. Haven't been to the closet or taken Brad up on his offer."

"How does that make you feel?"

Alice thought for a long moment. She knew you weren't supposed to think about your emotional reactions, just feel them, but Alice needed to think about her feelings, anyway. The death of her baby left a numb place inside of her that was no longer easily reached. "I don't feel as devastated as I did at first, but empty, which is literally true." She rubbed her left hand against her stomach.

"That is a step up, though it may not feel like it. Keep putting one foot in front of the other and let yourself mourn when you need to."

"I'm sure this pregnancy was never meant to be. It was some kind of freak thing that I got pregnant at my age. All for the best." Alice stretched the muscles of her face in an attempt at a smile. The look on Cindy Lester's face let her know it wasn't a very good attempt.

"It was rare, and that made it special," said Dr. Cindy.

"It still hurts deep in my bones, but I can't help think that I would not have been a good mother. My mother, for all her talent and her beauty, never seemed to want to spend time doing the mother thing. She did it, I guess. We never went hungry."

"You would have done the best you could, as we all do. Our children make choices that we can't control and..." Alice saw sadness in Cindy Lester's eyes. She set down the yellow notepad and said, "You keep doing the best you can and I will see you next week. You know you can call if you need before."

❧

Alice finished thirty minutes on her elliptical and headed to the kitchen to grab a can of dinner. She heard her phone make the sound for a text. She hit the message square and there on the screen were the cutest pair of basset eyes looking up at her with the words, "Somebody misses you." It was Barney's picture, but the words were Brad's. Maybe he was getting tired of dating the young stuff and felt like coming back to mature women like he once told her he preferred.

"What are you cooking tonight?" texted Alice.

"Grilling Salmon. Come on over," answered Brad.

Didn't she deserve a good meal and some masculine company? "Be there in forty-five minutes," she answered. He lived in Clayton, a ten-minute drive, but a girl had to take a shower before having dinner at a gentleman's house. Was she really ready so soon after… Maybe it was time she had a little fun, it was only dinner. *Could dinner with Brad James ever be just dinner?*

Chapter Fourteen

DANCING IN THE SHEETS

A lice stood on Brad's front porch in her very best white with spring flowers, Maggy London dress and silver platform sandals. She could never feel over dressed in this neighborhood of million-dollar brick Tudor homes. The maids probably wore clothes that cost more than hers.

"Wow, you look great," Brad said upon opening the door. He hugged her tight, smashing her breasts against his chest. Barney welcomed Alice by jumping up a couple of inches on his pudgy little basset legs and giving a woof.

"I think he remembers me," said Alice.

"He asks about you, often." And there was that look. Blue eyes sparkling as if the glass of wine he held was at least his second. He wanted her. The look made Alice want to throw him down on the marble of his foyer, but her ass and knees were glad she refrained. She bent down to rub Barney's tummy. The pink scar reminded her of the sacrifice the old dog had made for research. The new vessels that were implanted gave him several more doggie years, and Brad's adoption of him assured they would be spent in luxury.

Brad took her hand as if she were his high school girlfriend and led her through his home. They passed the elegant living room undoubtedly decorated using a talented interior designer to a dark wood French door. The door opened out onto a deck that ran the entire length of the house and overlooked a lawn of lush grass and wall of trees and shrubs blocking off the street. The overall effect…green serenity. Delicious scents float up her nostrils from a barbecue at the end of the deck. It was too large to be called a pit. It had cobalt blue tiled extensions where utensils lay and whitewashed maple cabinets below. Comfortable looking white metal chairs with blue and white striped cushions sat nearby and Brad motioned to her to take a seat.

"Need to check our dinner." He opened the grill, and the smell made Alice's mouth water. Brad bent down to open a small refrigerator and handed her a glass of wine he'd already poured.

"Thanks." She had no reason to turn it down and took a sip.

"Remember?" said Brad.

She smiled and raised her eyebrows, having absolutely no idea what he meant.

"It's J. Lohr Chardonnay." He smiled wide.

That had been the wine he offered her the first time they… Alice searched her mind for how to describe their past activities. Made love sounded too mushy. Fucked seemed a little coarse, though accurate. She settled for slept together because it sounded cordial yet a little sexy.

"It's delicious."

"Almost as delicious as you." He stood in front of her chair, looking down at her. She took a big gulp of the wine, set down her glass and thought, *Game on Mr. James.* Standing up, his arms went around her and his lips met against hers. A little moan escaped her lips.

"Is this what you want, Alice?"

"Yes." Her words a coarse whisper.

He took her hand again and led her back through the

house up a flight of stairs carpeted in thick white carpet and into what had to be the master bedroom. The pale gray paisley print covered king-sized bed held no less than twenty accent pillows. He must not have changed a thing since his wife left him. Brad didn't seem like the kind of man who picked out accent pillows in several different colors and shapes.

He sat on the bed and pulled her down to him. This kiss was different. No gentle caress with his tongue or tender teasing with its tip. This kiss, forceful and delicious, mirrored the action of his cock to come, filling her, owning her. Alice moaned and felt a strong contraction between her legs. She had not worn panties, maybe because the line would have shown under the thin summer dress and maybe not. He slid his hand up her thigh and she spread her legs.

Brad slid his rough fingers into her and Alice made a noise deep in her throat, her cries now louder as he teased her clit.

"Is that what my baby wants?"

"Yes." Her answer breathy and soft.

He moved his finger faster until Alice could hold back not a second longer and came hard and loud.

Brad laughed, with his lips still against hers. He stood up and removed his shirt, throwing it over a silver velvet upholstered chair. She knew what came next, but no matter how many times it happened, when he slid down his pants and his cock sprang up, she gasped. Brad reached down, caught the hem of her dress, and pulled it up and off over her head. He unhooked the clasp of her bra and it dropped on the bed. He filled his hands with her breasts. He squeezed, gently at first, and with his thumbs, he brushed each nipple until it was hard beneath his fingers. Alice moaned.

"What do you want now, Alice?"

"You inside me," she said. He put his hands under her hips and pulled her toward the end of the bed. Looking into her eyes, he gave her what she'd asked for.

"Oh, Brad." Alice wrapped her legs around him and

reached up to hold his ass in her hands, loving the feel of the muscles contracting as he slid in and out of her. The power of those muscles drove his thick hard cock into her over and over. His eyes full of her, he gave her what she wanted most, and he knew it. She heard herself cry out with exquisite pleasure as he groaned and stopped his movement, still looking into her eyes.

He smiled at her and continued to give her what she asked for. Brad made her come again with stamina worthy of a South Seas king. His eyes still locked on hers, he said, "Let's put our clothes back on and have that dinner. We can come back here for dessert," Brad said, pulling on his blue boxer briefs and then his shorts and shirt. He disappeared out the door and down the stairs.

Alice found her bra under some pillows, hooked it, and slipped her dress over her head. She stepped into the bathroom she found after opening several doors. The mirror above a stainless-steel vessel sink reflected Alice's silly grin and freshly fucked hair. She ran her fingers through her hair and headed down the stairs.

Guided by a delicious scent, she found the deck again and picked up her wine glass. Alice stood sipping as Brad slid a large piece of salmon off the grill onto a platter. With tongs, he placed perfectly browned spears of asparagus next to the fish. "Grab your wine. I like to eat in the kitchen."

Alice followed him to a white marble topped island with six whitewashed maple high stools. He had set the table already with plates and silverware. The kitchen didn't look like Brad's taste either, as it was white enough to make you shade your eyes. The only color, the stainless steel of the Viking stove and Subzero refrigerator. Nothing in this kitchen looked as if it had ever been used. The grill must have been Brad's domain.

The salmon tasted perfect; slightly crisp around the edges and deliciously moist. She had never had better asparagus, dusted lightly with some exotic spice. "Amazing. You're still an excellent cook," said Alice, setting down her fork after her last bite.

"I cook what I like…good food. Another glass of wine before dessert?" He smiled that smile that made her wet all over again.

"Yes, please." He refilled her glass, and she drank deep looking only at him. His expression was no longer hungry, but like he knew a little secret, one that would bring her more pleasure than any girl had a right to.

With her plate clean, she sat smiling at him,.Brad said, "Ready for dessert, baby?" He took her hand and planted a kiss on the palm.

"Yes."

Again they climbed the stairs to the master bedroom, but this time he pulled back the paisley silk bedspread revealing pale grey sheets subtly striped with silver. The perfect sheets for her favorite silver fox, she thought.

Alice pulled off her dress and threw it and her bra somewhere on the floor. Brad, naked, lay on his side, waiting for her by the time she slid under the covers. He took her face in his hands and kissed her soft and sweet. Then reached for her left breast with his hand and sucked the right nipple gently, now nipping with his teeth. He looked up at her slowly, licking and watching her enjoy the motion of his tongue. He pulled on the other nipple hard enough to cause those little moans deep in her throat.

"Want to suck my cock?"

"Yes, please." Alice got to her knees and took his luscious appendage in her hands. She slid her lips down the length, wetting it with saliva, so her fingers slid smoothly up and down as she sucked, her tongue teasing the little opening.

"So good, baby. That feels so good." Alice almost laughed. Men always seemed to say that, like she didn't know how good it made them feel. She loved sliding her fingers up and down as she slid her mouth over each vein and ridge. Tasting him, enjoying his pleasure, she felt that clenching between her legs that would make that hot cock slide in so easy.

"Ride me, baby. I want to look at you." She climbed astride him and he slid in hard and deep. He reached up and took her breasts in his hands. He squeezed and she increased her pace, sliding up and down the length of him. Alice leaned forward to feel the thick head of his cock hit that sweet spot in her that made her come so hard. "That's it, baby, come with me."

Alice gripped him with her thighs and rode his cock hard, ramming herself onto him. He closed his eyes tight, and she felt that rip in the universe of an absolutely cataclysmic orgasm. She made no sound, and she collapsed on top of him. He wrapped his arms around her and rolled them on their right sides.

They lay face to face, looking into each other's eyes. "This is my favorite part, holding you after you come hard." He kissed her forehead.

"I can feel my favorite part dripping down my thighs and messing up your fancy sheets." They laughed together. He pulled her head into his chest.

She lay content until she heard him snoring softly and a few tears leaked out of her eyes and dripped on the silver striped pillowcase. Their baby was gone. Nothing she said could change that. Telling him would not make her feel better. Some things were not meant to be, and the world would have to do without any child they made together.

Chapter Fifteen

WALK OF SHAME

Alice unlocked her office door the next morning thirty minutes late. She smiled to think that the boss would have been late too after the morning quickie turned into a mutual shower and…

"Hey, Stretch. You must have had some kind of night to make you late," said Ami Wen, who sat on Alice's office couch.

"How did you get in here?" said Alice. She walked to her desk, dropped her purse, and turned to Ami for an explanation.

"Hacked the door code to the outside door. The cats needed their grub and were not giving a shit about you sleeping in. Really should change that combination to the door. Four-digit codes are far too simple. Anyone can get in here."

"Obviously." Alice sat behind her desk and opened her laptop. "How is our little feral kitty colony?"

"All those we trapped and neutered are getting fat and lazy like they should. Elvis still won't go into the trap and Priscilla, the little gray and white tabby, is getting fatter every day. I think she will drop her kittens in a couple of weeks. Like her boyfriend, she won't go near the trap."

"We will get her once she has had those kittens." She looked up over the screen of her laptop at Ami. "Anything else I can do for you?"

"I did want you to know that the newest bone is growing in a layer thick enough to provide structural integrity, and I have all the pretty pictures and graphs ready for that meeting tomorrow. Were gonna need lots more dough to get the job done so you need to wow them."

"I will do my best. The data and models are impressive."

❦

Alice paced in the hall, waiting to go into the boardroom. The baby pink suit she had purchased for this important event fit well and said serious yet feminine, she thought. Her shoes were tall, four-inch heels, but black and conservative in style. She could care less what those misogynistic old farts on the board thought of her clothes, but this outfit exuded confidence, and she needed every bit.

Brad seemed to be taking his time setting the stage for her. Alice jumped when the door opened.

"You ready, Ms Hightower?" asked Brad. His smile conveyed his confidence and pride in her.

"Sure thing, Boss man." He held the door, and she walked into the room as if she owned it.

A half an hour later, she walked back out. She could still hear them clapping, but damned if she would stand there one second longer than necessary. There was little doubt that the board would approve her request for 750,000 more dollars to proceed with the vital research. Brad was CEO, let him stand there answering their stupid questions, she was leaving early.

"All 750 big ones. Great job!" said Brad's text. "Buy you a martini to celebrate?" said the next one.

"Sure." She texted in answer. Jonathan had always had expensive champagne on hand to celebrate with, but they were very different men. Brad was still here, and she never had to find out what he would have done when she told them about the baby. The thought had seemed like a silver lining until the stab of cutting pain in her chest reminded her it was too early to find anything good about the death of her child.

"Meet me at Tony's at 6:00 p.m." She texted Brad as she stood in the elevator. She wanted to head home and take a long soak in her tub and see if Mary at Vitality Spa had time to do her nails before this evening. A night with a handsome man in the nicest place in town felt like exactly what she needed after two weeks of late nights getting that presentation perfect.

❧

It seemed a little odd to see Susan's SUV in her spot in the garage as she pulled into her own space. Susan saw patients until 6:00 p.m. normally. A beat up Volkswagen Bug was parked in Susan's second spot. It looked like a car Susan's daughter Bailey would drive. She would have been at home in the seventies with her dress and style; a true hippy, five decades late. Susan had not mentioned anything about a visit, but Alice knew her friend would be thrilled. Bailey lived in California where she was working on her dissertation in some kind of physics that Alice had never heard of.

She stopped at Susan's floor in the building. She hadn't seen Bailey in ages and it would be fun to watch Susan fuss over her only child as if she was five, even though she was a grownup getting her doctorate. She might actually be baking and that could not be missed. Bailey answered the door. She had her father's light brown hair and height, but her bright green eyes were Susan's. The look on her face was not that of a daughter happy to be visiting. She stepped aside without a word and Alice walked in. Susan sat on Alice's favorite pink cloud chair.

"Oh God," said Alice in response to Susan's expression. "Is the cancer back?"

"David….is…he's…" said Susan.

"Dad is missing. His plane went down somewhere in Chad." Bailey's voice sounded robotic, as if she had shut off all feeling.

Alice knelt in front of Susan, whose eyes were wide, blank and dry. She wrapped her arms around Susan, who didn't move a muscle. Still Alice knelt, holding her friend tight. She felt Susan shaking slightly and heard the sobs she knew must come and was grateful for them.

The sobs continued for some time. When they slowed to silent tears, Susan said, "I want to go sleep for a week." Alice stood, took her friend's hand, and led her to the guest bedroom. She thought the bed she had shared with her husband might be too much.

"No," said Susan, pulling her hand away. "In our room, I can still smell him and pretend he'll be home tomorrow. He could be alright, couldn't he?"

"Of course he could. What can I get you? Tea? Water?" She tucked her friend into the bed and plumped the pillows.

"Gin, the good stuff…Not that dry crap you drink. I want to forget…for a little…"

Bailey still sat staring in the living room and didn't even look up when Alice walked in.

"Bailey, honey, can you show me where your mother keeps her gin. I've never seen her drink anything but wine, but she says she wants gin."

A light seemed to come on behind the girl's eyes, as if helping her mother might make her feel a little better. She climbed up on the counter and reached behind, far into the top cabinet. Her hand came out with the distinctive shaped black bottle of Hendricks gin. It tasted like perfume to Alice, but whatever her friend asked for she would get. She filled a short crystal glass with ice and then the gin.

She handed it to Susan, who took the glass, emptied it and said, "More." Bailey now stood at her mother's bedside.

"Mother, it will make you sick. Don't be unreasonable."

"Have you ever seen me sick from drinking?" Alice knew Susan could drink the entire bottle without getting sick from their experiences in college together. She poured Susan another glass and watched as she downed it like a sailor. She then closed her eyes and buried herself deep under the covers. Alice sat down in the deeply upholstered chair beside the bed and watched as her friend began to snore softly. She kicked off her shoes and closed her eyes for a few minutes.

ॐ

"Hey, hey," someone said as they shook Alice awake. Susan stood beside her, dressed in her scrubs for work.

"Do you think you should…" said Alice.

"Should what? Lay in my bed and cry all day, not my style. Work will keep me busy. I'm going to stay positive. They haven't found the plane. It could have landed somewhere. David always said his pilots could land anywhere."

Alice stood up and wrapped her arms around Susan.

"Really, I appreciate your staying. My life feels on hold, but there are people who need me."

"I'll be back tonight after work," said Alice, her eyes glistening with tears at her friend's pain and her courage.

The mask of bravery on Susan's face slipped a little, and she wiped away a tear. "Go on, you've got some place to be. See you tonight."

Alice picked up her purse where she had dropped it near the door and heard the tone for texts…Brad. She hadn't even called him. She wanted to apologize in person and took the elevator to her apartment, took a quick shower and drove to the office in record time. When she arrived at the twenty-third floor, Brad's administrative assistant did not look up from her laptop for at least two minutes.

"I'll see if Mr. James is available," said the girl without bothering to look up at Alice.

"I can see through the glass that he is in there." Alice walked past the desk and opened the door. Brad was on the phone. He smiled a smile that didn't reach his eyes and motioned for her to sit. He continued his conversation with someone that sounded like his signature sales pitch, and she was glad to hear him do what he did so well. Though he now had a sales force to handle such things, he was still the best.

"What can I do for you Alice" said Brad after ten minutes of conversation punctuated with head shakes and hand motions like always. He put down the phone, his face unreadable.

"I'm so sorry about last night I…"

"No worries. Wasn't alone for long." The look on his face was almost as cold and cutting as his words.

Alice didn't bother with an explanation, but stood up and walked out the door. How could she ever have thought… Things do happen for a reason.

&

Susan had left a text to say she would be heading off to spend time with Bailey, who always ran away from her feelings. Alice knew being a good mother was exactly what Susan needed. Alice answered that she was a text away if Susan needed her, hoping that David would be alright and that text would never come. She stood next to her car, staring at the asphalt. The weight of the last few days gathered on her shoulders. She heard footsteps and saw Vincent Torresi standing a few feet from her with a motorcycle helmet in his hand.

"You all right, Ms. Hightower?"

"Yeah, sure."

"You didn't show to our demonstration this afternoon. It was pretty impressive." His eyes looked blue against the sky and his smile was easy and warm, not at all what one would expect from someone who had been stood up.

"I forgot, I'm sorry." There were some advantages to an administrative assistant. Jonathan would never have let her miss an important demonstration.

"No worries."

"My best friend's husband is missing and may be dead. I didn't get much sleep and I guess I forgot to double check my agenda."

"I'm sorry." He stood there looking at her like he desperately wanted to help. He reached out and took her hand, pulling her toward him. "You need to fly."

"What?"

"Yeah, when the world weighs you down, you need to feel free from it." He led her between the few remaining cars to where his motorcycle was parked. It was a big shiny bright blue two wheeled "Donor Cycle" as everyone called them on her ER rotation in medical school. But when this kind and hot man held her hand, it did not look so scary to Alice at all. She knew that the little blonde girl in Alice's Adventure in Wonderland had been up for this adventure.

"I knew there was a reason I wore pants and flat shoes today," she said, smiling at Vincent.

He put his helmet on his head, then reaching out, took her purse from her. He then opened a little compartment behind the cycle's seat. Vincent removed a silver helmet, dropped in her purse and handed her the helmet. "See if this fits."

She pulled the plastic clip out of her hair, clipped it to her sleeve and pulled the helmet over her head. "It's tight." Her voice came back at her, muffled by the helmet.

"Good. Use this to step up." He pointed to a little metal loop and took her hand to help her up. Alice swung her leg over in two awkward moves, rather than the long smooth one she'd planned. Long legs did not always come in handy. Once seated, she found it surprisingly comfortable. "You have to hold on to me." She heard his muffled words muffled by his helmet and smiled inside her own.

He got on in one smooth move. Vincent leaned forward and threw his weight onto the starter, and they moved forward. Alice put her arms around his waist and held on like her life depended on it, because it certainly did. She felt her breasts pressed against him and knew he felt it, too. She shivered a little at that thought. The bike sped up and she tightened her grip and closed her eyes. *Be brave Alice, this won't be fun with your eyes closed.* She listened to herself after a few minutes.

Opening her eyes to see they rode along a two-lane road with fields on her right and rocky bluffs to her left. She must have had her eyes closed on the highway and now felt brave because there seemed to be no traffic anywhere. She let go her death grip, happy that she had not managed to cut off his breath and relaxed her arms, merely resting her hands on his thighs, hard with muscles beneath his pants.

The stone bluffs rose higher, and she looked out over the fields to her right. A large, winged soul circled the bluffs, casting a bird shaped shadow and dived into the cornfield. The sun hung low over the tassels and painted the sky pink and purple with evening clouds. The bike slowed as they reached a crossroads. She wondered if they would fall over, but they did not and turned left.

The bike began to climb a steep hill with ease that surprised her. The road wound through a canopy of trees as they came to the crest of a hill and turned off through a stone gate. Driving slowly on grass now, Vincent stopped in front of some tall stones marking graves. He got off, set the kick stand and offered her his hand without a word. Tripping over a tree root, she nearly fell on top of him, but managed to stay upright somehow. He removed his helmet, place it on the bike's seat and waited as she took off the silver one and placed it next to his. She smiled at him, feeling brave and exhilarated.

"Come on, I want to show you something you can't see from a car." He took off, and she followed. He stopped near a stone bench with the entire vista they had traversed spread out below. The clouds now streaked with orange at the horizon, the sun sank behind a distant farmhouse.

"Wow," was all Alice could think of to say. After several minutes, Alice asked, "Who are you, Vincent Torresi?"

"Just a guy giving a girl a motorcycle ride to watch the sunset."

"Wow." Vincent and Alice stood serenaded by crickets until the sun disappeared. Without a word, he walked back to the bike and Alice followed. Vincent helped her climb back on. She hung on tight to him as they rode back in the gathering gloom, her eyes wide open.

In silence they stood next to her car, and she could think of nothing to say, but reached up putting her arms around his neck. She kissed him slowly and tenderly, waiting for him to breathe and part his lips so she could softly tease the underside of his upper lip with her tongue.

"Wow," he said.

She let go and backed away. He turned and disappeared into the dark parking lot.

"Well, Alice, you ran another one off," she said to no one as she started her car and headed home.

Chapter Sixteen

MR. ROBATO

Alice couldn't help think of Vincent, who without a slick line or any game managed to seduce her soul a little. "I have the cure for that, Otis," she said to her cat as she ate her mini ravioli straight out of the plastic container. "The closet men may not be real, but they are always there when a girl needs a good hard…"

"Oh my," said Alice to tonight's offering. On the golden hanger hung an exquisite piece of bright aqua silk. White orchid appliqués decorated the hem and sleeves. The delicate center of each flower was embroidered with shiny silk threads that made the flowers look alive. On the floor, Alice found delicate white socks folded inside black velvet flip-flops with wooden souls. Something black lay folded on the floor. She took the lovely garment off the hanger and wrapped it around her like a bathrobe. "It's a kimono!" The thing on the floor had to be an obi sash. She had little or no idea how to tie the sash and hoped someone on the other side of her balcony door could help her. The socks were of the softest cotton and were like mittens for her feet with her big toe being the thumb. She tried to tie the sash around her waist and it ended up with little resemblance to any Geisha she had ever seen.

Alice took the clip from her hair and let it fall, having no idea what to do with her hair. She clomped on over to the balcony door and hoped a lot of walking would not be required in tonight's fantasy.

Alice stepped into a room lit by large, round paper lanterns. It smelled faintly like vanilla and pine. Three women stood in front of her. These were proper Geisha. Each wore a spectacular kimono with each sash immaculately tied. One wore a red kimono with black accents that looked like fans, one wore a bright pink and white number and the third one's kimono was pale blue with large dark blue and pink flowers splashed across the front. Their elaborate black hair dos and white make up covering their faces made them look more like dolls than women. Though they wore the same shoes with two-inch wooden blocks on the bottom as Alice, she towered a head taller than the three of them.

"Domo Arigato," said Alice. The three women look up at her and all burst into peals of laughter, covering their mouths with their hands as they laughed, bending nearly in two. The Japanese from her mother's old Styx album at least got her a laugh, but she was pretty sure saying Mr. Roboto would not get any reaction at all, so she smiled at them.

They straightened up and the one in the middle gave her a dark, disapproving look. They all began to speak what she assumed was real Japanese and Red Kimono untied Alice's sash.

"Ah," they exclaimed in unison as her kimono fell open. Evidently, her breasts were going to be a problem.

Pink Kimono shuffled off and Alice took notice of the correct way to walk in the strange wooden shoes. Tiny steps were the secret. Pinky bent down and removed a roll of what looked like gauze from a little black lacquer chest. Red held up Alice's arms and the other two wound the gauze around her, binding her breasts tight. When little evidence she was even a girl remained, they seemed satisfied. Now the lovely aqua silk bathrobe would close properly.

Wrapping her kimono tight, two of them fussed with the obi. Red stood looking at Alice and shuffled off, opening a door of the same paper screen as the walls. She came back with a large square red lacquered box. She set the box on the floor and very carefully removed a black wig, much like she and each of the others wore. This one had white birds fixed in among the jet-black hair piled into an elaborate chignon. The woman tried to stretch her arms enough to set the wig on Alice's head and now Alice burst out laughing. Again, she heard the mouth covering giggles from the other two. Alice stepped off the shoes and bent her knees, dropping her head to the woman's level. Red placed the wig on Alice's head, pulled at it arranging the bird ornaments in the hair and finally nodded in approval. The sash was so tight she could hardly breathe, but Alice felt like a proper Geisha, and made a little bow with her head. Blue Kimono said something, and Pinky produced lipstick from the folds of her sleeves and reached up to apply red lipstick to Alice's lips. She nodded, said something, and all three nodded in approval. Grateful no one offered to apply the white makeup to her face, Alice nodded back. It looked lovely on their small oval faces with delicate features, but she couldn't see it enhancing her high cheekbones and long nose. Blue kimono picked up an odd-looking stringed instrument, slid open the paper screen door, and they shuffled into a room with Alice bringing up the rear.

Three men sat at a low table. The Geisha in the bright red kimono, who always seemed to be in charge, walked to the table where a teapot and cups sat. Red Kimono poured tea into the cups and distributed them to the men. Pinky and Blue Girl shuffled off to a corner where four large white pillows lay and knelt on the pillows with downcast eyes. Alice did the same with her head down, but her eyes surveying the scene.

Blue Kimono began to play the stringed instrument. It had

a square body and an extremely long neck, but otherwise looked like a violin. She plucked the strings and Pinky sang. Her voice sounded sweet, but the tones were foreign to Alice's American ears and since she couldn't understand the words, she soon lost interest in anything but the men in front of her.

All three had jet black hair slicked back. Their wide lapels and thin ties of their suits gave Alice the impression that they were not men of modern Japan. The one on the left had a round face and the slicked back hair style accented the fact that his hairline receded nearly to the middle of his head. The blue suit he wore with a skinny black tie met with Alice's approval. The man on the extreme right looked barely out of his teens and seemed to be wearing his father's black pinstriped suit as it hung on him. It was the man in the middle that caught Alice's attention.

Taller than the other two, he looked directly at her. His face lean and angular and his black almond eyes seemed to drink her in. He wore a gray pinstriped suit with wide lapels. His skinny tie was blue. Dark hair gleamed silver at the temples in the soft light of the lanterns. The man said something in a quiet tone. Red turned toward Alice and nodded in response.

Alice surmised that he must have been the head of the group as Red poured his tea first. She dared to lift her chin, and he smiled at her. He made a motion with his hand and the other two men stopped talking. Red backed away toward the pillows. He suddenly stood and slid open the paper screen door and walked through, closing it behind him. Red took Alice by the hand, slid open the same door and pushed her in. Nearly losing her balance, Alice looked around. The room held little but a narrow pallet that she suspected was a bed. Alice smiled widely. Red clucked, said something in a hissing tone, shook her head and disappeared back through the sliding screen. Alice could think of nothing to do but kneel on the pallet. Very shortly, Mr. Robato came through another door carrying something and stood over her.

"I am very pleased to be honored with your lovely presence."

Whoa. "You speak English, great."

"This house is known to provide exclusive company much different from the usual."

"That's me, Alice the different."

"Ah, Alice. I am Hiko and I could not be more pleased by your difference from the common pleasure Geisha." He set down something black and square, knelt next to her, and reached around to untie her sash. He did it with the skill of one who had done the same a thousand times. He opened her kimono and began to unwind the gauze binding her breasts. When at last they fell free, he gasped again. "Why would they do this to such beauties?"

Reaching over, he took her breasts in his hands. "I am here to bring you pleasure, Alice." He squeezed gently and Alice moaned.

"That's a pretty good start."

"I come here for meetings and a little entertainment. As I love my wife, I have promised her not to take sexual pleasure from other women, but she said nothing about the giving of such ecstasy." He smiled at her.

"Would you like to taste them?" She looked down at her breasts. He leaned forward and took her left nipple between his lips. She moaned louder this time when his tongue moved like butterfly wings against her nipple as he squeezed the other one hard. "You know what you are doing, Hiko."

She felt that clench between her legs that always meant she was wet and ready.

Hiko stood up and placed a black leather bag that looked like one a doctor would carry on the floor near the pallet. Opening the bag, he removed a pair of white gloves, and slipping them on, returned to kneel close to Alice. "The touch of your magnificent flesh with my bare hands would bring me too much pleasure." Alice assumed nipple sucking didn't count in his agreement and was glad of it.

"I won't tell your wife if you won't." They both laughed.

With the sash untied, Hiko slid the heavy silk off Alice's shoulders. She watched as he began to stroke her slowly. The gloves looked identical but had very different textures. One felt like smooth velvet and the other rough, more like a combination of terrycloth and Velcro. He began at her breasts, slowly caressing them. Alice couldn't decide which she liked better, the smooth glove or the rough one. Each breast was enjoying completely different sensations, and she began to moan and breathe heavy. Hiko smiled, not bothering to hide his teeth.

As he slid past her belly, she opened her legs and wondered which he would choose to make her come. He answered with the soft glove sliding inside her and the rough one teasing her. Brushing the rough finger against her clit, it took very few strokes to make her moan and cry out in a loud climax.

"I doubt Madam Eno's house has ever been privileged to enjoy such a melodious climax."

"I am loud for sure. These paper walls must be tougher than they look." As Alice lay catching her breath, she wondered what would come next. Hiko went back to the black bag. "Oh, goody," she said, watching as he produced three ivory phalluses.

The lovely objects were in three sizes and he held them up for Alice. "Oh, the big one please," she giggled. He put the small one and medium ones back in the bag. Alice noticed it was a nice large size, but not anatomically correct. It was a gently curved cylinder without the delicious head that she enjoyed in just the right place. "Oh well, it is the Indian, not merely the arrow." This could not have been Hikos's first attempt to please a woman.

Alice watched as Hiko rubbed the hard white phallus against her nipples, one and then the other. The cool ivory brought each one to stiff attention and a low, deep moan from

Alice. Without warning, he quickly inserted the ivory phallus into her. It slid in easily and he began to rub her clit with the smooth glove. The rough glove had made her clit especially sensitive, and he slid the ivory cock in and out of her with a speed no flesh cock could match. This time she held herself back, watching his face as her pleasure mounted. The expression on his face looked as if he were about to come, too. As the wave of pleasure washed over her, his eyes closed and he stopped his movement.

His mouth was slightly open, his eyes still closed, and she wondered if he could climax by making her come?

"That is the secret we must never tell my wife." Hiko said, answering the question she had asked only in her mind.

"Wow."

"I will let you rest a bit as I do have some business to attend, but perhaps a repeat performance would be desirable, yes?"

"Oh yes, please." He left, and she closed her eyes for a minute.

"Thank you all for preparing so well for this morning's meeting," said Alice to the other four people seated around the long black marble conference room table. Louise sat next to Alice and looked proud of her engineers. Each report had been both thorough and concise. She knew that was Louise's touch. Though engineers in general were thorough, the "short but sweet" was all Louise. She could blabber on for twenty minutes about nothing in particular in conversation, but her work reports were beautifully to the point.

Alice watched Vincent as Yeshia read her report on matrix tolerances which could have been tedious, but was, instead, informative. Vincent's eyes were on Alice. He wore a deep green sweater that hugged his chest and biceps. *Who said men looked hottest in suits?* Today his eyes looked green. The color was called hazel because it reflected nearby colors. The sudden silence reminded her that she was head of R & D and these were her monkeys and her circus.

"Dr. Wen, continue please," said Alice, forcing herself to concentrate.

"I've got nothin'. These guys are on it. I do want to introduce Dr. Karen Mariani from The University of Missouri. She will be helping us with the surgeries we will need to implant the first trial knees. I'm no kinda surgeon and Karen has taught veterinary surgery for ten years.

"Hello," said a lovely mahogany haired woman. Her large, dark eyes looked intelligent and intense. She had the delicate, small-boned, elegant look, the complete opposite of Alice. Alice guessed she was somewhere in her forties, but had that ageless look that kept you guessing. "As soon as you get a completed prototype, I will be happy to perform the first replacements. Your facilities are amazing. I agree that the larger the breed, the more successful the result, more comparable to human subjects."

"There is one rather large problem." All eyes turned their attention solely to the speaker of those words, Vincent Torresi. "No dog weighs 300 pounds. The average knee replacement patient weighs over two hundred pounds. Many are 300 and over. If you get approval in dogs and fail in humans, what good is that?"

Alice sat up straight in her chair. She noticed that Louise's eyes had narrowed. One of her ducks had broken from the flock. Not something Louise appreciated in her orderly shop.

"Do you have a suggestion as to how we could avoid such a disaster, Mr. Tericci?" said Alice, now leaning forward in her chair.

"You need a simulator than can test the design at higher weights. We used one at Stryker to test tolerances. Mostly for new materials, but the concept would work to test design strength, too. This wouldn't guarantee success, but it might reduce the odds of failure."

"Bringing out any new product comes with risks. Can you email me a proposal ASAP?"

He smiled a wide smile. "I thought you'd never ask."

Alice laughed a nervous laugh with little mirth. "Okay team, same time next week. So glad to have you help us out, Karen." Alice sat typing notes from the meeting when she noticed Louise had stayed behind and still had her narrow-eyed angry look on her face. She sat with her arms crossed across her exquisite black suit that looked like vintage Channel.

"I know, Louise. Why didn't he bring this up before now?" Alice didn't look up but kept typing.

"I know why, showing off for the boss. It was a good point, but you know I don't like surprises. He looks at you like it's only the two of you in the room."

"I think he is cute and smart as hell and brave enough to buck you and come straight to me."

"Uh huh."

"What? Wasn't it you who extolled his virtues to me as dating material, which is neither here nor there. Failures in human trials would mean human beings would suffer. And if he saves us time to clearance, that's money."

"Yeah, you're right. So do you want to know his deets? He isn't into cradle robbing as an Olympic sport like James." Alice kept typing.

"He is 52 and single. Wife died two years ago after a long illness. All the production people like him. He tells a great joke. What's not to like?" "And he rides a motorcycle to work," said Alice.

Louise stood up and headed to the door. "And he gives you that thirsty look. Pretty soon, you'll have him and James fighting over you in the cafeteria." She laughed and disappeared out the door.

Chapter Eighteen

HELTER SKELTER

Susan hadn't responded to any of Alice's texts in days. Dr. Cindy had told her that to be supportive of someone grieving, you should let them know you are there, but make no demands and do not make it about your own grief. She would continue to send supportive messages and let Susan tell her when she needed her friend.

Her own grief for a child she had never even met was definitely not going away. This Friday evening, as she sat on her couch watching the tears fall onto her white couch, those tears almost felt like someone else was crying them. She found it less and less possible to sit still with every passing moment and even her favorite form of self-soothing and pacing, did nothing to soothe her. It had felt like a long time since her Bipolar Disorder had been a problem, that part of her thought it had gone away like a bad cold. Usually a hyper state came with a positive feeling, not this evening. Alice felt certain that Vincent Tericci's concern would be correct and the project would end in a terrible disaster.

Susan wasn't answering her texts because she had stupidly said the wrong thing and hurt her. Brad had turned to younger women because she was too old to keep him interested. She could see all of this so clearly when, an hour ago, everything had been fine. Something was terribly wrong. If she called Dr. Cindy's emergency number, would she answer? It was 5:00 p.m. on a Friday night. Something deep inside her made make that call.

⁂

"I am so sorry," said Alice. She sat on Dr. Cindy's couch. She couldn't keep from tapping her feet and she put her head in her hands and sobbed.

"Please don't be. This is most likely a mixed episode. They can be terrifying. All the depressive thoughts are hitting you at once and rather than shut down, you are hyper."

Alice raised her head and took the tissue Dr. Cindy offered and wiped her eyes. "How can I make it stop? It has been so long and I hoped…"

"You are doing well. Unfortunately, Bipolar Disorder is not something you have, but it is a part of who you are. The life-style changes have helped and can again. This will pass."

"I feel so…so…hopeless."

"Those negative thoughts are not reality. Let's examine them. Tell me what you are afraid of?"

"My friend Susan's husband may have died and she won't even answer my texts. I must have said something…."

"She will in her own time. Haven't you and she been friends for years?"

"Yes, twenty-two years."

"And in all that time you must have managed to say the wrong thing once in a while and isn't she still your friend?"

"Yes. I get it. But my new project could implode. Our design doesn't take high weight stress into consideration. Brad doesn't even want me. I'm too old for him."

"How do you feel right this minute?"

"I still feel like I could run a marathon, but I am afraid

134

of…everything." Alice lifted her head and opened her eyes. "I think… these fears… aren't real."

"That's great. The intelligence that creates those fears is your best weapon against them. Know that nothing has really changed but how you feel about things and that is caused by your brain chemistry. I suggest you increase your efforts. Work out a little harder. When did you last eat?"

"I can't remember." Alice's voice sounded stronger now.

"Well, that alone will seriously mess with your brain chemistry. Continue your self-care and this will pass. But stay safe. You can call me anytime. Call a friend and have dinner. Be around people. If you feel you can't handle it or you want to hurt yourself, call me day or night. If this continues for more than a day or two, we may want to consider medication for a short time. It can act to slow down your thoughts so your reasoning ability can take over, nothing more."

"Thank you."

"This is my job. I'll be in the office catching up on some paperwork tomorrow afternoon. Why don't we have a session?"

"I've already ruined your Friday night…but sure."

Alice took a deep breath and began scrubbing her kitchen floor once more. The pretty gray-green Italian ceramic tiles still seemed to have a haze on them. When she finished, she dusted everything on the counter, though Lourdes, her housekeeper, had done a thorough job yesterday. Since her usually spotless apartment now gleamed operating room clean, she decided to get a start on Monday's emails. Wouldn't it be nice to walk in Monday morning to zero emails in her inbox? This internal happy talk was not really slowing her down, but she did feel more in control and less afraid of the negative feelings that popped into her head after two sessions with Dr. Cindy. She wasn't a complete failure. Her project would move forward even if the design needed to be altered. Susan would call when she was ready and if Brad wanted twenty-five-year-olds instead of her, it was his loss.

The first email she pulled up was from the Excellcardia Engineering Group. The Subject line said, "The Answer To Your Prayers." It was from Vincent Tericci. Attached, she found ten pages of diagrams, specs and a complete budget on the last page. "All this in three days," said Alice to the laptop screen. She wondered if the contact number at the end of the document was his personal cell? Why not offer him dinner as a reward for his quick and excellent work. She would be following doctor's orders after all. Maybe dinner with a nice intelligent man might feed her hyper brain cells some nourishment that would slow her down. She would keep her phone on in case Susan called.

Vincent had suggested that they meet at LoRusso's. She arrived right on time at the cute little Italian place where the food was extraordinary. Of all her favorite places in St. Louis, this one had roast duck. Indulging in extra calories when she felt hyper seemed to work out as often as she forgot to eat entirely. It boded well that Vincent had chosen a place she was familiar with and enjoyed. He was sitting at a table for two in an intimate corner when she arrived. He had a glass of something bubbly in his hand and another flute shone in the light of the artificial candles on the table.

"I love this place, thank you," she said. "I am happy to reward your amazingly speedy work with dinner at one of my favorite places." She beamed at him. She could see her choice of black leather leggings and a long black tunic sprinkled with silver stars met with his approval as his eyes swept over her and his smile widened.

"My pleasure," said Vincent. He set his glass on the table.

"I am amazed and duly impressed at how quickly you pulled that proposal together." Alice tucked her chair in and dropped her napkin in her lap.

He raised his eyebrows, narrowed his eyes, and said, "Kinda seemed we needed it in a hurry." His eyes looked dark blue and had a sparkle in them that gave her the tiniest shiver.

"Well, we needed it detailed and complete, and you accomplished that." Alice couldn't read the look on his face. It was pleasant, but his brows seemed to knit together with some concern. He reached down beside the table and produced a bottle. "I like prosecco better than French Champagne." He poured her a glass after asking with the lift of those dark brows if she would like one.

"I'm not sure I know the difference. If it's bubbly, I like it." Alice took a long sip and felt the tightly wound fibers of her mind relax a bit as the alcohol hit her bloodstream. She knew using any mood-altering substance to handle her moods could be unwise, but she planned to eat dinner, and it was just a little bubbly. She was not drinking to alter her mood, but to accompany a lovely meal with a very talented and hot engineer.

Alice ordered the duck and Vincent the cioppino, which he told her was a house specialty.

"Tell me, who is Alice Hightower and what does she want out of this life?" said Vincent.

He had kept her glass filled and chatted about the weather, never looking at her directly. Now, waiting for her answer, he trained his dark fringed eyes on hers and the storm clouds that were his brows lifted a fraction.

"Well. I am Head of R&D. I used to be CEO, but when industrial espionage severely damaged Excellcardia's bottom line, I was sacked." He listened intently as she spilled the whole sordid story. He refilled her glass twice, but did not pick up his or take his eyes from hers. Finally, she stopped talking.

"That's a complete company history of some pretty dark

shit, but that doesn't tell me who you are or what you want?" The corners of his generous mouth turned up.

"That is a question I am not sure I can answer." Alice drained the last of her prosecco.

"Why? Don't you trust me, Alice."

"It's not that." She hesitated a minute and as she looked into his eyes, she felt certain she could trust him. "I can't answer because I don't know the answer. I am a work in progress." Why was she telling this man she barely knew the truth of her? Had she lost her ability to be casual and flirty? Did she ever have that skill? Obviously not. She was mercifully interrupted by a tall young man in a waiter's black pants, white shirt and black server's apron, delivering their food.

The duck was delicious as usual, and Vincent shared over his dish that he grew up in St. Louis and was the youngest and only boy in a family of five children. Alice smiled and ate her dinner like she hadn't eaten in weeks. It might have been a day or two.

"With all those sisters, I'd guess you understand women better than most men," Alice said finally over a little sip of port. Vincent had suggested she have a small glass of the cordial as dessert. She had never tasted the darkly sweet, delicious stuff, but quickly realized she liked it very much.

"I don't think any man can ever understand women. Too much mystery."

"I don't think there is any mystery to me. I try every day to do the best job I can. I am a loyal friend and try hard to be a good boss." What would he think if she told him she made up crazy fantasies where she travelled in time and enjoyed a lot of men in very naughty adventures?

"Oh, I think there is a lot more there than that," he said.

She tried to pay for dinner as she had asked him, but he had told the waiter to bring him the check and not accept any payment from her beforehand. He walked her to her car and stopped a few feet away, not close enough to kiss her, to her great disappointment. "Thank you," said Vincent, standing out of reach.

"For what? You bought dinner?" Her cheeks were warmed with the delicious food, bubbly and port.

"For your company." He then took a step toward her and reached up to touch the side of her face. His hand caressed her cheek and then he stepped back into the darkness.

"Huh?" said Alice, still enjoying his simple touch.

Chapter Nineteen

THOSE SHOES

A lice was relieved to feel the scary mixed bipolar episode run out of fuel in another twelve hours. She read in *The Journal of American Psychiatry* that most suicides in bipolar individuals occur during mixed episodes, and she could definitely understand why. Dr. Cindy had helped her with both the hypo manic and depressive episodes, but feeling both hyper and depressed all at once was a lot to handle. It wouldn't sneak up on her again. Susan texted that she was home the next Saturday morning and Alice took the elevator to Susan's apartment.

"Well, that was fast," said Susan, opening her door. She wore sweatpants and a sweatshirt far too large for her. *Probably David's.* Susan's voice sounded normal, but the muscles of her face were slack with the weight of her worry.

"Still no word?" asked Alice. Susan merely shook her head. "It is a beautiful day and we are going to walk to breakfast," said Alice

"It's cold." Susan's voice was flat and sad.

"Get a coat. The sun is shining and we need the fresh air. I know you do. Your office has that gross clove oil and formalin smell of all dentist offices." Susan walked to her coat closet without even defending Alice's crack about her office.

Alice made happy chat about work and Vincent the interesting man she worked with, and Susan simply put one foot in front of the other, not commenting.

When they arrived at the Benton Park Café, Susan said, "I'm not hungry, really."

"Well, I am, so you can watch me eat." She ordered her favorite Eggs Benedict. Alice continued her cheerful banter. Her food arrived and Susan looked up from her latte.

"Does smell good. I'll have that too, please," said Susan to the server. Alice smiled, proud of her little scheme. She knew the power of something delicious to make a person feel better. Susan managed to eat most of her food but didn't add much to the conversation.

"So everything in my life is just peachy," said Alice, smiling at her empty plate.

Susan gave a little laugh. "You are the absolute worst at happy talk."

"Hey, I am trying to be appropriately cheery without being self-absorbed, and you know that's not easy for me."

"Yeah, I know." Susan's weak attempt at a smile was thanks enough. They walked back to Susan's apartment and Alice spent the afternoon tidying up as Susan sat staring at the floor. Alice made Susan a cup of tea with fancy clover honey. When it got cold without a sip, she made another setting it on a coaster next to Susan.

Alice had been the neat one and Susan the slob in college. Alice's hyper cleaning jags had always kept the little apartment they shared, orderly. Susan had evolved and normally had things in their place, but Alice was still Alice. It appeared as if Susan's suitcase had exploded all over the living room. Clothes were draped on chairs or lay in piles on the floor. There seemed to be no distinction between clean and dirty clothes. *The horror.* Normally Susan wouldn't have let Alice arrange her things as she saw fit, but Alice was happy to do it.

&

The weekend spent keeping her best friend company had been oddly satisfying, Alice thought, opening her laptop Monday morning.

"Who sits smiling at their laptop," said Vincent. He stood in front of her desk, sexy eyes looking at her through the dark fringe of his lashes. He wore a sky-blue sweater and black jeans. Louise always dressed as if she was about to walk some runway or another, but allowed her team to be casual.

"Me. I love emails," said Alice.

"Nobody loves emails." He looked down. Is he here because the weight trials are proving disastrous? Thought Alice.

"I was wondering if...if...if I could make you dinner at my house." She found it adorable that he would be nervous asking her out.

"I would love that." She gave him her widest and most gracious smile.

"Don't you want to know if I can cook?"

"Everyone cooks better than me and you're Italian, right? Isn't that in your genes?"

"Pretty much, but I enjoy it." Now he grinned at her.

"Does Friday work?" she asked.

"Sure, is there anything you can't eat?" He shifted his weight and Alice noticed his thick leg muscles straining the fabric of his jeans.

"Nope, I like everything." Brad wasn't the only man who could cook.

&

The week passed without any new disasters. It had become her new after work ritual; stop in, make sure Susan ate something, and sleep on Susan's comfy couch in case Susan needed. She found herself thinking about her dinner date with Vincent as she warmed Susan's dinner. He didn't look at her with sex ray eyes like Brad, but he was cute and extremely bright. There had to be something good beneath those jeans. A suit could hide a paunch, but that blue sweater made it easy to imagine what was beneath it.

When she let herself in to Susan's apartment Thursday evening, she smelled something delicious and smiled. Susan was cooking. The something delicious bubbled in the crock pot and turned out to be chicken cacciatore. While Susan hardly beamed when she dished up Alice's portion, her face looked closer to normal. Her features no longer seemed heavy with grief. It was not fair to compare her grief for a child she never got to hold with possibly losing one's husband of 30 years.

"What do you think? Some chicken parts and jar sauce," said Susan.

"It is yummy," said Alice, dripping red sauce on Susan's dining table and quickly wiping it up with her paper towel napkin.

"Tell me more about your date tomorrow," said Susan. Alice had told Susan about Vincent over breakfast when she was still deep in her grief and worry, but was not surprised she hadn't paid attention.

"He is lead engineer on the Excellosteo project. He is a widower for two years and he cooks."

"Are you really ready to give up on Brad?"

"He gave up on me. He's freshly single, I get it, but I don't need to sit around waiting for him to act his age. He is two years older than me, if young women are what he wants…whatever."

"Yeah. I will have plenty of leftovers for tomorrow night so you can enjoy your engineer without worry over me. I am resolved not to grieve until I know for sure. He could be okay."

"I won't stop worrying about you, but I will have my phone with me so…"

"I might wait until you are having Vincent for dessert and call you." It was wonderful to hear her friend make a joke, much more like herself. Alice knew Susan would be okay eventually, no matter what happened.

§

This date called for the heavy artillery—cleavage. Alice wore a sheer to the point of being see-through v-necked black blouse. This required she pull out the pretty Victoria Secrets bra, complete with spangles, from the back of her bra drawer. No safety pinned straps of a faded glory bra would peek through this blouse. Her skirt was plain and black, but the shoes she chose were spectacular. The faux Prada pumps were black alligator with spangles decorating the ankle straps and four-inch stiletto heels. The real ones these were a copy of cost a month's pay and were no more gorgeous, she thought, admiring them on her way to the garage.

Alice typed in the address Vincent gave her and let her navigator guide her. It took her far outside the city down Highway 55. When finally her guide told her to turn left, it was onto a narrow gravel road. She drove slowly, her Porsche wasn't fond of flying gravel.

"Easy Girl," said Alice to the car. The road led between tall trees to a clearing where she found a large log home. It was hardly a cabin with dormer windows and a front porch wrapping around the house.

She climbed out of her car and searched for a sidewalk in the twilight. There were only smooth stones a small step apart leading to the house. Vincent must have heard her car approach and gave a little wave from the porch. Alice held her head high and planned to strut right on down that path and up onto that porch, but her left foot slipped off the stepping-stone. The heel of her shoe sank deep into soft ground, depositing Alice on that same ground on her ass with a thud. Vincent stood beside her in an instant, extending his hand and helping her to her feet. The beautiful, spangled heel was still buried in the ground, no longer connected to the shoe.

"It can probably be repaired," said Vincent, carefully inspecting the shoe she now held in her hand. He pulled something from his pocket and stood up with the heel in his hand. "Looks like a clean break, easily reattached." Alice walked barefoot the rest of the way down the path and up the stairs. "I'll be right back," he said, heading back down the steps and around the side of the house with the heel and injured shoe in his hand. Alice stood in the twilight wondering if bears lived in these woods.

When she decided she could probably bare foot fast enough to get inside and shut the door if any bears did show up, Vincent reappeared. Handing her the shoe with the heel now held on with a little clamp.

"It'll be set up enough to walk on in an hour, good as new." He opened the front door, and she followed him in. The foyer was magnificent. Drywall formed the walls to about eight feet and the logs forming the ceiling were exposed the rest of the way to a twenty foot vault. A black wrought iron chandelier hung from the highest point. He led her into a large living room again with the same cream-colored walls and exposed log ceiling.

"Thank you for the repair, Vincent," said Alice. She gave him what she thought was her most seductive smile. The look he returned told her nothing. *What's not to adore about a hot man who can fix shoes?*

Through an open doorway, Alice could see the kitchen and smell something much better than canned spaghetti.

"Would you like a drink before dinner?" This time he smiled at her and his eyes swept over her form as if he liked what he saw.

"Sure." She stood looking around the room as Vincent clinked ice and glasses behind her. Two walls of his house were glass from ceiling to the floor. The windows formed a glass corner, looking out on nothing but trees outside as if Vincent lived in a tree house.

The glass wall required no decoration; the gorgeous green canopy outside painted the loveliest scene. Alice watched the red sun disappearing between the trees far in the distance. A room this large and might seem bare if each furnishing was not particularly unique and interesting. Two chairs of some beautiful light wood with swirling grain graced the corners. Alice had never seen anything like them in any furniture store. The cushions were deep blood-red cloth, creating a vivid contrast to the light wood. In front of each chair sat a unique small wooden table and, beside each, a wrought iron floor lamp. Alice chose the leather couch on which to plop her derriere.

One whole wall was a bookshelf, made of unpainted wood and filled with books separated by framed photos and knick-knacks. A picture of three handsome young men with their arms around one another sat on the coffee table in front of her. They were most likely brothers and two of them had Vincent's eyes. The table itself was as interesting as the picture. It was made of a single horizontal slice through a tree trunk. The wood was reddish, and the edges were deeply scalloped as the tree it was cut from must have been. The table felt smooth as glass to her fingertips, but unlike glass, the wood had the faint warmth of a living thing. The dark and light swirls of the wood's grain were interrupted near the center with an oval window three inches long. It looked like the tree had grown around a diamond that had been sliced along with the wood. It was as smooth as the wood and her fingers lingered there.

"That's resin. I fill the flaws in the wood with it." Vincent sat a martini glass down on a coaster.

"It looks like a jewel, beautiful."

He smiled a wide, warm smile, and she thought she saw a bit of heat in his eyes. The martini glass held three olives and a sip revealed it was indeed Tanqueray with a hint of vermouth. "How'd you know?"

"I have my sources." His eyes narrowed with mischief. "I stirred it rather than use a shaker which bruises the gin." He sat down on the couch next to her and took a sip from his own short crystal glass that held something brown.

Alice chuckled with joy that anyone would go to so much trouble to discover what she liked to drink.

"Hmm. It's been a long time since anyone has laughed in this house." He smiled at her without any trace of sadness.

"I'm sorry."

He looked away from her at the exquisite Tiffany style lamp on the end table next to him. "My wife was sick a long time. Astrocytoma. They'd think they had it under control and then another tumor would pop up on a scan. She just faded away more and more each time they—she had a lot of surgery."

Alice reached over to take his hand. He looked into her eyes and this time she was certain she saw desire. She wanted to lean into and kiss those lips, but he picked up his drink and stood up.

"I hope you like Italian."

"I like everything Italian." She couldn't tell him she enjoyed her private chef, Boyardee, nearly every evening.

He served her delicious lasagna with salad and warm crusty garlic bread in a dining room empty of anything but a large and magnificent glass-topped table and another huge window made up one wall. The thick glass of the tabletop, eight feet long, gave a unique view of the four pieces of wood supporting the glass. The supports formed two Xs. Each X was of a grayed wood that, as it neared, the floor seemed to disintegrate. The wood became split with black veins and green lichens coloring the grey as it reached the floor. The flaws were filled in with resin so all the character was visible, but the support was a solid rectangle. It was almost a shame to put anything on such a table. Six plain black wrought-iron chairs with wooden seats sat around the table in perfect contrast to the spectacular table.

"Did you make this?" said Alice, tapping on the table.

"Yep. I made almost every stick of furniture in the house. Built the house too."

"Wow." She wiped her mouth with a red and white checkered napkin. There was a lot more to a man who was so good at his day job. Never had she tasted such delicious lasagna. In this case, the calories were worth it. Who was she to turn anything down? If her life ended tomorrow, she would think of the lasagna and not the size of her butt.

"I can't eat another bite," Alice exclaimed after her second piece of garlic bread.

"Too, bad. There's key lime cheesecake for dessert." Then he gave her his little narrow eyed look of mischief that she was beginning to enjoy. She would definitely not turn down any cheesecake. It was as good as it sounded, both creamy and tart. How good in bed must a man with hands that could create such masterpieces of wood and calories be? She hoped she wouldn't have long to wait to find out.

As they sat drinking tiny glasses of port, back on the couch side by side, Alice leaned close to Vincent and gave him an unmistakable look. She wanted him and she was pretty sure he didn't cook for hours for nothing. He took the hint and kissed her soft and sweet, teasing her lips with the tip of his tongue.

"Where is your ladies room, please?" she said.

"It's in my house, so it's the men's room, but you're welcome to it. Left through the master bedroom." She had seen a little powder room off the kitchen, but sending her through the bedroom was the sign she had been waiting for.

After making use of the restroom, she perched herself on the end of a king-sized bed with a plain brown bedspread, two pillows, and zero decorative throw pillows. She slipped off her blouse, unhooked her bra, crossed her legs, and waited. Vincent showed up as expected. His eyes devoured her and then he closed them, inhaling audibly. Walking to the end of the bed, he knelt in front of her. In his eyes, she saw only sadness, not desire. Her cheeks burned.

"I'm so sorry, Alice. It has been years since I've…I'm… don't think I… I'm not even sure I remember…"

She grabbed her bra, hooked it, then pulled on her blouse and buttoned it up. Had she really misread the situation so badly? Now fully clothed, she said, looking at her knees, "I'm sorry. I thought…" Her cheeks felt as if they were on fire with embarrassment and she could not meet his eyes. He still knelt in front of her.

"You have nothing to be sorry about. I want this, I want you, but I need some time."

She looked into those eyes, this minute the color of the deepest part of the ocean, and she believed him.

Chapter Twenty

WHISKEY IN THE JAR

A lice still felt the fire in her cheeks as she sat on Dr. Cindy's antebellum couch the next day. "I'm usually not so wrong about these things."

"How would you feel if the situation had been reversed, if he were the one sitting on the bed exposed?" Dr. Cindy had stopped writing and peered at Alice over her chic, red-framed readers.

"Fine with me. That's what I wanted."

"What about getting to know a man before you are intimate?" She wrote furiously and her voice sounded doctor-neutral without a hint of judgement.

Alice thought for a long moment, but said nothing. Wasn't settling on one man and really getting to know him how you got your heart broken? The long dinners and Sunday walks with Jonathan didn't keep him from dumping her, and it made it hurt a hell of a lot more when he did.

"Do you think you could be treating men as sex objects? If this man is special to you, it might be worth knowing him better before you know him biblically." Dr. Cindy smiled. Her little joke warmed Alice's heart a little.

"I knew Jonathan for three years before we…"

"You were his boss. You only knew his work persona. You never got to know him on equal footing before you had sex with him. It is similar with Brad. You had sex with him, knowing him almost entirely from work. Sex is a powerful motivator. It may lead you into a relationship that ultimately might not be healthy, just for the sex."

"I am technically Vincent's boss too, but he's not my direct report," said Alice. "Huh. Something to think about." *Vincent might be worth spending some time to get to know.*

❦

Alice couldn't help thinking about a certain engineer in between her emails. Her schedule of meetings was a light one today, and she thought she would take the time to visit her charges in their natural environment. It had been a while since she had been to the tenth floor.

"Hey, Alice." Ami Wen shot Alice a glance over her shoulder as she poured some liquid from a tall glass flask into several small tubes that sat on a platform continually shaking them. This was how you grew cells, Alice knew. The gentle shaking kept the cells from clumping, which, though sometimes desirable, was not good before they attached to a matrix. It would be an artificial knee this time rather than heart blood vessels, but this principle was the same in Exelosteo as in Biocardia.

"Baby osteoblasts like to hold on to each other, hinders attachment to the matrix. Wait a sec." Ami wore a complete isolation suit, with plastic gown, hood and face shield. Bacterial contamination was death on cell cultures. Alice had donned a yellow paper isolation gown and booties and was careful not to step too close without a bonnet and face shield. Ami worked under a hood in this clean room where no one could enter without protection.

"How are they doing?" Alice asked from a safe distance.

"Cooking up a new batch of babies to apply to engineering's latest design." Ami closed the opening in the hood and walked over to where Alice stood. "To what do me and my teeny cells owe the honor of a visit?"

"Wanted to see how things were progressing." Alice could see a large bruise on Ami's cheek through her face shield. The yellow color indicated it was old and healing. Ami didn't seem in pain and flashed her wide Bugs Bunny smile at Alice.

"Are you okay?" asked Alice.

"Sure. Have you seen Pricilla's kittens? I think she must have dropped them in the woods sometime in the last three weeks. She was skinny when I fed the cats this morning."

"Wouldn't they still be too small to walk?" Bringing up kittens would not chase Alice off the scent.

"Yeah, but sometimes mama ferals bring their babies to show you. I was hoping."

"But how are you, really Ami?"

"What I do on my own time is my business."

It was none of Alice's business if she had a boyfriend who like to play rough, unless it was against her will. Battered women often kept the violence a secret. She had never mentioned any man and often stayed at work until midnight. Security had strict orders not to let anyone up to the tenth floor without Alice's approval. *How could she help if Ami wouldn't let her in?*

Ami turned away and fiddled with the temperature controls on the hood. "All peachy." There was something in her tone, not quite genuine. However, clearly, Alice would get nothing else from her today.

Alice intended to visit the engineering lab to see the new weight testing machine in action after she finished her reports. An email marked URGENT insisted she open it and changed her plans. Colonel Bill, from security, warned that someone had downloaded the Tor browser on a company computer. "A clear violation of company policy, which could seriously threaten the security of the entire company."

Two minutes later, Alice stood in front of Colonel Bill's desk for an explanation.

"Tell me what is so dangerous about this," said Alice without bothering with any conversational niceties.

He continued typing on his laptop, while Alice steamed. He was a disrespectful jerk but didn't seem addicted to any substances that could be manipulated like her last chief of security.

"Well, Ms. Hightower, since Mr. James has instructed me to share all security concerns regarding the new Excellosteo project, I'll tell you." His little dark eyes reminded her of some reptile or another. "Tor is a browser used primarily for accessing the Dark Web. There are unsavory characters on the Dark Web looking for secrets to steal. Using Tor is like opening up the door of our hen house to a pack of wolves."

"What! Wouldn't our firewall protect against that?"

"Someone seems to have bypassed the firewall. They could not have down loaded Tor without some pretty serious hacking skills."

"Where exactly did this breach occur?"

"Tenth floor lab. Hard to pinpoint the exact location since there are too many PCs there. Every time I shut one down, another one pops up."

Ami. Alice knew she was as bright as they come and there was definitely something going on with her. If she was jeopardizing the company's safety, genius or not, it would stop.

Ami stood in front of Alice's desk fifteen minutes after Alice summoned her. Without the protective face shield, the bruise covered most of Ami's left cheek.

"I get it. I'm sorry," said Ami, after Alice confronted her with Colonel Bill's discovery.

"Sorry will not cut it. Security will block the browser and you will not download it again. Is that understood?"

"No one can get into our data. I was…."

"Is that understood?"

"Sure. Didn't mean any harm. I have some family in places where standard communication isn't possible. Installed a separate monster firewall to protect the company." Ami's eyes were wide and serious beneath her glasses.

Alice accepted Ami's explanation at its face value. Still, a little nexus of fear took up residence in Alice's rib cage, next to her heart. It felt small, but she could not ignore any risks to this project. She might never get another chance at such an important discovery. She did not want to be head of R&D forever; she was a CEO.

§♣

When this long, strange day neared an end, and all the feral cats were fed, Alice collapsed on her faux leather office couch with a sigh. She would visit Vincent another day.

"Tough day?" asked Bradley James, who seemed to delight in startling her. Maybe she could get a bell for her office door.

"Just a day." She sat up straight. He sat down dangerously close to her. She scooched into the corner of the couch.

Brad laughed. "Are you afraid of me? This couch…" He caressed the black vinyl with those hands she had so loved caressing her.

"I am not afraid." Her voice cracked a little. He wore a suit so dark green it nearly looked black, a snow-white shirt and a pale greenish blue tie with the company logo on it. Alice used the breathing techniques she'd learned in Susan's yoga class to try and ignore his effect on her. In slow, out slower.

"I've a proposition for you." He lowered his chin slightly and looked at her in that way that usually made her panties wet and her knees drift apart. The knees stayed tight together, but still she felt his eyes toasting her like a marshmallow at a girl scout cook out.

"I am not interested in being another notch on your bedpost. I am too old for that." Alice kept her expression neutral and hoped he caught the reference to his rumored obsession with younger women. "You may be wise, but never old. It's a business proposition. Come with me to Dallas. I'm making a presentation to huge a hospital group."

"Don't we have a very capable sales force for that?" Alice's distrust of Brad's motives came through in her voice a bit more than she intended.

"Some things can't be left to amateurs." Brad smiled.

Alice knew he was right, his sales skills were beyond compare, his arrogance didn't change that. She held his gaze, determined not to let him melt her into a little wet puddle of want.

"Along with our cardiac lines, I don't think it's too early to spark enthusiasm for Excellosteo. This is a big important group. I know the CEO personally and I'd like you to help me pitch us as a one stop shop for 'all your implantable needs.'" Excellosteo is your baby. I need you.

$\approx$

She had not given Brad a definite answer, and the trip was still weeks away. What could take a girl's mind off difficult decisions better than an escape to who knows where and when? Whoever waited for her on the other side of her balcony door would certainly distract her for the evening.

A plain dress of soft moss green wool hung on the magic gold hanger. A soft cotton under shift was folded neatly on the floor. Next to the shift sat an adorable pair of lace up cordovan leather booties. She had learned from experience and Google that this probably meant the middle to late eighteen hundreds. The rectangle of green, gold and black plaid wool folded next to the boots gave her some idea as to where. She wasn't entirely certain how to wear the plaid wool triangle that she learned from a quick check of the internet on her phone, denoted a certain Scottish clan. Alice decided to throw it over her shoulder and walk out her balcony door in search of hot kilt wearing men.

Squinting in the bright sunshine, she found herself standing in front of a large formation of craggy grey stone. The ground sloped gently down covered with purple flowers she thought must be heather.

"Mornin," said a man who stood leaning on the rocks with his arms folded a few feet from her. Alice gasped at the sight. A man in a red and black kilt towered over her. Legs seemed to sprout like the trunks of trees from the kilt and long black socks encircled substantial calves. A wide chest strained at the buttons of a white shirt.

"Good morning, sir," answered Alice.

"Ach, I'm Ian Killkenny no English Sir." Dimples decorated his wide ruddy face. Alice swallowed and tried to keep her eyes on his, instead of following the curls on his chest that disappeared into that shirt.

"I'm Alice." Alice took two steps toward Ian and inhaled the scent of leather and wood with a hint of something sweet.

"I dunna ken the McReas to have fair haired women and you're handsomer that most of that lot." He walked around her and looked her up and down. "You'll do." He took two steps to stand very near her. She could not identify the strange, sweet smell, but mingled with the man scent of Ian, it was delicious.

"I'm glad of that."

"'T'ain't every gal worth ten barrels of Killkeny's best." Ian reached up and gently stroked her hair. His deep green eyes looked into hers and she longed to run her fingers through the wild mahogany hair that curled around his wide shoulders. Ian stroked her cheek, flashing dimples. "Though you're mine by law, I'll not take you if this be not your will." He lifted her chin with his index finger. "You can sweep the barrel hall for the next year instead." His green eyes sparkled.

"I'm not much of a sweeper," said Alice. His lips were on hers and he tasted of salty fish and again the hint of sweetness. She would have to try anchovies on her next pizza, she thought as he pulled her down with him to his knees. He let go of her to reach into the leather pouch at his waist and held up a flask.

"You should at least taste the reason you're here."

Alice took the flask, pulled out the cork and took a sip... whiskey. But this was not the sticks and rubbing alcohol she had always thought whiskey tasted. She took another sip. It tasted slightly sweet and richly woody, with a dry finish that made you crave another sip to make certain it was real. Her expression must have shown her appreciation as Ian's smile widened.

Ian replaced the flask and undid his thick leather belt, pulled off his white shirt and reached down to remove the dagger shaped pin that held the kilt closed. The kilt slid to the ground.

"How could a girl turn down that?" said Alice appraising a delicious, thick erection. The dimples were gone and his eyes half closed with desire. He reached over to take her breasts in his hands, caressing her through her dress. Alice gave a soft whimper.

"Nor a man resist these. It would'a been more torture than payment to watch you sweep." He reached around to undo the buttons on the back and pulled the top of her dress to her waist. The shift did little to contain Alice's double DDs and the look of wonder was his this time. As if he read her mind he placed one hand on her left nipple and began to suck greedily at her right. Alice felt the spasms between her legs that had first began when he dropped his kilt, increased in frequency.

"Oh God, Ian, I want you inside me." She lay back on the soft heather and he lifted her skirt and answered her prayer. His thrusts were slow and delicious, not what she expected at all. The sounds he made against her ear were soft, almost whimpering sounds, again a surprise. With each thrust, Alice's pleasure built until the sounds of her coming chased the crows from their perches in the rocks.

Ian laughed softly against her ear and began thrusting harder now, balancing his weight on his arms so he looked directly into her eyes. The look in those green eyes stirred her to follow each stroke with a deep moan. The pace and the depth of his delicious thick cock inside her caused him to climax with a soft sigh and collapse on top of her, holding so tight she could hardly breathe.

Ian propped himself on one elbow and dimpled at her. "Will ye have a bit more Killkeny's before we go again, if that's yer want?"

"Oh yes, please," said Alice. She took a sip. "I have never been fond of whiskey, but this…." She shook her head, unable to find words to describe the flavor.

"A wee drop of wild honey is the secret to the sweet beginning. Not another like it." He searched through the pile of his clothes and held up a small, dark glass bottle. Setting the bottle on the ground, Ian pulled her dress over her head and tore off her thin shift. His eyes devoured her with a hunger she had rarely seen in a man's eyes. She liked it.

He picked up the bottle and slowly poured thick amber liquid onto each of her breasts. He dripped a trail down her stomach and stopped after pouring a generous amount between her legs. When he was finished, he slid a thick finger between her legs and then to her lips. It was honey. He began to lick the honey slowly from her breasts. The viscosity of the honey made it take a good deal of effort to remove it all, both licking and sucking to get every drop of golden sweetness. She watched his lips and his tongue devour the honey and her flesh, little by little, make his way down her body. By the time he reached the honey between her legs, all it took was a few strokes on her clit and a finger inside her for her to climax hard.

"Honey is the secret, huh." Alice said laughing. "Is there any left?"

"A wee bit. But I'd try the whiskey." He lay back, filled his navel from his flask and handed the flask to Alice. She emptied the tiny but delicious cup formed and licked every drop from the auburn curls that led to her heart's desire. Filling her mouth from the flask, she took his cock in her mouth and bathed it with the whiskey. He gasped. She swallowed and began to slide her lips up and down his shaft, lubricated now with her saliva. Alice used only her tongue and lips and this time he was not so quiet as he filled her eager mouth. Even his semen was sweet.

Ian pulled her on top of him and held her tight against him, breathing heavy. "Am I worth the ten barrels?" she said with her head on his chest.

"Ach, was not a price, but a forfeiture for a crime committed. Your kin made off with ten barrels in the dead of a winter's night." He caressed her back and kissed her forehead. "Our clan is civil. Most would have shed blood for such a theft."

"I am quite happy to help keep the peace," she said drowsy, Ian's arms around her, the warm sun on her bare skin and whiskey in her belly. Alice closed her eyes.

Chapter Twenty-One

PHENOMENAL CAT

With her groceries purchased and put away, everything perfectly in its place, Alice intended to cap her Saturday with some crockpot delicacy or another at Susan's. Opening her door, she saw a man standing in the hall with his back to her. He was tall with dark hair and wore a long gray wool overcoat. He turned and smiled at her with her father's smile. Her brother Sean looked so well put together she nearly didn't recognize him.

"Alice. Glad you opened your door. I won't have to bother somebody else in this building trying to find you." He took a step toward her and opened his arms. Alice froze in place.

"I don't blame you. I was in pretty rough shape the last time we met."

"You tried to rob me." Alice did not open the door further but stood looking at him with her hands on the door.

"Yeah, I did, didn't I? You know that wasn't me. It was the coke. I never would have…"

He always blamed someone else. He looked good. Wasn't this what she had always wanted for him?

"Aren't you going to invite me in? I have been knocking on doors in your building for a half an hour."

Alice opened the door wide and took a step back. "It's great to see you looking so…."

"Sober. Cause that's what I am." Sean put his arms around Alice and hugged her tight. She let him but did not return it. "This time rehab really changed my life and I know I have you to thank." He took a step back and put his hands on her shoulders. "I met a guy at rehab in real estate and we hit it off. I'm going places and I'm gonna pay you back."

"Great." She hoped her voice sounded more hopeful than she felt.

"Let me take you to dinner. We can catch up." He walked into her great room, pulled off his overcoat and plopped down in the middle of her couch.

"I have plans." Alice closed the door but did not move toward Sean.

"Cancel them." He flashed her that smile that she never found genuine on her father or her brother. It was wide with big straight teeth and not one ounce of warmth.

"My friend Susan already made dinner. Her husband disappeared and is feared dead."

"Invite her."

Alice picked up her phone and texted Susan. *Sean showed up. Sorry about dinner.*

"This is some place." He looked up at the exposed beam in the ceiling." I'll be looking for a place like this soon, but in Chicago. St. Louis real estate is small time. Three bedrooms?"

"Two." Alice walked around the couch and sat in the black leather chair across from him.

"Oh, too bad. Tough resale. Need three bedrooms at least in this market."

"I am proud of you," said Alice. She had not seen him look this healthy in decades. He usually sought her out when he was in deep and heavy trouble with the law, a drug dealer or someone big and mean. He didn't look as if he needed money for the first time since she could remember. He stood up, handing Alice his coat to hang. She draped it over a chair. He wore a sharp navy-blue blazer and nicely cut khaki pants. His black shoes looked expensive and had a shine you could see your face in. Alice heard Susan's knock on her door and let out an audible sigh of relief.

"Hey, I made enough food for an army and I haven't seen Sean for ages." Susan stood holding her crockpot with two oven mitts. Walking past Alice, Susan set the crockpot down in the kitchen and began to open drawers and cabinets, pulling plates and utensils.

"I had planned to take my sis out to someplace classy, but home cooking can't be beat."

"Susan is a great cook. What's in that magic pot tonight?"

"It's my famous Beef Au Italian dressing." Susan's smile was a little weak, but her eyes reassured Alice that she was making an effort and Alice appreciated the rescue. Sean did look wonderful, but left alone with him, Alice might find it difficult not to bring up all his past failings. Which would change nothing except destroy any chance at a possibly good relationship with her only brother. Susan's company was more than welcome.

"It smells delicious," Sean said.

"It's always wonderful. I have salad." Alice opened the refrigerator door and pulled out a bag of pre-chopped salad and a bottle of blue cheese salad dressing.

"How old is that stuff?" asked Susan, placing plates on the bar.

Sean laughed. "Alice was never much of a cook." He perched himself on one of the stools at Alice's black granite bar and waited to be served.

"That hasn't changed, but I bought the salad two days ago," said Alice. She filled three bowls from the bag. Susan nodded, as if impressed that Alice's healthier eating habits had stuck. "I have another stool in my bedroom. Be right back."

She could hear Sean's voice and it was good to hear Susan

laugh as she dragged the stool up to the bar. She could see that Sean was using his considerable charm on Susan, who now sat on the stool with her shapely legs crossed, dishing up beef onto plates. Susan knew all of Sean's history and had once helped Alice drag him inside when he had passed out on the steps to their apartment. Still, it was nice to see her friend smile.

"You lived with Alice in college. Did she still lay in her bed whispering to imaginary people like she did as a kid?"

"Nope." Susan stopped smiling at Sean and set down her fork.

"Yeah, our parents spent a fortune on shrinks for her when we were kids," he said with his mouth full. "They even sent her away to some camp to deal with...

"How was rehab? Any celebrities getting sober with you?" Susan said. Her eyes narrowed.

"Nah, it was a great place, but mostly regular folks. I did meet a big real estate mogul. Teaching me the ropes," said Sean.

Susan nodded with raised eyebrows. Alice wanted to be happy for him. But she had heard how he was on his way to fame and fortune many times in the past. He looked healthy and calm. Alice smiled and returned her attention to her plate.

Alice's father's smile and her mother's clear gray eyes, in the form of Sean, seemed to brighten Susan's mood. Perhaps this time the check she wrote for Sean's rehab had been well spent.

Otis sat in the middle of the kitchen floor meowing. Alice could see his bowl was full. She made the universal cat calling kissing sound, and he walked toward her.

"So when are your cat's kittens do. She looks ready to explode," said Sean.

"He's just a little portly." When Alice looked down at Otis walking toward her, she knew immediately something was wrong. Otis's sides bulged as if he were pregnant. He had always been a little round, but this had happened overnight. She realized he had not touched his food from this morning.

His usually round emerald eyes were more green slits. "His belly feels full of fluid and he looks like he's in pain," said Alice as she knelt next to the black cat, clutching him to her.

Susan hopped off her stool and headed to the door. "I'll grab my coat and call the emergency vet to let them know we're on our way," said Susan.

Alice retrieved the cat carrier from the coat closet and Sean held it up on its end as Alice gently dropped Otis in. It felt comforting to have her brother's help like when they were children and her big brother had been her staunchest ally.

"Thank you, Sean I…"

"Glad to help." He picked up her cell phone where it sat on the coffee table and handed it to her. "My number is 816-960-4920. Text me so we can keep in touch."

Alice entered the number, and a tone sounded from Sean's pocket.

"Perfect. I can carry the cat…"

"I've got him. Thanks. Talk to you soon." Sean let himself out.

❧

"I'm afraid it's not good," said the young vet whose name tag read Dr. Diesel. "The radiographs reveal a large tumor and it involves several organ systems. We could do surgery, but I doubt…"

Alice petted Otis's shiny black head, and he purred his chainsaw loud purr.

"Is he in pain?" she asked the chubby vet in blue scrubs. The look on his round pink face was grim. He ran his fingers through wispy blond hair.

"Could be. The incessant purring can be a form of self-soothing."

"He always purrs like that."

Susan reached over and took her hand and she knew what

she had to do for her other best friend. If he were human, they would do debulking surgery and chemo which might buy him some time, but he's a cat. Her little friend wouldn't understand the pain and sickness of treatment and deserved more than a little more time in misery.

"He is too good a cat to suffer. Let's put him to sleep."

Dr. Diesel blinked back tears. Alice guessed he hadn't yet learned to accept an important part of a vet's job without feeling. It comforted her.

Dr. Diesel turned and removed some supplies from a drawer. Next, he drew up some liquid in a syringe. His eyes now dry, he said, "This will relax him." He pinched some skin on Otis's flank and injected the fluid. Otis continued his purring but his head bobbed as if it was hard to hold up. Alice knelt down, took his paw with one hand, and held his head with the other. She talked softly into his ear, "You're a good boy and I love you." The cat's eyes closed, and the purring stopped.

Alice could see that the vet had placed a small catheter in Otis's leg and administered the drug that stopped his heart. Tears streamed down her cheeks, but no words would come.

"Do you want to take him to bury or we have a cremation service?"

"I don't have a place to bury him."

"We will call you in a couple of weeks. I'm sorry. You gave him a good life." Dr. Diesel's face was composed now and his smile genuine and comforting.

Susan cleaned up the table and kitchen as Alice sat on a stool, crying. "He was just a little tripod cat, but he has been my rock for the last decade." She wiped her eyes. "I know it's not the same as possibly losing your husband, but I can't…"

"It's okay." Susan closed the dishwasher door and walked

over to her friend. "Losing someone you love hurts. The fact that he was covered with fur doesn't change the pain. You loved him and he's gone. Go ahead cry as much as you want." She handed Alice a piece of paper towel. "I'm not ready to give up and cry yet. Maybe I should be, but I'm not ready to give up. I do cry, though. I think crying is good."

Chapter Twenty-Two

OOPS!...I DID IT AGAIN

O n Monday morning, Alice felt that the weekend's tears had helped a little. She felt a small cat shaped hole in her heart, but she would be okay. Work was the perfect distraction. Dr. Mariani had planned to do some actual transplants of prototypes on living subjects this morning.

The bell she had installed on her office door rang and she looked up from her emails to see Brad James standing in front of her desk. "So, should I email you some pertinent facts about Dallas Regional? The meeting is two weeks away, but I know you like to prepare." He wore a black suit, pale lavender shirt and a deep purple tie. His expression was all business, but those eyes…

There was really no reason not to go, she told herself. Excellosteo was progressing beautifully and generating some industry buzz was a sound strategy. "Sure." She could control herself. If Susan got bad news about David from Africa, she could be back in two hours.

"Great," said Brad. After a long moment of silence, he turned and walked out her door. Alice called Doris, who arranged all the travel and made sure two hotel rooms were booked in Dallas.

❧

"So tell me again why Excellosteo implants are better than the standard titanium?" said Brad James as soon as Alice had clicked the seatbelt closed on her window seat in the 747 to Dallas.

"They are far more bio-compatible because they are made of the patient's own cells. Our revolutionary design insures placement will require minimal bone prep, which is easier for the surgeon and less trauma for the patient. Both factors contributing to faster patient recovery. Surgeons love anything that cuts down on their work. We hope to get the price per unit far below the old-fashioned implants after a short time. You know how expensive titanium is?" She looked only at her laptop, but wished she would have told Doris to make sure their seats were in different rows. She could feel the heat of his skin through his dark gray pants. Damn those tiny airplane seats.

❧

The meeting with Dallas Regional went unbelievably well. She had worn her most serious gray suit and shiny patent stilettos. Watching Brad present to the group reminded her why she had hired him four years ago. He talked to the CEO, CNO and CFO like they were old friends. His manner was easy, as if they had all gone to the same middle school and happened to be sitting around a large conference table on a Thursday morning. It was a thing of beauty. She had her own more formal style, which had been successful countless times, but how smart was anyone who could not learn?

Today, she followed Brad's lead and talked to the three men and two women like she knew them well, making eye contact and smiling often. Anytime she glanced Brad's way, his expression let her know he thought she was right on target.

The heads of the hospital system agreed and requested another meeting to work out the particulars of a potentially huge deal and seemed intrigued by the possibility of Excellosteo. They might have to add an extra shift on the pacemaker line for this group alone.

§.

"You made a damn fine presentation, Alice." She could find no place to look but at him as they sat in the back of the Uber, heading to the hotel. He beamed his look of pride in her and she melted a little.

"Thanks. This was not my first rodeo," she said, this time looking him straight in his eyes.

"I know." His eyes searched her face, smiling. "It's early yet. There are some fun places we can walk to close to the hotel?"

Didn't a girl deserve a drink after possibly the best presentation of her career? She had to admit she had made a better presentation after watching Brad, but not out loud. "I'll change and meet you in the lobby in half an hour." Alice had brought some skinny jeans and a baby pink tunic top. It wasn't sexy, but then this wasn't a date. She tugged on her favorite fake cheetah booties. She was merely celebrating a successful afternoon with a colleague...a very hot one who had seen her naked on more than one occasion. Was it worth spending some time getting to know Brad like Dr. Cindy suggested? Brad was a real cheetah and though extremely fast, probably could not be tamed.

§.

"I do know how capable you are," said Brad as they walked across the fake cobblestone courtyard. There were restaurants, bars, and boutiques along on either side of the street made to look like an old western town. "I know you should still be CEO, but I think I have done a decent job." He shot a sideways glance at her.

Alice looked straight ahead as she walked, but couldn't contain a small smile. She should still be CEO. She enjoyed her R & D job and crushing it, even though it was definitely a step back down the career ladder. She had agreed to go on this trip to keep her skills sharp. It wouldn't hurt to keep her name in front of a large hospital group like Dallas Regional. She stopped in front of a place called Dirty Dicks. *How appropriate.* "This looks fun," she said.

"Looks good to me." Brad opened the door for her. At three in the afternoon, the place looked deserted. It had a long bar across the back of the place, with wooden trestle tables scattered around the room. There was only one group of twenty somethings drinking pitchers of beer in the far corner. Looked like it might be packed later this evening, but Alice didn't mind the quiet of Dirty Dick's at this hour. They sat side by side on two empty bar stools. There were every kind of mounted fish over the bar, which suited her fine since she loved seafood of all kinds.

"Little early for dinner. Why don't we grab a drink and…" He reached over and caressed her butt through her skinny jeans. "…head to my room?"

Alice ignored the caress that would normally make her shiver in anticipation. She shivered a teeny bit but kept her eyes on the menu. "I'm hungry, and I have my own room."

He removed his hand from her posterior. "I guess I deserve this. I did leave you hanging after that night at my place."

"I get it. You are fishing in a younger pond these days," she said, glancing up at the fish over the bar.

Brad laughed. "I don't know what you heard, but I didn't want to feel tied down. It hasn't really been that long since Olivia left."

Still pretending to study the menu, though she had settled

on something long ago, Alice said, "Far be it from me to tie anyone down." She turned to look at him and her little smile was gone.

"I am sorry, Alice. I didn't mean to hurt you."

"I'm not hurt. Just smarter."

"I think I know you better than…."

"Oh, do you?" She turned to him. "What's my favorite color? Where did I go to college? What was my major?" Alice didn't want him to think she was angry, so she widened her eyes and lifted her brows.

Brad signaled the bartender, who had been drying glasses, standing far enough away to pretend not to hear their conversation. "A Tanqueray martini up with three olives for the lady and I'd like a Modello."

The cute young man with a mane of black curly hair and a neatly trimmed beard smiled at Alice and answered Brad. "Yes, sir."

Now Alice laughed. "I don't intend to stay head of R & D forever, you know."

"The best employee is the one who wants your job." He lay down his menu and looked at her. "I have some amazing news and I wanted to tell you myself. Hold on to your hat." He smiled an ear to ear smile. "Legal has managed to not only get a permanent cease and desist against Patterson for Biocardia, but it looks like the patents formerly granted to Patterson, will be transferred to us."

Alice hopped off her stool and wrapped her arms around Brad in elation. She couldn't believe he was telling her she might soon have her pet project back. Biocardia was revolutionary and would yield large profits much sooner than the still experimental Excellosteo.

"I'm betting you can handle both projects at once." He picked up his glass. "Here's to implantable device dominance."

Alice clicked her martini glass with his, took a sip of pine flavored goodness and began to run over the details in her head. The principal research on Biocardia was finished. Ami could handle the small details. She hoped Dr. Mariani could handle the additional dog bypass surgeries and if she couldn't, she might know someone who would.

Brad reached over and put his hand on her shoulder. She didn't move. "Hey where'd you go," said Brad. "I think we have some celebrating to do."

She took another sip. Whether it was gratitude, genuine joy or gin, she did feel like celebrating. They ordered an appetizer to share and Alice outlined some things that had to be done to get Biocardia up and running again. Brad listened and his beer disappeared, as did the mini crab cakes they had ordered. As she outlined, Brad's initial look of interest morphed into the one she knew too well.

"I...I..." He was doing it to her again. Her heart sped up and her cheeks got warm.

"Your favorite color is red. You went to St. Louis University and majored in biology with a botany concentration." He grinned.

"Very good." All she wanted as she took her last bite and sip was Brad. Did alcohol cause bad judgement, or was she born with it? She leaned over and kissed him. He didn't say a word, but threw two twentys on the bar, took her hand and led her back to his room.

"You look beautiful," Brad said as she sat on the couch in his room. He dropped down beside her and took her face in his hands. Kissing her softly and teasing her lips with the tip of his tongue. "Better than twenty-five in every way."

He pulled her against him, holding her tight and stroking her hair. "I care about you, Alice," he said softly against her ear. "Always have."

"Yeah," she answered. Leaning against Brad enfolded in his arms felt like the most comfortable place in the universe. She could have stayed there forever. Brad had other ideas and his lips began to slide down her neck. A little moan escaped her lips.

"I'll be right back," said Brad, and headed to the bathroom.

Alice quickly threw off her clothes and got under the covers on the bed, striking a pose she thought seductive. She tucked the covers below her breasts to leave them exposed.

Brad returned. "Now that's sexy," he said, and reached up to loosen and remove his tie. Slowly unbuttoning his shirt, he kept his gaze only on her. His pants folded over the chair, Alice couldn't wait for her favorite part, the unveiling. Standing in only his black boxer briefs, he walked to the bed and slid them down.

Alice gasped. She would never get used to the beauty of him.

Brad laughed. "It's all for you, baby." He lifted the covers and slid in next to her. Kissing her this time deep, and delicious. Now focusing on her breasts, he sucked one nipple hard and pulled gently at the other.

Alice moaned and spread her legs.

Brad reached down, sliding his fingers into her. "And that's for you...baby," she said. In seconds, he was inside her. She wrapped her legs around him, pulling him in deeper. With each stroke she cried out until reaching her usual loud climax, Alice hope she hadn't awakened any napping children in the next room. Brad collapsed on top of her, holding her tight. When finally she whimpered softly, he lifted his weight off of her and reached down to take her hand and wrapped it around his cock. "I want to watch you please yourself."

Alice obliged. Taking his exquisite thickness in her hand, she began to stroke her clit with it. His width covering the most sensitive parts of her, his hardness the perfect friction until the pleasure of Brad split the universe inside her. She made not a single sound as she came apart beneath him, exploding into a million shimmering pieces. He slipped inside her once more and each deep stroke seemed to create its own climax as she lost herself in his eyes. He closed them and pumped hard into her, making the hissing growl she knew meant she would soon feel his climax gather in a pool beneath them. Rolling on his side, he took her with him. They lay face to face, still locked together by his arms tight around her.

"I love pleasing you, watching your face when you come," Brad said.

"You are very good at making that happen."

"Still early. Want to get some dinner?" He propped up on one arm, smiling at her with the other still holding her tight.

"Not sure I want to leave this bed."

"We'll be back. Let's get some oysters."

"I love oysters." Alice wiggled out of his arms and sat up.

"Hooters has the best ones around here." He grinned at her.

"Right, because anyone goes to Hooters for the food." Her face must have reflected her words.

"Really? I asked at the front desk and he said Hooter's had the best oysters in the whole area."

"Well, a good burger would be fine, too. That western looking place probably has one of those." Alice had little interest in watching Brad smile at the adorable twenty-year-olds serving food and liquor in little orange shorts and tiny t-shirts. Besides, she had always felt Hooter's entirely too exploitive to ever be patronized.

"Put your clothes on, Alice. We are getting those oysters." He looked at her like she was the most beautiful girl in the world and she could deny him nothing.

As Alice sat sipping her second martini of the day, a rare occurrence, Brad looked only at her. Around the bar sat a dozen men ogling the servers whose bounty overflowed their too small white t-shirts. Brad sat beaming as if he knew he was the only man at that bar not going home alone.

"You would look as good as any of those girls in that outfit," said Brad.

Alice laughed, but his sincere tone touched her. "I would never earn my living exploiting myself."

"You use your talents and so do they. Women are too hard on each other."

The server, with a mane of red hair and a dazzling smile plus the other required Hooter's attributes, set the tray of oysters down in front of Alice. Smiling widely at her, the server said, "They are kinda gross, but I love them too. They taste like the sea and you don't get much of that in Dallas." Their eyes met and Alice realized Brad was right. This was just a woman making her living with what God gave her. It was hard work and who was she to judge?

They finished two dozen oysters and headed back to Brad's room. Why had she insisted the company pay for two rooms? Brad's idea of dessert was every bit as delicious as the oysters and she fell asleep laying on her side, the little spoon to his big one.

Chapter Twenty-Three

EVERY DAY IS A WINDING ROAD

"I am proud to turn this part of the meeting over to our head of R&D, Alice Hightower," said Brad, sitting in the spot at the long black conference table from which Alice had led hundreds of meetings. Every chair was occupied for this meeting. He smiled as proud as a papa peacock. His smile didn't make her want to trade places with him any less, but she did remember why she still liked him.

"Thanks, Brad," said Alice. She closed her laptop and stood up. "It is with great pleasure that I announce today that the Biocardia project is ours again thanks to the incredible efforts of our legal team. Stand up, you geniuses." The two lawyers hired specifically because of their experience with industrial espionage, stood looking embarrassed. Both wore nice blue skinny cut suits, had similar dark hair and haircuts, and appeared about the same age. Alice thought she would keep them straight by the fact that Jones wore glasses and Garcia did not. Everyone around the table broke into applause. Jones and Garcia both smiled widely and sat down.

"Alright, now let's talk specifics. Excellosteo needs to proceed, but it is pretty obvious that we are a long way to market with this one," said Alice. Ami Wen frowned.

"Dr. Wen, I am hoping you can handle research on both projects. The principal research on Biocardia is finished, but I am certain your talents will be needed to help put Petrus's work into some usable form as we move forward." Ami's frown faded, and she gave the nervous little teeth-hiding smile to the large group.

"Louise, I will let you organize your department as you see fit to bring Biocardia closer to production for human trials as soon as is feasible." Alice telling Louise how to do much of anything was a waste of time. She was as competent as she could be difficult.

"Dr. Mariani, How comfortable are you with canine cardiac surgery?"

"I taught that before I switched to orthopedics," said Dr. Karen Mariani. The woman's pretty little features seem to light up at the thought of greater challenges for her.

"Great. Mr. Guri, How soon can production retool to produce vessels once again in numbers great to move toward human trials?"

An intense middle-aged man with wild black hair and a hawk's eyes took a minute to answer. "We can be ready as soon as engineering gets us the specs."

"Alright everyone, thanks for your attention. I know very well we can walk and chew gum, so let's get on with rocking the bypass world with Biocardia as we continue to bring Excellosteo along." The table burst into applause. Alice nodded and smiled. It did feel good to sit at the big black conference table and lead the show.

Brad stayed behind when the others filed out of the room. "A little brilliant to get all the principals at one meeting, give them the news and secure their cooperation all at once." He sat smiling across the table at her and she couldn't help feeling the heat from three feet away.

"Why thank you, sir. I am glad you were pleased." She was

sure he caught the entirely unprofessional tone in her statement.

Brad laughed. "I would love to discuss that further at my place tonight. Now I have the rest of the company to attend to."

Alice enjoyed watching his dove gray suit pants hug his scrumptious ass as he left the room. She was glad he had left the lovely jacket in his office for this meeting. His pale-blue shirt and shiny silver cufflinks were more visible this way. She smiled, picked up her laptop, and headed down to her office. She was a good leader and now, with Biocardia back in her portfolio, she doubted that she would be stuck R&Ding forever. The success of two such impressive projects would go a long way to impressing some company to hire her as CEO when she was ready.

Typing up her notes from the meeting, Alice heard the bell on her office door and was happy to see Ami.

"Pretty awesome, about Biocardia." Ami gave Alice her big bunny smile.

"Thanks. I am pretty sure that the task of growing cardiac vessel cells is cake compared to bone."

"Yeah, the complexity of bone metabolism makes it particularly intriguing, but that's my jam. I will be happy to tackle any problems that might arise on Biocardia, if you let my main focus be on Excellosteo and the knee team."

"Agreed," said Alice.

"Priscilla will bring the babies up to say hello soon. One of them might help you forget Otis."

"I will never forget Otis. But I will be happy to see the cute little guys. Who knows?" Ami headed out the door. *Had Ami always walked with a limp?* wondered Alice.

Chapter Twenty-Four

THE SOUND OF SILENCE

"I t was perfect," said Alice, answering Dr. Cindy's opening question about her last week. "Work is proceeding brilliantly, better than I could have hoped. I spent an evening with Brad and we actually streamed a movie and talked instead of burning up his sheets. I think I like the man and he seems to like me."

"You don't look like everything is fine," said Dr. Cindy. She crossed her long legs, currently wearing knee-length silver-gray ostrich skin boots. The boots matched her gray leggings and tunic and were magnificent. Alice's pulse didn't even race at her proximity to fabulous footwear. She stared at the floor with her hands folded in her lap.

"Everything still feels dark and empty."

"Depressive cycles often seem to come out of nowhere." Alice heard the doctor's pen scribbling on the paper but didn't look up. Her head felt so heavy.

"I thought since it had been so long since…."

"You have been managing beautifully, but unfortunately depression happens to good people when least convenient. You know what to do. Keep up your healthy patterns and it will pass. If you need the medication, it can be used short term."

"Yeah," said Alice. She could hear Dr. Cindy speaking more words, but the words could not break through the heavy black clouds still gathering in her head.

She wasn't certain how long the session had lasted. Alice found herself in her car and could not bring herself to go anywhere. The leaden fibers of darkness seemed to wrap her neurons tighter with each breath. Dr. Cindy's office was in a small medical building in a residential neighborhood. Sitting alone in the only car in the parking lot with her head in her hands would not look good to the police officer. Someone would soon be calling.

With all her concentration, Alice put her key in the ignition and started the car. "Hello darkness my old friend," sang Simon & Garfunkel from the oldies radio station. She didn't have the energy to turn it off when she parked. At the bottom of her darkness, Alice could not ignore the irony and she laughed. And she laughed. She would get herself home and like Dr. Cindy said, her old friend would pass or she would call and get the medicine Dr. Cindy mentioned. This bipolar cycling couldn't be cured evidently. Human brains were too complicated, but she could manage it. She had to.

After twenty-four hours of lying in bed, Alice forced herself to get up and get dressed. It was Sunday and Susan would be knocking on her door for breakfast and yoga soon. She determined to remove Otis's food dish and water bowl, but she found they had already been removed along with all the cans of his favorite food and his litter box.

"Come on, we're burning daylight. The Benton Park Café needs our money," said Susan, standing in Alice's doorway.

Alice attempted a weak smile. "I'm not really hungry."

Susan walked to the closet, took Alice's coat off the hanger and slipped it on each arm. Alice would have to pull it up the rest of the way, which she did.

The walk from their building in the crisp late winter air filled her lungs and helped clear the darkness that had already begun to lift. The smell of good coffee and bacon at the café aroused Alice's drowsing senses. "Thanks, Susan. I needed this."

"You drag me, I drag you. How it works."

"My life is going well. I really have nothing to be depressed about." Alice picked at her veggie omelet.

"Maybe this stuff is cumulative. You did lose a child and a very dear furry friend not that long ago." Susan had set down her fork. Alice wondered how Susan could be so chipper as each passing day increased the chance that her husband was never coming home. If it made Susan happy to pretend everything was alright, she could go along with it.

"Yeah, I still feel those losses, but I have moved on from the intense pain. The depressive episodes happen with no warning, like a gust of winter wind that knocks me on my ass."

"Kind of poetic."

Alice smiled at Susan. "I guess something good can come from my downs, poetry."

"I don't think you will be reading poems at a coffee house anytime soon. How's your boss, Mr. Hunky Suits?"

"Brad is well. We've been spending some time together. He is away on a golf trip with some friends this weekend." Alice was glad not to have to explain about her mental issues yet to Brad. She had finished her entire omelet and started on the fruit she usually took home in a box.

"I'm glad. That is one man too good to waste." Susan waved the server over to refill her coffee.

"I was never wasting him. He needed some space after his divorce and wanted to waste himself on twenty somethings."

"Not very original, but I'm guessing he came to his senses and recognizes women closer to his age are much better company."

"So he says."

Breakfast with Susan and yoga had invigorated Alice, and she hummed as she put everything in her home back in place in preparation for the week to begin tomorrow. Her phone sounded the text tone, and she picked it up.

"Miss You," said a text that her phone identified as James. She felt her pulse quicken.

"Me Too," she typed and returned to straightening her shoes.

The darkness had lifted as Dr. Cindy had reminded her it would. There was no doubt it would be back, but not today.

Chapter Twenty-Five

WALK LIKE AN EGYPTIAN

After a long day of researching and developing, Alice couldn't help think of rewarding herself a little. Who might she find to indulge with her in a little meaningless fantasy sex courtesy of her guestroom closet? She knew Brad was extremely busy with the relaunch of Biocardia, but he had made a point to send her cute little texts at least daily.

She stood at the window in her office watching the kitties devour their evening meal. Snow fell, gathering on the dormant grass and dusting the naked trees. The cats seemed to be eating as if they knew the weatherman had called for three to five inches of snow. The empty parking lot at 3:00 p.m. demonstrated the average St. Louis resident's terror of winter weather. It snowed almost every year, but people never seemed to lose their fear or learn to handle the winter weather any better. The highways would be packed with twisted metal smashed together as people headed home at top speed as if they could outrun precipitation. Alice preferred to watch the snow and the feral cats until anyone who could destroy her precious Porsche was off the roads. There were plenty of emails to get a jump on for tomorrow and reports to finish. The clothes from some delicious time and place would soon transport her.

Her office door's bell tinkled. Figuring it was Ami stopping by to update her and watch the kitties, she did not turn around. Arms encircled her waist and lips found her neck.

"Brad," purred Alice. The arms fell away, and the lips were gone.

"No," said a voice that definitely was't Brad's.

She turned around to see Vincent Terreci. Alice thought the look of surprise on Vincent's face almost comical, but she did not laugh. "I'm sorry I…"

"Was expecting someone else. I get it." Vincent smiled at her, but his eyebrows told another story knitted together tight.

"Yes." She hoped the smile she gave him looked apologetic.

"I told you I needed time, and I couldn't really expect a woman like you to wait around." His face relaxed.

"And what exactly is a woman like me?" Alice leaned against the door.

"Smart, beautiful and sexy."

Her heart hurt a little as she looked into those gorgeous eyes. "Timing is everything."

"Yeah, and mine has never been great. I saw you looking out the window, and you looked so lovely and everybody had gone home early, fleeing Snowmageddon. I couldn't resist."

"I don't know what to say." Tempted though she was to melt into those strong hungry arms that showed through his burgundy sweater, she had to admit dating two men simultaneously was never a good idea, for her anyway. She was not Scarlet O'Hara and a bevy of beaux courting her was too much.

"There's nothing to say. Mama Torresi didn't raise an idiot. I'm not going to mess with the boss's girl." He headed to the door. There was nothing she could say. Scarlet O'Hara had ended up alone, after all.

Alice heard the tone for a text come from her phone buried deep in her purse as she buttoned her coat.

"Hey, baby. I'm beat from pushing cars out of the parking lot. Dinner tomorrow night? I'll cook you something amazing," read the text from Brad. They hadn't had a firm date. But for the past few weeks, they'd spent some weeknights and most Friday and Saturday nights together.

"My favorite dish needs no cooking. See you tomorrow." Alice smiled at her own wit as she answered him. She had been neglecting her fantasy men. Falling into Vincent's arms would definitely have been a betrayal of Brad, but some imaginary hottie from another time would never tell tales.

Mini ravioli and a little green salad downed, 30 minutes on her elliptical and she slid the closet door open.

A white sheath hung on one hanger. She could see her fingers through the soft cloth. The other hanger held an elaborate collar made of beads attached to straps made of the same beads of black, terracotta and deep blue strung on golden threads. On the floor sat a black lacquered box. On top of the box sat a small round glass object. Curious, she picked it up... It had a lid and when she lifted it off, she found a deep red substance. "Lipstick?" she asked the little jar.

Inside the box, she found a wooden head with a wig sitting on it. She had found wigs in her closet before, but this one came wearing a circle of gold and blue beads.

Pulling back her hair and setting the wig on her head, she could see the wig's shiny black hair hung in tiny braids to her shoulders. Alice could see it on Elizabeth Taylor's head as she rode in to Rome on a golden sphinx. Cleopatra was one of her mother's favorite old movies and she had seen it a hundred times as a child.

She picked up her phone and the picture she found googling women's clothes in ancient Egypt told her that the sheath went below her breasts and the straps covered them and attached to the wide beaded collar. With the help of the picture on Wikipedia, Alice slipped on the sheath, which fell slightly above her ankles and would not slide over her breasts. Since the clothes always fit her perfectly, she did not force it higher. The straps were wide enough to cover her nipples and little else. She tied the beaded straps to pieces of thread on the sheath she assumed were there for that purpose. The fine weave of the sheath's fabric allowed it to cling to her as if it were made of spandex. Google also told her that red lipstick was primarily worn by prostitutes that were highly revered during several of the Egyptian dynasties.

"Being revered sounds fun," she said as she dabbed on the dark red, waxy lipstick. The effect in the mirrored closet door made her want to break into the Bangle's ditty. Disappointed there were no shoes, Alice stepped out the balcony door.

The bright sunlight made her long for ancient Egyptian sunglasses. The dry sandy soil beneath her feet felt warm. A few feet in front of her rose ten pillars twenty feet high. Each pillar was decorated at its base with brightly painted frescos of Egyptians engaged in various activities. The figures walked, rode horses or chariots and either wrestled or had sex, Alice couldn't tell which, all done in the stylized profiles of ancient Egypt. Two enormous, winged creatures guarded an even larger doorway. The buff-colored walls of the building looked like they could have been made of concrete only smoother.

Alice inhaled a rich spicy scent, heard someone singing and a flute playing. She walked through the doorway into a small room. Two men stood in front of another large doorway, this one with a huge wooden door. The figure of a man wearing a tall hat like the Pope's miter was carved into the door. She knew that hat was a crown. The two men wore nothing but short skirts made of a material similar to her dress, but unfortunately for her viewing pleasure, it was pleated in the front before disappearing into a wide woven belt. A collar of black and gold beads hung around each man's neck. Their heads were shaved and their eyes ringed with heavy black eyeliner. Slender muscles decorated their delicate frames.

"Hey, dudes," she decided to say, figuring they did not understand English and having no idea what else to say. They fell to their knees and put their faces to the floor with hands outstretched in front of them. The man on her right lifted her foot gently and put it on his neck.

"Let the revering begin." She beamed. The men scrambled to her side, and each one took an arm, holding gently as if to guide rather than restrain her. One opened the huge door but never let go of her. They led her into an enormous room. Alice struggled to focus in the dim light.

There were clay vessels set in sconces on the walls that must have held oils as flames came from them and lit the room with adequate soft light once her eyes adjusted. At the back of the room, on a raised platform, sat two people in golden chairs. As she moved closer, she could see they were beautiful. Their smooth, tanned faces and the fact they both wore eye make-up, made it hard to tell their sexes. The one who wore a pope's hat had a shaved head, so Alice assumed he was male. The one by his side had hair very much like her wig and must have been a woman. The queen wore a circle of gold much thicker than Alice's, with large sparkling stones. Both wore similar linen outfits with long sleeves and ankle-length skirts. Golden sandals decorated the pair's feet. The regal duo inclined their heads slightly in a little bow in Alice's direction and her escorts led her to the left side of the room. On each royal face, Alice thought she saw boredom.

Along the long wall were cushions a few feet apart on the floor and on almost every one knelt a woman. There were beautiful dark-skinned women with close cropped hair who wore collars of straw and nothing else. Many were dressed like Alice but appeared to be of all ages, from those who looked barely out of puberty to several whose plaits of dark hair were streaked with silver. Some wore less and some more. All sizes and colors of womanhood knelt. Tiny slender nymphs knelt next to corpulent women whose rolls of fat hung over their knees. Most were somewhere in between, like Alice. Each woman held her head high, wore a gold circle and red lipstick exactly like Alice's. A quick count told her there were twenty-seven.

"Looks like a female buffet." No one responded to her words as she expected. Alice wondered who might be partaking of this banquet as they led her to the last cushion in the line obviously meant for her. She knelt.

In the middle of the room, a young woman sat on a cushion playing the flute softly. The royal duo maintained a dazed and completely disinterested expression. Alice's knees began to ache a little from the kneeling. Just when she decided to try straightening out her legs, the huge wooden door opened and a line of young women filed in. Each young woman wore only a belt around her waist and carried a small woven basket. The women all had long hair tied in a braid that hung down her back. All were slender with small perky breasts and seemed made of the same living light brown silk as most of the people around her.

The first in line stopped at Alice, set her basket down beside Alice and stood smiling at her. Alice nodded and smiled. The serving girl, as Alice had decided they must be after watching their actions, dropped to her knees and seemed to be appraising Alice with a cocked head and narrowed black eyes. She began searching through her basket and brought out a small golden bowl and a pouch and handed it to Alice. In the bowl, Alice found figs covered in honey that turned out to be as delicious as they looked weird. The pouch held a sweet drink that packed an alcoholic kick. The young woman waited while Alice tasted the figs and took a drink from the pouch. When she could see Alice was pleased, she gently pushed Alice into a reclining position and motioned for her to keep eating, and drinking. Alice happily obeyed.

"Thank you, my knees were killing me," said Alice. The girl didn't answer but produced another small golden bowl and a several strips of cloth from her basket. She leaned toward Alice and pulled up Alice's skirt. "Hey, you are not my type at all." The girl paid no attention to Alice's comments at all and began to slather some warm goop onto her pubic hair. It smelled delicious and felt wonderful. When the girl lay the strips over the goop, Alice got the picture. "Okay, if you need the playing field bare, have at it."

Alice sipped the wine and as she began to feel relaxed and drowsy, her new friend quickly removed one of the strips. It stung a little, but she drank deeply as the next two strips came off and she marveled that the one time she had gotten a Brazilian bush wax, it had hurt a hell of a lot more.

Her waxer removed a tiny jar and applied an oil that smelled of flowers to Alice's forehead, feet and groin, gently massaging the oil into Alice's skin. Sitting back on her heels seemingly satisfied, the girl took a small cobalt blue bowl from her basket, set it down next to Alice and taking her basket, scampered away. Alice lay on her cushions, sipping wine and downing figs, her freshly smoothed pudenda ready and willing for whatever was to come. She raised up on one elbow at the sound of a trumpet blaring. A tall, muscular man with skin the color of mahogany set down the long instrument he had been playing and made some sort of announcement in Ancient Egyptian, no doubt. In walked a line of men.

To Alice's complete delight, the men wore only very short snow-white linen skirts tied up between their legs. An elongated triangle of something stiff hung down in front of the skirt, obscuring Alice's view of their masculine goodies. Each man wore a small skull cap of some material, possibly leather, on his head and carried either a long spear with a bronze tip or a huge curved blade.

"Soldiers," said Alice. "One of my favorite flavors."

She heard excited cheers and giggles from her fellow

cushion sitters as the men lay down their weapons in front of their monarchs and headed their way. Each man walked along the line of women until coming to a stop in front of a woman evidently to his liking. The women let out excited shrieks at being chosen.

Alice waited as man after man chose his prize. Finally, a particularly tall and muscular man stopped before her. His skin was darker than most of the others and as he moved near, she could see his eyes were topaz rather that deep brown. Dropping to his knees, he dropped a coin into her little blue jar and removed his linen. His groin was as bare as hers and a gorgeous cock still only half erect greeted her as she lay down on the cushions. He smelled delicious, spicy and masculine. He reached over to stroke her cheek with one hand, while his other hand freed her breast from the beaded straps and squeezed her nipple. Gently at first, but as she moaned, he increased the pressure, rolling and pulling her nipple until she dissolved into a moaning puddle and opened her legs wide. Now the lovely cock between his legs stood at full attention, begging to be touched or sucked. Alice longed to taste this beautiful manly delight and slid down to take him in her mouth. Now he moaned and gave her a look of delight and surprise as she slid her fingers over every inch of him. Teasing the opening resulted in a loud moan from Ramses the Delicious, and strong hands pushed her away and flat onto her back.

With some words she couldn't understand, he whispered into her ear, then entered her. He pumped fast and hard and did not miss a stroke as she came with her usual loud cry. Close behind her climax, he let out an equally loud cry and slumped on top of her, breathing hard. He rolled over and pulled her along with him and they lay facing the other cushions.

Alice watched as her sisters of the cushions enjoyed their own rewards. A few cushions down, a woman at least sixty swallowed a man's cock whole while he fingered her and she whimpered. Several cushions over one woman enjoyed sucking on her soldier on her hands and knees while another man pumped into her from behind. "Lucky Dog," said Alice. Ramses seemed to understand her desire and motioned to a man still standing in the line. He lay back and his cock rose under her wet mouth and she felt the other man push into her and fill her to the brim with his hardness. She caressed, Ramses moaned, and she moaned in delight as both men managed to climax within seconds of each other. She followed shortly and her men laughed at her loud exclamation.

Ramses, as she had dubbed her original soldier, sat up and began to lick and nip softly on her left nipple while she could feel a slick strong tongue lapping at her clit. She impressed them once more with her climax and lay back on the cushions to watch. A few cushions down, one hot warrior on his knees howled with pleasure as another pumped into him from behind and one of the ladies in red lipstick sucked loud and hungrily on the man's cock.

The woman directly next to her seemed in a daze, brought on by extreme pleasure, no doubt. Each of her breasts received the attentions of its own soldier, and another soldier pleased her with his tongue between her legs. Her eyes were closed and her mouth open, not making a sound.

"What do you think, Ramses? Do you like a lady loud or quiet?" He did not answer but held her tight against his chest. Her second to command had moved off down the line where someone else needed to be revered. One pair of smooth muscular arms felt like enough for right now and Alice closed her eyes for the littlest nap.

Chapter Twenty-Six

WHY CAN'T THIS BE LOVE

I t had been a productive day, with both her projects moving closer to profitability. Alice was proud of her teams and headed to her car, feeling satisfied that all was well in her little work world. She would be on her way to Brad's for dinner and delicious dessert of the masculine variety. She decided to leave for home out of her private entrance for a change. The cat colony had been fed earlier, but as she glanced toward the woods, she saw a little dark shape dart back into the brush. Priscilla's kittens were getting big enough to explore. She would talk to Ami about the possibility of taming one. Maybe it was time.

Still no word from Susan about David, but she had her phone on and nearby for when the news came. Every day that passed made Alice less hopeful, but not Susan. She was certain he had survived. Denial was Susan's new best friend.

❧

"You know I care about you don't you, baby?" said Brad as he held her still breathing hard against his naked body covered by his lovely silver sheets.

"Yeah." She settled into her favorite place with her head on his chest, nestled between his silver chest curls and his arm around her.

"Making love to you is like nothing I have ever…but I like and respect you, too." He kissed her head.

"I would hate for you to fuck someone you didn't like." She made a little snort giggle she rarely let anyone hear. It amazed her that he had used the term making love, when before he always used the more coarse but completely accurate term fuck for their activities.

"Stop that. I'm trying to tell you how important you are to me." He sat up, leaning on one arm.

"You are important to me too," she said, a little shocked that she had said those words out loud.

"I've never felt this way about anyone. It's like you are my best friend and my lover. I think this is special… maybe for keeps."

"Yeah." She smiled a small, satisfied smile and fell asleep feeling happy and special, no matter what words Brad used.

The sex the next morning in the shower wasn't hot and raging like usual, but tender. Brad carefully soaped and rinsed all his favorite parts of Alice, after he had made her come loud enough to make Barney howl downstairs. As she dressed, he kissed her neck while he zipped her skirt. She could have done it herself, but who could turn down those hands and those lips on her one more time?

❧

Had she imagined that Brad said those amazing things to her last night? Could he really mean them? She gripped the steering wheel nearly hard enough to leave permanent dents. Dr. Cindy would know what to do about Brad's revelation. She drove straight to her office for an early morning session after texting Ami to feed the ferals this morning.

"Can't you believe he really cares about you?" said Dr. Cindy, who wore jeans this morning and a black cardigan Alice was sure was cashmere.

"I want to." Alice gave the little half smirk that always meant she had serious doubts about something. "I really want to, but Jonathan told me he loved me ten times a day and still bailed."

"What would Brad have to gain by not telling you the truth?" Dr. Cindy peered over her black reading glasses.

"Nothing, I guess. I never asked him to say these things." Alice chewed her bottom lip.

"Do you love him?"

"I'm not sure. I can see myself with him, growing old maybe." She felt surprised by her own words.

"I want you to ask yourself what you want from a relationship and if Brad checks those boxes for you. We will examine that next time."

❦

Alice texted Susan on her way to her car that evening after work, Big News. You busy?

Nope. Got news myself. David has been found alive and fine. Come over, answered Susan.

She stopped to change into a pair of jeans and a sweatshirt and stood at Susan's door thirty minutes later. Susan opened the door and handed Alice a tall glass full of ice, some effervescing liquid, and two lime wedges. "Let's get drunk," said Susan. Strange behavior from a woman who just found out her husband was still alive after all this time. But people had different ideas of celebrating.

"Sure." It was Friday night, and she had no idea when Brad would get back from his trip. She took a sip from the glass and found it to be full of gin and tonic.

"It's Hendrick's gin but I have that diet tonic you like and your favorite hors d'oeuvres." Susan's voice trailed off as she disappeared into the pantry.

"Thanks. Why don't you look happier about this wonderful news?" said Alice. She took a long draw on her drink.

Susan reappeared carrying a bag of Doritos. "Look on the mantle." Susan pointed with her own glass that contained no ice and no limes.

Alice saw a cell phone. She picked up the phone and handed it to Susan, having no idea why she had it or what Susan wanted her to do with it. "So is this David's?" Alice sat her drink down on the end table and sank into the pink cloud chair.

Susan dropped the bag of corn chips into Alice's lap and sat down on her quilt draped couch. "The head of Doctors Without Borders called himself to tell me David was found alive and unharmed and that they had sent his things when they thought he was dead. Take a look at his screen saver." Susan took a cell phone out of her pocket and handed the phone to her friend. There on the screen was a photo of David with his arm around a skinny brunette wearing a pith helmet, khaki shorts and a bra or bathing suit top. Alice had no idea what to say. That was definitely not Susan he had his arm around.

"Yep, the asshole was cheating on me. He'd left his phone charging in his quarters when he flew into the bush, so they sent it when they thought there was no hope. It's full of pictures of her and texts too. Dumb shit always used his birthday as his password."

"Oh, sweetie. I don't know what to say." Alice reached over and put her hand on Susan's shoulder.

"Nothing to say. Now I am angry instead of sad. Son of a bitch." She took a drink and half emptied the glass she was holding. After all these weeks hoping and praying by some miracle, he would be alright. Falling asleep every night after praying on my knees. My prayers are answered, and I discovered he was off in the bush playing hide the salami with his assistant.

"Has he tried to contact you?"

"A little hard when I have his phone. I'm guessing he found out they sent me his phone and knows what I'd find. For all his life saving, David is basically a coward when it comes to anything emotional."

※

Alice understood David's reluctance. Emotions had always scared her too. "Men suck," said Alice, downing a serious portion of her drink. "Is that straight gin?"

"I'll drink to that and limes and tonic get in the way of my buzz." Susan took another big slug and poured more gin from the black Hendricks bottle sitting on the wooden coffee table Susan had painted robin's egg blue.

"She's got bird legs and a big, beaky nose," said Alice, still looking at the screen. "Was she at least on the plane when it went down?"

Susan laughed, spitting gin everywhere. "I sincerely hope so. Her name was Meredith from the texts. David finally left me a message on the landline and he didn't sound sad, so I am guessing she survived, too."

Alice opened the chips and offered them to Susan who shook her head. "When we are properly wasted, we can take an Uber to Ted Drewe's and completely drown our misery in frozen custard."

"Great plan," said Alice, stuffing a handful of chips into her mouth. Susan knew that while Alice loved the crunchy orange triangles, she would never buy them for herself. She could not trust herself not to eat the entire bag. *Why did they taste so much better with alcohol in your bloodstream?*

"Want to read their texts? They really were not very imaginative." Susan snatched the phone from Alice's hand. Alice reached over and put her hand over the phone's screen. "I don't think that's a good idea."

"She sound's English. Probably some kind of surgeon, too."

"Susan."

"What?"

"The fact that what he did hurts you doesn't change what you shared for all those years." She took the phone and Susan let her. She would throw it down the incinerator shoot on her way to the elevator.

"Yeah." Tears rolled down Susan's cheeks. She put her head in her hands and ugly sobbed. Alice sipped her drink and let her friend cry. After a few minutes. Susan raised her head, took a sip of her drink and said, "You said you had big news. What is it?" She reached for the tissue box on the end table and dabbed at her eyes.

"I...I don't really want to…"

"Oh, come on. Is it something good or bad?" Refilling her glass she said, "Cause I could use some good right now."

"I'm not really sure." Alice bit her lip and leaned forward to the edge of her chair.

"Spit it out. I'll be very understanding until the gin wears off." Susan giggled.

"Brad told me he cares about me. That maybe this is for keeps." Alice crammed another handful of chips into her mouth, never taking her eyes off of Susan.

"That's fantastic. Why didn't you tell me the second you walked in the door?"

"Because men are dogs and…."

"Wait. As mad and sad as I am about David, I wouldn't have missed a second of it, except maybe his cheating shit." Susan started laughing and Alice joined her for several gin fueled minutes.

"How can I trust that it will last?" Alice cocked her head

sideways and looked into the bottom of her glass at the two lime wedges.

"Nothing lasts, Chica."

"Yeah." Alice turned the empty bag of chips upside down. "You only got the one teeny bag?"

"You know, that's about seven billion calories."

"Nah, only a couple hundred thousand. Good thing one of us is good at math."

Alice and Susan consumed half of the bottle of gin. In less than an hour. Susan lay curled up on the couch. Alice was glad to see Susan sleeping peacefully even though tomorrow would include one wicked of a gin-on-an-empty stomach hangover. She wondered, sitting in the pink cloud, if she could spend the night in the chair or if somehow she could possibly get up and drag herself home.

A knock on the door made the decision for her and she pulled herself into a standing position miraculously.

"You didn't answer your phone, so I took a chance," said Brad. He wore his CEO face, which was a more serious version of his Vice President of sales face. The veins in his temples stood out and his jaw muscles were tight as a pencil skirt ordered online.

"Shush. Susan's sleeping."

Brad made a face that suggested he was not enjoying Alice's Hendrick's breath and walked in the door. "You guys having a party?"

How could he smile and still look so tense? "They sent her husband's cell phone back today," whispered Alice. "Turns out he is okay, but the phone is full of pictures of some other woman."

Brad's expression softened. Alice took a step toward him and stumbled. He caught her and, with his arm around her shoulder, guided her to the pink chair. He then walked to the couch, slipped off Susan's work brown leather shoes, unfolded the quilt at the end of the couch, and covered her. Taking

Alice's hand, Brad pulled her gently to her feet and with his arm around her waist once more, guided her out the door toward her apartment.

"Wait, wait, wait," Alice shouted in the middle of her hallway. Brad let her go for a second and she lurched into the wall. She reached into the pocket of her jeans, removed David's cell phone and dropped it into the shoot that led to an incinerator in the basement of the building.

She put her finger to her lips and she weaved toward him. "You didn't see that."

"No, I did not." Brad smiled the sort of smile she had seen him give to Barney the basset, kind and tolerant. She was certain she didn't look hot in her jeans and Cardinals sweatshirt with a very inebriated smile on her makeup free face.

§

When she opened her eyes the next morning, she became acutely aware that she was naked but in her own bed. Odd. She always slept in pajama bottoms and a tank top in case the building caught on fire or some middle of the night emergency required running out of the building from bed in a hurry. Even when she woke up after a closet adventure, she had on her pajamas. This morning, she was completely naked.

"Good morning," said Brad. Alice smelled coffee and rolled over to see an angel that looked exactly like Brad with a coffee mug in his hand. He was dressed in the same pale blue shirt and black suit pants as last night. His shirt was rumpled, but his gorgeous cornflower blue eyes looked at her with tenderness. He handed her the coffee.

"Bless you, sir." She took a big gulp. It was black. Though she usually took it with several sugars, the strong, bitter brew felt like what she needed. "Did you sleep here last night?" Alice raised herself on one arm and tried to look fetching. She was pretty sure she failed.

"Yeah, in the guest room."

"I don't blame you. Drunks are not very attractive."

"You were pretty cute, but I thought you needed a good night's sleep without my snoring."

"Liar, but thank you. Your snoring never bothers me." In truth, she enjoyed the sound of his little snores. They never actually woke her, but reminded her he was there, which always made her smile as she lay next to him in the dark. *Oh, who has it bad now, Alice Hightower?*

"How do you like your eggs?" said Brad.

She sat all the way up, but pulled the covers under her chin. "You're not a breakfast guy."

"I'm not making them for me. You only have two anyway."

"Scrambled."

"Okay, you need some food in your stomach so you can take a couple of ibuprofen. Your head's going to split open in about an hour." He turned and walked back to the kitchen.

Was that wonderful man actually going to cook her breakfast? Was she still drunk or did that flowery gin Susan drank give you hallucinations? She leaned back into the pillows and the room spun a little. She must have closed her eyes because the next time she opened them, Brad sat on the edge of the bed holding the tray she kept on her counter for decoration under her coffee pot. On the tray sat a pretty plate with deliciously fluffy looking scrambled eggs and two pieces of toast with jelly on them. "Where did you get the bread and the jelly, and the plate, for that matter?"

"Susan showed up already way down the hangover road ahead of you. I asked her if I could borrow some stuff to make you breakfast. I think she likes me."

Brad sat on the edge of the bed as she ate. "I came last night to tell you the good news about the Dallas Presbyterian deal. They went for it—the whole damn thing." He waited to see the look on her face. "I would love to get you back down there now that we have Biocardia back. Nobody can sell it like you. They have a gigantic new Heart Hospital associated with the university. They're really interested in breaking new ground technologically. I think that may be the perfect place to do our first human trials."

"That is wonderful," said Alice. "To think we are actually talking about human trials for Biocardia when only a few months ago we didn't even have the patents and clearances."

Brad leaned in and kissed her lips softly. "I like to see you all excited." She kissed him back and dropped the sheet she had tucked under her chin. He reached over, taking her breasts in his rough hands. Alice inhaled. "Gotta get home to let Barney out. Hold that thought until tonight."

"Tease," she said.

"Always leave them wanting more," he answered on his way out the door.

Chapter Twenty-Seven

HIT ME WITH YOUR BEST SHOT

A mi Wen texted she was ecstatic to hear Alice might be interested in one of Priscilla's kittens and insisted on meeting Alice at the office even though it was Saturday morning. After Brad's delicious breakfast, three ibuprofen and two large glasses of water, she was pretty sure she would live and who didn't want to see baby kittens? She put on her cutest skinny jeans, a pair of adorable if impractical red heels, and her favorite red cashmere sweater. She would be heading over to Brad's later and it was nice to dress only once.

Ami was already standing outside the back door wearing jeans leggings and a long gray sweater. Alice realized she had rarely seen her in anything but scrubs. She had a nice slender little figure, the kind Alice would have ordered if she hadn't been blessed with her Scandinavian ancestor's height and her English ancestor's sturdy physique.

"Four of them came to the bowl yesterday morning," said Ami as she and Alice stood looking out into the trees, the feral colony called home. "I picked one up and I think I could have grabbed all four of them. There are two tabbies like their mama and one gray and one black. Pookie and I are still discussing whether or not she would appreciate a cellmate."

Ami set the bowls down and called the cats. Elvis came running first like always, followed by the one tabby, the two black ones and the orange one that seemed to have doubled in size in the last month or so. Finally, Priscilla, the fluffiest of the tabbies, walked out slowly followed by a tiny black ball of fur, with its head held high and its little legs working hard to keep up with Mama.

"Now stay still. This is the one that came first yesterday. There is usually one in the group that's the bravest. This little guy must be it," Ami said quietly.

Alice watched as the black kitten walked behind his mother and came right to the food bowl. Alice and Ami stood still as statues. When he got to the bowls, he dove into the middle of the biggest one and began crunching the food and growling. Ami reached over and picked him up by the scruff of his neck. His little eyes, still blue, were wide and round and he gave a squeak that served as his meow. She handed him to Alice.

Alice hugged him close against her. His little body felt bony, with a hard round ping-pong ball stomach. He relaxed against her.

"Priscilla does the best she can, but they're skinny and their tummies are full of worms."

The kitten hung on hard with his little razor-sharp claws. Alice took it as a good sign that he didn't seem to want to leave.

"He likes you. Usually they squirm like mad trying to get away," Ami said, beaming and reaching over to rub his fuzzy little head. "Colder than a witch's mammary at night out here. Let's see how he does inside?"

They walked inside and sat down on the couch. "Ami, can I ask you a personal question?"

"Well, that depends. Personal information is by definition personal. You can ask, but I decide whether to answer, got it?"

Alice continued to pet the kitten, who snuggled into her

sweater as if looking for a place to nurse. "What's the deal with your money troubles? You make a decent salary and yet you need to borrow money? And what is the deal with those guys that trashed your office?"

"Yeah. That is pretty personal." Ami sat staring ahead, and the smile disappeared from her face.

"I don't mean to pry, I care. I feel like if there is something I can do to help, I want to."

Ami sat saying nothing for a long moment. "I help people. I help them escape a bad situation and it costs money. I started with a cousin and it sort of grew. I can't stand by and let some things happen."

"What kind of bad situation?"

"I would tell you, but there are some bad characters involved and I can't put anyone else in danger."

"Bad characters? Is that how you got the black eye a while ago? We can go to the authorities if you let me in."

"Absolutely not!"

"What are you so afraid of? Are they some kind of Yakuza mobsters?"

Ami gave a quick laugh, the kind devoid of any mirth. "These guys make the Yakuza look like girl scouts. This really isn't my story to tell, but I have everything under control now." She turned and gave Alice a sincere smile. "I really appreciate your concern, I do. I haven't used the Tor browser at work and I won't. Everything is fine, so butt out, please."

"Okay. I am sure this little guy likes me." Alice kissed the little black head.

"He has really big feet and the way he loves the chow, he ain't going to be no teeny, little dude."

"Is he big enough to be away from his mom?"

"Will be in a couple of weeks. I think they need their mamas until they're eight weeks. Pretty sure they're only six."

Alice held him up so they were face to face. "You grow up

a little and you can come home to be my kitty, okay?" The kitten blinked at her. When she set him down in the grass, he darted back to the safety of the trees. "I like him. He's brave and smart."

§

The tone of Susan's text six days later made Alice risk speeding on the way home. It really wasn't easy to speed in the heavy traffic Friday afternoon on 270, but Susan had said she needed her and with all Susan had been through in the last few months, if her friend texted, she would go. Brad could sleep alone once in a while. It might be good for him to miss her occasionally.

She knocked on Susan's door, having no idea what to expect, but she was there for her friend, no matter. She hadn't even stopped to change out of her navy pin-striped work suit.

"Wow, you must have used every one of that Porsche's horse's to get here so fast."

"You said it was an emergency," said Alice.

"It is. A dating emergency. I have a date." Susan stood still in her blue work scrubs with hot curlers in her short brown hair.

"I'm not going on a date with you. Are you sure it isn't too soon to…" Alice spread her arms wide in frustration as she walked into the living room.

"David has moved on. Why shouldn't I? I need you to help me get ready since I have no idea what men like."

"Why do you think I know?"

"Because you are almost never without one."

Alice had to admit, even in different times, men seemed to appreciate her. Alice followed Susan into her bedroom, where her king-sized bed was strewn with clothes. Susan's adjoining closet was a mirror image of her own, one floor above, but without shoes around the entire perimeter. Her master bath was exactly like Alice's except it was painted a bright peacock blue with navy accents and Alice's was white with black towels, of course.

"Let's start with makeup."

"I did my eyebrows, watched a YouTube video."

Alice tried as hard as she could not to laugh at her friend's efforts. She failed, but managed only a small chuckle. Susan's eyebrows resembled Groucho Marx's. They looked to have been drawn on with a fat black Sharpie and had the exaggerated arch of Gloria Swanson in Sunset Boulevard. She doubted any man was a big enough old movie fan to appreciate them, though. The earnest look on Susan's face made her sorry she'd laughed. "A little bold for a first date. Here, wash your face. You don't need that much, you are naturally gorgeous."

"The video said…"

"The video can't see that your natural brows are perfect." Alice examined the makeup Susan had spread out on the vanity in her master bathroom. She must have spent five hundred dollars on makeup. Choosing mascara, a raspberry lip liner and lipstick, a pale blush and some sparkling finishing powder, Alice said, "Here you go. This is all you need, really. The influencers on the internet want to sell stuff you don't need. Besides, you don't want to seem like you are trying too hard. Are you really, really, sure you are ready for this?"

"No, but I need to get my feet wet and maybe take my mind off that cheating son of a bitch. Thank you for coming to save me. I was going to put one of the darkest shades of every one of those, thinking it would make me look younger."

Alice was extremely glad she had come to Susan's aid. What her friend didn't need was to be laughed at by the very first man she tried to interest. "Now for hair. I really am no expert at that, but take out the curlers."

Susan pulled the curlers out, dropped them onto the pile

on her bed, ran her fingers through her hair and looked in the mirror. Her hair stuck out in an odd choppy way that made them both laugh. "I think Sonic the Hedgehog hair is what this occasion calls for," said Susan, still laughing.

"It's not that bad. Wet a brush and sweep it back and it will rock." Susan followed Alice's instructions. "Perfect," said Alice when Susan finished. "Pat Benatar would be jealous."

"Hit me with your best shot," sang Susan to her image in the bathroom mirror. "I need you to go along in case he is a serial killer or worse, boring. I met him online, as if that is a good idea."

"That's how people meet now. You can do it. I would be in the way."

"Please, please, please. I will never ask for another favor in my life."

"Right."

"Okay, I have narrowed it down to this tunic," Susan held up a red crushed velvet top that she must have worn in college twenty years earlier. "With these black pants or jeans?"

Alice wrinkled her nose. "Lose the pants. Show off those legs, wear that tunic as a dress with some black tights."

Susan's eyes widened. "You are a genius. I'm not sure which of my shoes will…"

Alice looked over the three pairs Susan showed her. All were low heeled and sensible.

None were date worthy. "Put that on and let's go to my place. I want to at least change my shoes for our date. I have a pair of black booties that will be perfect for you. Your feet are a half size smaller. Should work. Can't have you stretching out any of my preciouses. Though for a good cause…"

&

An hour later, Alice and Susan walked into Bar Napoli. It was a posh place in Clayton, the toniest congregation of offices and eateries in all of St. Louis County. Alice had changed into her red suede platforms with an adorable ankle strap. She had chosen to stay in her work suit as this was not her date, but she would not go out on a Friday night in Clayton wearing ordinary shoes. Susan balanced on Alice's black stiletto booties gracefully.

"George says he will be wearing a red sweater," said Susan, sipping an over-priced Hendricks neat.

"Ugh, George, really?" said Alice over a Tanqueray martini. The waiter had brought the drink with only one olive when she specifically asked for three, and for this she had given up an evening with a very delicious man.

"I think the sweater is a good idea. He will be easy to spot —practical."

"And that's what you want for your first date in twenty-five years?"

Susan eyed the door nervously and hardly touched her Gin Ricky. "I think that's him," she said. "Do not turn around."

Alice did not listen. The man in the red cardigan sweater looked like a version of Mr. Rogers that loathed every single member of his neighborhood. He was slender, with thinning dark hair, but there is where his resemblance to Fred Rogers ended. This guy's face was one gigantic scowl and his nasty look got worse when Susan waved at him.

"George?" Susan said sweetly with a smile Alice thought terribly generous.

"Susan, no doubt." The man gave a little bow of his head that seemed more hostile than respectful. "I see you brought a friend," said George. He stared at Susan's lovely legs crossed demurely on the high chair of the bar's table. While her skirt was short, it merely showcased her lovely legs rather than gave off any slutty vibe. The expression on his face was not appreciative, but disapproving. The look he gave Alice was menacing.

"I am meeting someone and was happy to run into my friend," said Alice.

"Sit down. Have a drink," said Susan.

"I don't drink…alcohol." George sat on his chair as far from the table as he could manage. "You look a bit older than your picture." He squinted at her, tilted his head and pinched his thin lips tight. Alice hoped he wouldn't attempt a smile. How awful must that be? She was pretty sure bats would fly out of the gaps between teeth the color of a gravestone. Though there seemed little danger that Alice or Susan could do anything to make him smile.

Susan, who until this moment Alice thought was the epitome of politeness, now looked as if she would burst into tears at any moment.

"I think I am going to be sick. Susan, come with me, please." Alice grabbed Susan's hand and dragged her through the crowded bar to the ladies room. Once the door closed behind them, they began to laugh. "We are going out through the kitchen. You are not spending one more second pretending to be that gargoyle's date."

"Maybe he's just nervous and…."

"Right, a beautiful woman smiles at him and he looks like that. Screw him. We're out of here." A smile spread over Susan's face and she followed Alice through the kitchen.

Having dropped Susan off after a pep talk on not giving up on men, Alice opened her door and realized it wasn't really that late and it was Friday night. She wondered, would Brad still be up or should she see what fantasy man might tickle her fancy this evening? She texted Brad.

Alice: Susan's emergency handled. You still up?

Brad: Nope. Let yourself in. You know the security code. Wake me.

Alice used her key to open the front door to Brad's house and punched the code into the keypad on the wall inside. She smiled when she heard Barney snoring in his crate in the kitchen. His snores were a little louder than his master's, but just as cute. As she climbed the stairs to the bedroom, she heard Brad's softer snores. She undressed as quietly as possible and climbed into his bed. He lay on his side, facing the wall. She studied his silhouette. His wide shoulders tapered to a narrow waist where the covers barely covered that butt she loved so much. Rock hard muscle covered with the smoothest skin. There were babies with rougher behinds than her lover. She loved to caress the smooth muscle as it powered his cock into her. She slid her arms around his waist and softly kissed his shoulder. The snoring stopped. He took her hands in his and kissed them.

"Laying here thinking about those beautiful breasts of yours." He rolled over, pulling her to him, her breasts crushed against his chest. He kissed her, still tasting of Colgate Xtra white toothpaste. She could feel his erection pushing into her groin, and she opened her legs. He slid his index finger along her cleft until he stopped at her clitoris and she made a low moan. A few strokes of that talented rough finger against her and she cried out in a quick orgasm. He slid his finger into her. "That's my wet baby."

Alice opened her legs, and he slipped inside her. They lay locked together in the dark. With each slow, delicious stroke, Alice moaned softly. Brad kissed her face and took each of her lips into his mouth nursing it softly and teasing with his tongue while his hands caressed her back, her hips, her buttocks. When she couldn't take one more gentle stroke, he worked his hips against her hard and faster now. Just as she felt his every muscle tense with his climax, the earth shattered for her.

Brad rolled her over onto her side and wrapped himself around her. His hand found her breasts, and he caressed them. His head on her shoulder, he began to snore softly. Alice fell asleep feeling satisfied and cherished. Her fantasy men could manage only the former. She knew tonight she had chosen wisely.

Chapter Twenty-Eight

MOTHERLESS CHILD

A lice had made an appointment with Louise's administrative assistant to see her. She knew she didn't really need one and could have shown up anytime to talk to her head engineer, but Louise deserved the extra respect. She was handling both the Biocardia and Excellosteo, as well as any and all engineering needed for the rest of Excellcardia's product lines. As she sat waiting for the appointed time, Alice surveyed Louise's office décor. The outer office walls were painted a warm coffee brown. All the chairs were black lacquered wood. A spear, a shield and a mask that must have been from Africa hung on one wall and on the other was a beautiful painting of three black girls jumping rope. A bust of Martin Luther King sat on a pedestal made of exotic zebra striped wood. Her outer office displayed the pride and passion for her heritage Louise exuded in her person in a subtle way every day.

Alice waited for Mildred, Louise's terminally serious admin to tell her that her boss would see her. She had been in Louise's office many times, and no matter how she had tried, Mildred had never smiled. She was a small shadow of a woman who always wore black or gray to match her short, curly hair. Alice had once found out the date of Mildred's birthday and brought her some convenience store flowers to see if she could get a smile out of the woman. It did no good. She thanked Alice and returned to her typing without changing her expression. She wondered if perhaps Mildred wasn't entirely real, but was some spirit sentenced to sit unsmiling at some desk in the Excellcardia building for eternity.

Louise stuck her head out of her door. "Get on in here. Since when do you need a damn appointment?"

"Since I came to pay tribute to the Queen of all things engineering." Alice gave a little bow, laughed and followed Louise into her office. There were huge potted palm trees on either side of her ebony carved desk. The chair behind the desk had a back of a woven fiber in a huge sun ray pattern that framed Louise like a halo.

"Um, huh." Louise gave a little chuckle.

"Seriously. This news deserves an appointment, and a brass band." Alice gave Louise a wide, appreciative smile.

"Spill it."

"We will be starting a human trial on Biocardia within ninety days." Alice couldn't help beaming with pride.

"My sweet Lord." Louise stood and her face lit up with a joy Alice had rarely seen. "You know my mother died from complications after a bypass."

"I didn't know."

"She had terrible varicose veins in her legs, threw a clot from one and died two hours after her surgery. Biocardia would have saved her life. That's why this project has always been close to my heart. You brought more than Biocardia to us, but this one means something special to me." Louise closed her eyes briefly and then sat back down.

"We are going to make the bypass procedure easier for a whole lot of patients."

"And make a good deal of money, too."

Louise laughed. "Of course, that too."

"Thank you for telling me." Louise's warm, dark eyes searched Alice's face. "How are you really?"

"I'm pretty good."

"Our boss seems to have a smile on his face and a spring in his damn step. That's you, isn't it?"

"I have been seeing Brad, yes."

"Tericci doesn't look too happy lately. That surgeon, Dr. Mariani, finds every reason in the world to come to engineering and consult. She asks endless questions, bats eyelashes and he won't give her the time of day. You didn't break his heart?"

"I did not. He isn't ready for a relationship and the timing was—I have nothing to do with his unhappiness. Maybe you're working him to death?"

Louise narrowed her eyes and gave Alice a sideways glance. "Uh huh. I know James is pretty, but do you really think you can trust him? He doesn't seem like one to settle down to me."

"Who says I want to settle down?" Alice kept her face neutral.

"Have fun, then, and thanks again for bringing this news to me in person."

❧

A day full of meetings finally came to an end and as Alice took the elevator to her home, a smile spread across her face. Brad was visiting his children in Phoenix and it would just be her and her closet this evening.

She inhaled a spaghetti and meatballs and a container of mixed fruit. It seemed too much trouble to make the little spinach salad she usually had; someone, somewhere in some time, was waiting for her.

On the golden hanger was a long blue dress. The material was soft cotton, thin and covered with tiny pink and blue flowers. No bra, but a pair of white cotton bikini panties lay folded on top of a pair of leather sandals. A piece of leather lay on top of the undies with a feather attached. When she pulled on the dress, she found the style empire with a large ruffle around the bottom. The dress had a tag "Mod Girl." She didn't bother to google it. She felt sure she knew this one. "Sounds groovy. The seventies or late sixties maybe?" she asked the girl in the mirror. Alice slipped on the sandals, and taking a guess, pulled the clip out of her hair and tied the leather cord around her neck.

She stepped out the door onto the grass at dusk. She smelled smoke from wood fires and cigarettes mixed with whiffs of marijuana; and people, lots of them. Sweat, sweet incense and weed wafted up her nostrils. A cheer went up, and she realized she stood in the middle of a huge crowd. Someone took her hand and pulled her down onto a red plaid blanket.

"Where'd you come from?" asked the man holding her hand. "Want some grass."

"Sure," she answered. The man let go of her hand and passed her the joint he had been smoking. She took a long, deep drag. She held it in until she absolutely had to cough.

"Whoa, Girl. Easy. That's the really good shit." The man next to her smiled an easy crooked smile at her and she passed the joint back to him. His brown hair fell to his shoulders in soft curls the way Alice always wanted her poker straight blonde hair to look. She could not resist reaching over and running her hands through it.

A slow dreamy, relaxed feeling she remembered from college and even once on a rock band's tour bus, washed over her. In front of her, a few hundred feet away, she could see a stage. Guitars and drums twanged and pulsed. A throaty voice sang out, "Motherless, motherless, motherless child." And the band pounded rhythmically. Right this minute, amidst all these people, with the weed caressing her brain cells, she still felt like a motherless child. "Sad song," said Alice. She turned toward him.

"My mom died when I was in Nam. Guess I'm a mother-less child."

"Yeah, mine's gone too, sad." Alice looked past his wire-rimmed glasses to brown eyes that looked both young and old. The lines around his eyes belonged to someone at least forty; the freckles sprinkled across his nose made him look seven.

"Yeah, bumming me out." His eyes slid down from Alice's face to her low-cut dress with no sign of a bra. "Nice to meet somebody my age here. Most of these people look an awful lot like the kids I used to teach."

"You're a teacher?" asked Alice.

"Was, before Uncle Sam sent me off to kill our little brown brothers."

"Let's have some fun." She put her hand behind his head, pulled him to her, and kissed him. He tasted like spearmint gum and weed. She couldn't help but wonder what the rest of him tasted like?

"Want to go swimming? There's a pond over there." He motioned with his head. His broad smile promised he was indeed interested in some fun.

"Sure," said Alice.

"Not big enough for a real swim, but still fun to splash around." He stood up and took her hand, pulling her to her feet.

"My name is Alice, and I love anything fun," she said, standing eye to eye with him.

"I'm Ben." He leaned in to kiss her quick and they weaved between the people sitting and laying all over the ground. She stepped over a couple under a blanket who seemed to be having a little fun themselves. Finally, they came to a clearing, and the promised pond. The crowd roared.

"The bands here are far out," said Ben.

"Yeah," said Alice, standing near the edge of the pond smiling at Ben. He pulled off his red t-shirt with a peace sign across the front and stood looking at Alice with a smile that dared her to take something off. Alice grabbed the hem of her dress and in seconds stood naked except for her sandals, in the bright afternoon sun. She kicked off her shoes and stepped into the water.

"Warmer than it looks."

Ben unzipped his bell bottoms that looked faded by a thousand washings to the shade Alice knew could not be reproduced by any modern jeans manufacturer. He pulled them off and followed Alice into the water. When they had waded in up to their waists, she turned to him. He took her in his arms and she could feel something hard against her groin. She reached down and wrapped her fingers around his hard cock as he slipped his tongue between her lips. Ben moaned. Alice slid her fingers up and down the length of him.

"This looks fun," said Alice.

He reached over, splashing water on her breasts and rubbed his palms against her hard nipples, slippery from the water. "These feel as fun as they look."

Alice closed her eyes and enjoyed the warm water and the hot man touching her. "Come on." Ben grabbed her hand and pulled her across the little pond to the other side and down onto a patch of mossy bank. A stand of reeds blocked the crowd, though Alice didn't care who watched. She dropped on to the moss and as he stood in front of her, she took his cock into her mouth. It was long, not overly thick, but with a slender beauty she had to enjoy. Her fingers slid up and down as her tongue slid along the underside. He put his hands on her head and shortly he filled her mouth. She smiled up at him.

"Jesus H. Christ," said Ben, gasping and dropping down beside her.

"Nope, plain old Alice." They lay face to face on the soft moss. He caressed her breasts as they kissed his tongue filled her mouth, completely. "I know just the place for a good, strong, lovely tongue like that." She took his hand, and opening her legs wide, placed it between them. Ben, obviously an astute learner, dragged his tongue slowly down her body, looking into her eyes. His was as long and thick a tongue as she had ever encountered, and she wanted it.

Ben granted her wish and stuck the beautifully long and slick bundle of joy that was Ben's tongue into her. Alice cried out.

"Damn, honey, you taste like sunshine," he said into her crotch as she moaned. He moved his lovely, slick tongue up to her clit and she gasped. She heard him laugh as he licked her firm and wet. She had never had any man deliver such incredible oral pleasure. Often the pressure of a man's tongue was not enough to make her toes curl, and she usually guided the teaser to another area she wanted tongued—not so, Ben.

He stopped and surprised she still lived, Alice lay breathing hard. He lay down on his back, pulled her astride him and then slid her still damp body down his until she straddled his face. "I want to taste you as you come, Alice." He stuck his tongue out to its full, magnificent length, and she moved against it. Ben slipped a finger deep inside her and she moved faster until the frogs in the pond grew silent rather than compete with Alice in her usual fine voice.

Alice froze, not wanting to ever be separated from Ben's deliciously talented tongue. "Let's put our clothes back on and go dig the tunes," said Ben. "A black cat named Jimi something plays soon and I want to hear that."

"Whatever you say, teacher, Ben. I'm eager to learn." Alice pulled on her dress, somehow found her sandals in the tall grass, and followed Ben back to his plaid blanket.

In the gathering dark, she could see three people now sat on the blanket. "That's cool, man," said Ben to the three young men who had appropriated his blanket. "We can share." The three scooted over, making room for Alice and Ben. They sat down and an awesome guitar wailed. With her head on Ben's shoulder, Alice fell asleep.

THIS NIGHT

A lice had finished her Saturday apartment straightening routine when she heard her phone make the sound for a text.

Ami: Please come to the office. I have a BIG surprise.

Had it been two weeks already? Maybe the little black kitten was ready to be her kitty.

Alice: Sure. Be there in a few.

Alice changed into a clean shirt and slipped on her Jimmy Choo strappy sandals. They were not really appropriate for walking much of anywhere, but it was a short hike from the parking lot to her office and special occasions required special shoes.

On this gorgeous bright spring afternoon, Alice breezed down the Highway to Hell, not missing the week-day traffic. The sky was free of the usual St. Louis humidity haze and shone bright blue. The white dogwoods and lavender red buds scattered along the side of the road made her smile. What a perfect afternoon to take home a new little friend.

Alice hummed as she punched the code into the side door's security lock, a little surprised that Ami wasn't enjoying the cats in the sunshine. The door opened, a hand grabbed her wrist with an iron hold and yanked her into the room. She fell to her knees. In front of her, Ami sat on the couch with her hands behind her and duct tape wrapped around her head covering her mouth. Her eyes were wide, but she could make only little muffled sounds.

Alice screamed as long and as loud as possible and someone fast and strong slammed her to the carpet face down. A foot on her back kept her flat on the floor by crushing her ribs to keep her from making another sound. She felt cracking and lightning bolts of pain shot through her.

"Scream again and I will break the ribs on the other side too," said a man's voice. Pain ripped through her chest like a chainsaw as he kicked her. The pain told her he knew how to break ribs. She tried to breathe in, but her lungs wouldn't expand all the way and it now felt like a knife stabbed with each breath.

She dared to lift her head slightly and saw a man sitting at her desk with his shiny black combat boots up on it. A black turtleneck and pants replaced the suit he had worn in the video, but it was the same man she had seen on security tape, one of the two who had tossed Ami's office and given her a black eye. The foot on her back must be the other one.

"Hello, Ms. Hightower. So good of you to come," the man at her desk said in a flat, unaccented tone. His features were handsome. He had a chiseled look and bright black eyes, but there was a cruelty in his mouth as he smiled at her without a trace of warmth. "Thank you very much for coming to our little party," said the man.

Wasn't that what all the villains in James Bond movies said right before they attempted to beat or torture him?

"The party is in Miss Wen's honor, but what is a party without a guest?" Alice saw a black case three feet long sitting on the floor a few feet from where she lay. She felt sure it did not contain a slide trombone or anything musical. "Miss Wen has been seriously interfering with a client's business. She was warned, and now she must pay. But first, she will watch the entertainment we have prepared."

"We have discovered, though you are technically Miss Wen's boss, she thinks highly of you and you seem the perfect special guest for our party." He uncrossed his legs and stood up, taking a few steps closer. "You will assist us in a demonstration for Miss Wen's benefit. She will watch everything we do to you and know what is to come for her...to anticipate." He squatted down close to her and said, "I hope she will enjoy watching my darling cut you into pieces and finally remove your head from your shoulders while you still breathe. I know I will. So, no matter." He chuckled again, low and without humor.

The foot on her ribs briefly let up and pain ripped through the side of Alice's head. Another bolt of pain shot through the back of her head and her world went black.

Alice regained consciousness sitting on her office chair, which had been rolled into the middle of the room. She couldn't see Ami on the couch behind her, but heard the sound of a long strip of duct tape being pulled from a roll. She knew it would soon be wrapped around her. In front of her, the man in black knelt over the long black case now open to reveal something gleaming deadly in the office's florescent lights. She watched as he ran his fingers along the blade of a sword with tenderness and a look far beyond admiration. He loved the sharp and murderous thing.

"Isn't she beautiful?" He looked only at the sword. "She had been in my family for ten generations and is made of steel folded seven hundred times. The Japanese normally have very little I desire, but their swords are incomparable."

Alice tried to take a deep breath, but again the pain stopped her. She heard grunts behind her and wondered why the tape was not yet restraining her. She had to act fast. Now! Through her pain and fog, she stood up and grabbed the only thing on the desk that she could use as a weapon—her first edition of Alice's Adventures in Wonderland. Thank God she kept it in a heavy teak box to protect it. She hit the kneeling man squarely in the jaw hard and he toppled over on to his side. Alice raised her leg to kick him, aiming for his neck. He turned his head as her heel struck him and it sank into his eye socket. The man struggled to shake her off. She lost her balance, falling forward. The whole of her body weight drove the heel deep into his skull. He stopped struggling and Alice crumpled to the floor. She lay still, barely able to move. She had fallen on her ribs and each breath was ragged agony. She could feel his body beside her and tried to move her leg and remove the heel from… Her leg felt twisted at an odd angle and would not budge. A wave of nausea and relief, a deafening crash, and she fell into the darkness.

§.

The dark held on tight to Alice. She was aware occasionally that people moved around her. Sometimes she heard voices and felt someone touch her cheek or her hand. Time must have passed, but to her, there was only darkness and pain. Slowly, she became more aware. She thought she could see light through her eyelids but opening them would have taken far more energy than she could yet muster. She smelled alcohol, and Cidex disinfectant.

Her neurons began to fire, processing the input. *I am in the hospital!*

"Alice. I know you are still in there. I am going to sit here and talk to you until you answer," said Susan. Alice listened as

Susan spoke word after word, making little sense of anything else she said. The pull of the darkness still too strong.

Soft snores were the next thing she heard, and they soothed her. Someone held her hand and sat snoring in the chair beside her. Brad. The strong, rough texture of the hand holding hers confirmed it. Alice struggled to climb up out of the dark, to move toward the comforting sounds. She squeezed Brad's hand. The snoring stopped and Brad dropped her hand.

"She squeezed my hand. I felt it!" Alice heard Brad say to someone. Someone else was touching her, now standing near.

"Her EEG does look like she may be waking up," said a voice Alice did not recognize. Alice felt someone pull open her eyelid, and she saw a bright light. "Her pupils are reacting," again the voice with obvious medical knowledge spoke. "Talk to her."

Brad took her hand again, and she felt his breath against her ear. "Alice, baby, come on, wake up. Her eyelids are moving!"

Alice wanted to smile at Brad's excited tone. Not possible yet, but she did manage to open her eyes the teeniest amount. Brad stood over her. His pale gray suit looked rumpled. He had removed his tie and unbuttoned his shirt.

"Brad," she croaked through desert dry lips and a throat set on fire with her effort. "Water." This time, it was a little easier.

Someone placed a straw between her lips and said, "Just a small sip." Alice obeyed. It took a lot more effort to suck on the straw that she could ever have imagined. The effort it took to climb up out of the dark had been exhausting, and she sank into a deep sleep.

Chapter Thirty

BACK IN BLACK

W hen she woke, it felt like morning. Turning her head to where she remembered there had been a chair when she first woke up, she saw Susan reading something on her kindle. "Susan," said Alice, proud that this time her voice sounded more like a voice that the whispering of dry bones in a graveyard.

"Oh my God. You are awake. Brad called to tell me." Susan leaned in and hugged her.

Alice winced. "I'm sorry. You've had surgery, one of your ribs punctured a lung, and you had to have the lobe resected."

"Brad..."

"He finally went home, but he'll be back."

"Tell me everything. How am I still... Those guys where..."

"Okay. The North Korean thugs that did this to you are both dead."

"Ami?"

"She's fine. They hadn't done anything but tie her up and slap her around. You got the worst of it. The ribs and a subdural hematoma. You have been in a coma for thirteen days."

"How did I get…"

"Ami had notified the police somehow, and they broke in the door. But when they got there, one guy was dead and the other lay unconscious, strangled by Ami evidently. You are two badass women."

"Brad's been here?"

"Yeah, he comes after work and sits in the chair 'til visiting hours are over. He held your hand and talked to you. It was pretty touching." Alice was touched by Susan's smiling face.

Alice smiled. Her chest hurt a little with every breath, and her head felt like it had been split open with that guy's sword, but she knew she would eventually be okay.

Susan pointed out the glass window in the ICU room. "Yeah, Brad was here every day, but that guy has been in that chair every time I've come."

Alice lifted her head to see Vincent Terrici smiling at her.

"Only one person at a time in an ICU room, but he dragged that chair over from somewhere and set up camp outside the window."

"He is a good guy."

"I'd say so," said Susan.

Her day nurse, Jackie, helped Alice to sit up and hang her legs over the bed. Night nurse Jack helped her to the bathroom for the first time, but after the first day, Alice was on a mission to get the hell out of that hospital. Physical therapy and dogged determination made that possible five days later.

Brad wanted her to come to his house to recover, but Susan overruled that suggestion. He would have had to hire a nurse to stay with her during the day, at Susan's she would have the care of her best friend.

"Are you up for a visitor?" said Susan as Alice woke from the nap Susan insisted she take, once she settled into Susan's guest room.

"Sure." She hoped it was Brad. He had texted her, but she hadn't seen him since that first day when she woke up.

Ami Wen stood in the doorway to Susan's guest room that had been converted into Alice's recovery ward. Susan managed to drag Alice's favorite pink cloud chair to sit beside her bed and there were at least three quilts piled on top of her. Ami held the handle of a cat carrier. Setting the carrier down next to the bed, Ami said, "I don't know what to say."

"I wish you would have told me sooner how serious the trouble you were in actually was."

"Yeah, you can see now why I didn't want anyone else brought into this." Ami's usually pleasant face was grave.

"Those two were both killed?"

"You stilettoed one to death and the one I strangled didn't wake up."

"How did you…"

"Strangle that guy? I couldn't let him… I'm pretty limber. I pulled my taped hands over my legs to the front, then slipped the tape around his neck, put my foot in the middle of his back and squeezed as he was concentrating on taping you." Ami smiled, covering her teeth. "I doubt it will affect their disgusting business much. I gave all the information I could to the guys from the State Department and the Interpol agents. I hope it helps. They told me there were no other operatives in this country and I should be safe."

"What exactly was their business?" Alice leaned forward on her elbows until the pain forced her to drop back into the pillows.

"Their syndicate kidnaps children and sells them to the highest bidder."

"Oh my God." Alice closed her eyes. "I can't help be happy those animals would never hurt anyone again."

"Animals is exactly what they were. When I messed with their business, I had to go. Sorry you got sucked in. They sold the children they kidnapped on the dark web, mostly for sex. I found kids as young as four for sale. Dickered the price down and queried all other prospective buyers by threatening to expose them. That way, I could afford more. I'm pretty good at hacking."

"Child protective services found people to adopt the ones that couldn't be reunited with their parents. I called them right away once I got them. I know nothing about taking care of kids."

"How many have you managed to save?"

"Twenty-seven over the last five years. The first one was my cousin Kni's little girl that was kidnapped right out of her stroller in Seoul. Kni came to me begging for help and I couldn't exactly go get her."

"I thought you were Cambodian?"

"I am Vietnamese and Cambodian, half-breed, don't ya know? Stupid Kni, fell in love with a Korean guy when we were at Oxford."

"How did someone come to…"

"Oh, I had my phone set to call 911 if I didn't check in every half an hour anytime I wasn't safe and secure at home. Those animals were mucho scary. After a recorded message that my life was in danger, I set the microphone to turn on so they could hear what was going on and find us by pinging the phone. As soon as you went down, I started screaming and telling the cops what was going on and where to find us." Ami was a genius, after all.

The carrier at Ami's feet gave a hearty meow. Ami bent down, opened the carrier and handed Alice a little black ball of fur. Round emerald eyes looked at her. She clutched it to her chest. The kitten relaxed against her and little pops of purring warmed her heart.

"He looks a lot like my sweet Otis."

"Maybe Aretha, Whitney or Diana would be more appropriate since this one's a girl."

"Otis came with his name. I will need to think about it. Can you keep her a while, not quite up to scooping litter boxes yet. Just seem to want to sleep?"

"Sure, Pookie likes to bat her around, but she sticks up for herself. Won't mind babysitting. She's a sweetie." Ami put the little black kitten into the carrier and sat down in the chair beside the bed.

"How are our projects going?" asked Alice.

"Everything's fine, now that we have Terreci back. Spent the last two weeks burning vacay at the hospital watching you coma. I came a time or two, but it wasn't much of a show. Biocardia is still on track for human trials and we are implanting ten doggie knees next week. You should see these things, Alice. They are sweet...."

Alice couldn't keep her eyes open any longer. When she awoke again later, in the dark, she was hungry as a bear. Susan brought her home made split pea soup. The stuff was thick and green, full of ham and shredded carrots, surprisingly delicious for healthy stuff. She ate every bite and fell asleep once again.

The next time she opened her eyes, after venturing to the bathroom by herself, she decided to sit up in the pink chair.

"What are you doing out of bed?" said Susan.

"Shouldn't lay flat all the time, especially after lung surgery. I feel like walking a little. Can we go sit in the living room?"

"Brad is coming by in about an hour, so you have time to shower and fix up." Susan helped her out of her nightgown and walked her slowly, gently, to the shower.

"Thank you." Alice ran her fingers over what she expected to be a whopper of a scar on her left side.

"It's not so bad, really," said Susan, who insisted on standing near as Alice showered.

"Oh, come on. I have seen thoracotomies. It has to be hideous."

"Not at all, really." She handed Alice a hand mirror. The angry red line was only four inches long and flat.

"That was one good surgeon. I'm glad to be alive. I thought when that guy kicked me the second time..." Alice began to shake, standing in the stream of water Susan had adjusted to perfectly warm. "Oh, God, he kicked me and…"

Susan wrapped her in a big fluffy towel and helped her to the bed where she had laid out some jeans and a pretty purple long-sleeved t-shirt. She had stopped shaking and smiled at the fact that her skinny jeans were no longer tight. Before Brad arrived, her hair was dry and Susan had helped her with a dab of lipstick and some mascara.

Alice burst out laughing, holding her ribs when she walked into Susan's living room. Every horizontal surface was covered with flower arrangements. There were four on the coffee table, two on the end table, and she counted six on the counter that separated her kitchen from her living room. "It's like a funeral parlor in here." Alice kept laughing. "Reports of my death were greatly…whatever the rest of the quote is."

"Half of them are from Brad, the roses. The rest are from people at your work. I think there is one from Sean too."

"The white lilies are from Louise O'Neil, of course," said Alice, as she walked stiffly to the counter and confirmed her suspicion by checking the card. There were red roses, pink roses and two vases of mixed colors. "Feel better soon, baby," said the card on one of the vases of roses.

❦

"You look great." Brad kissed her lips but held off on one of his passionately tight hugs. He wore a pale blue suit with a white shirt and a deep red tie with the company logo on it and looked as handsome as ever.

"Thanks. Fill me in on the sales projections for Biocardia."

Brad smiled the smile of pride she had come to love. "I didn't bring the figures with me. I think it will be a while until…"

"It's not like I lay bricks. I sit most of the time, anyway. She held up her right hand. I can type. Please have someone deliver my laptop. There's a lot I can do before the doctor clears me to go back to work."

"Yeah, that's my baby." Brad sat down very close to her and wrapped his arm around her. She stiffened at his touch.

"I'm sorry, baby. I didn't mean to hurt you." He softly kissed her cheek.

"It's okay. A little sore still." She lied. It was not pain, but his touch…any man's touch she could not bear. She stood up too quickly. The room spun, and she fell back into his arms. This time it felt all right for him to hold her.

ॐ

Dr. Cindy volunteered to make a house call when she learned what Alice had been through. She looked out of place in a sleek black pants and a black blazer seated in the pink cloud chair that Alice insisted be moved back into Susan's living room. Alice sat on Susan's quilt covered pale blue couch. She had asked Susan to bring some of her own clothes from her apartment and was delighted to find them all loose. She sat on the edge of the chair with her back straight and her head up.

"I really appreciated you coming here, but I feel pretty good," said Alice. She leaned back and said, "Grateful to be alive and glad those two guys could never hurt anyone again."

"Alice, you have to realize the trauma is not only to your body. It will take time…"

"I don't have time. I have two huge projects and, actually, I am feeling fine." She had nearly shouted and felt a little guilty to take such a tone with someone who cared enough to make a house call.

"No nightmares or flashbacks?"

"Nope. Don't see the point." Alice stood up and began to pace slowly across the room. "I am getting stronger every day and the surgeon and my GP say I can go back to work next week. I can't let this incident wreck my whole life. "

Dr. Cindy narrowed her eyes and sat listening as Alice paced.

"I need my work. It makes me feel whole." Alice tried to stand up straight as the physical therapist had suggested. It hurt a little, and she winced.

"Going back to work when you feel up to it is good. Don't let your work distract you from dealing with your feelings about your attack."

"I do not see how reliving that horrible thing will help. The monsters that did it are dead. It's over, I'm healing. I want to go on. Dwelling on a bunch of bad feelings is not going to help me." Alice stopped at sat back down.

"I am glad that you are feeling well. My concern is that you stay this way as you process what happened to you. I think we should up our sessions to two per week for a while."

"No! I am not going to have time for that. In fact, why don't I call you when I do have time?" Alice had walked to the door and opened it.

"Alright." Dr. Cindy stood looking at Alice for a minute and then picked up her leather briefcase, stashed away her notes and said, "Please call me as soon as you have time. Ignoring your feelings can be dangerous. Call me anytime."

"I will. As soon as everything at work is under control. Thank you so much for your concern." Dr. Lester stopped at the doorway and looked into Alice's eyes. Alice attempted a reassuringly sane look.

"I'll call soon, promise," said Alice and she closed the door.

❧

Alice insisted on moving back to her own apartment the next day. Susan knew better than to try and move the immovable object that was Alice when her mind was set on something.

Susan moved into Alice's guest room for a few days until she was certain Alice did not need her. She still delivered dinner each night and checked on Alice several times per day by text.

Alice got up every morning at her usual time and moved through her day as she would have if she had actually gone to work. She held departmental meetings by Zoom while dressed as she usually would from the waist up, anyway. She processed her emails, surprised that there were so few. Someone must have placed a notice that she would be out of the office for a while. When her day ended, she climbed on her elliptical. At first, she hung on with both arms and managed only five minutes, she could now manage twenty. Brad had brought her laptop by personally but seemed in a hurry to leave and she had seen relatively little of him since. Fortunately, at the end of her days, she was too exhausted to fret about Brad's absence.

The day came, and with her doctor's approval, Alice went back to work. She wore her favorite black suit with silver pinstripes and her scarlet peep toe pumps. She walked in the front door and received a standing ovation from fifty people who stood waiting. In the front of the group stood Brad James. He took her breath away in his deep blue suit, pale blue shirt and dark blue tie. He put his hand on her waist and escorted her personally to her office.

When she walked through the door, she thought she was in the wrong place. Gone was the cheap short blue carpet replaced by hardwood and a lovely oriental rug under her beautiful new desk. *Couldn't get the blood out of the old carpet.*

A gorgeous new black modern desk with a white leather chair replaced her old inexpensive Office Max model. The faux leather couch had been replaced with a seating group of four white leather chairs and two low glass tables. Very chic and entirely to her taste. Alice suspected Louise had a hand in the decor.

Brad followed her into the office and pointed out the new security features. "There are now cameras on the inside and outside of the doors, as well as retinal scanners for entry."

"That cost a pretty penny," said Alice, trying out the new chair behind her desk.

"You're worth it." Brad smiled and looked at her like she was the most important person on the planet.

"Why don't you cook dinner for me tonight? I don't want to be a burden to Susan forever."

His face looked strained. "I'm sorry. My girls are in town. I'll take you somewhere nice later in the week." He smiled a smile she had seen him give someone he was pitching a sales deal to, not the woman he had said he cared about.

Alice dove into her day deep. Three meetings and 120 emails later dragged herself into her apartment feeling old and tired. She microwaved one of the containers Susan left in her freezer. Still insisting that she eat properly, Susan had filled her freezer with plastic containers of home cooked food. She wondered what she had done with her prepackaged delicacies that had previously filled her freezer. Tonight was a chicken and rice casserole with some broccoli thrown in and tasted delicious. Even though her body felt tired, with her successful first day finished and a belly full of healthy food, Alice thought it couldn't hurt to at least see what was in her guest closet. Maybe her head injury had eliminated her ability to conjure fantastic clothes. She had to at least take a peek.

There were clothes on the magic golden hanger, after all. A pair of jeans and a long-sleeved shirt that looked vaguely familiar. A bra and panties lay in a pile on top of crock sandals that looked very much like a pair she owned. Not original, but she had to see where these would take her. Looking through her the closet in her bedroom, she found that she did not have those clothes even though they looked familiar.

She slid open the balcony door into the bright sunshine of a spring day and found herself standing in front of the side door to her office. Her heart beat wildly, and she backed up, turning to go back through the balcony door. The door leading to her apartment was gone. She wore the same clothes she had the day of the attack. Of course, they weren't in her closet. They'd cut them off in the emergency room. All she had to do was open that door and she would relive the whole terrible thing. No way in hell would Alice go through that again, no matter what Dr. Cindy said about processing.

She walked a ways into the trees in the little park next to Excellcardia until she came to a small clearing and sat down on a fallen log. The moss covering it provided a comfortable place to rest. When her heart settled down, she realized she was exhausted. If she closed her eyes, she could leave this nightmare behind.

She opened her eyes sometime later and found herself right back in her own bed. She closed her eyes and there was the door to her office again. This time, she could not stop herself from opening the door. A hand yanked her through the door and the whole scene began to unfold in all its technicolor horror. The pain, the terror, the fear in Ami Wen's eyes—all of it happening again.

The man kicked her, and she felt her ribs break. With every bit of concentration she could manage, she forced her eyes open. She lay safely in her bed, breathing hard and laying in a pool of cold sweat. *This must be the flashbacks Dr. Cindy had mentioned.* Part of the process, but rather than go through that experience again, Alice got out of bed, picked up her laptop and worked on emails. A few hours later, Alice tried the bed again and managed a few hours of dreamless sleep.

Chapter Thirty-One

I THANK YOU

T he next morning, she shook off her awful night and decided she needed to visit Engineering to express some long over-do gratitude. She opened the door to Louise's office and Mildred waved her into the inner office. She knew Louise had not forbidden the woman to smile.

Seeing Alice, Louise motioned for her to sit in the comfy woven fiber chair and wrapped up her phone conversation. She had worn one of her favorite suits for Louise. Today, Alice wore a thigh length soft white wool blazer over a matching dress, a very nice copy of a Channel. Louise would know it was a copy because designers never made anything over a size 8 and Alice, like Marilyn Monroe, wore a twelve. It had been a little snug when she bought it, but now fit like part of her fantasy closet wardrobe.

Louise beamed at Alice. This was a wide warm smile that the gorgeous, highly intelligent, and incredibly competent engineer rarely shared. "Wonderful to see you looking so fantastic."

"I want to thank you for your decorating efforts and the gorgeous flowers."

"I couldn't let James do it, though it was his idea. It would have been all clear acrylic and chrome."

"Well, thank you. It is beautiful and exactly my taste, only better."

Louise nodded. "You are completely welcome."

"I need to see Torresi and I have to admit I have no idea which is his office. I don't want to just summon him. Doesn't seem right to do that to someone who sat outside your room every day while you were in a coma."

"Yes, he did." Louise dropped her chin and looked at Alice as if she had something to say, but thought better of it. "Second door on the right. 314. I saw him go in a few minutes ago."

Alice knocked on the door to 314 and Vincent opened it. His face lit up. "Come in, please." His office was neat and organized, as one might expect of an engineer. He sat down behind the desk and his eyes shone deep blue, reflecting the golf shirt he wore. On his wooden desk sat nothing but his laptop. The wood on the top of the desk had the color of maple with incredible black lines swirling across it like smoke crawling up a wall. Alice couldn't help but run her hand over the pattern of the wood.

"It's called spalted maple. The pattern is made by a fungus in the wood before its cut. Only a thin veneer, though, would be hard to find enough to make a solid desktop."

"It's gorgeous." Her fingers caressed the wood.

The chair behind the desk matched the desk with a high round back with wooden spindles. A similar chair with a round back sat in front of the desk.

"Have a seat," said Vincent.

Alice sat down gingerly, a little cautious of the hard wood against her still healing ribs.

She found the chair's contours fit her butt as well as if it had a cushion on it. The spindles on the back gave a little as she leaned into them, cradling her.

"This chair is…" Alice settled into it like no wooden chair she had ever sat in.

"It's my own design. Comfortable?" He said, brows raised.

"Very. It feels padded, but it's wood." Alice wiggled in the chair.

"Yeah, each slat flexes independently." He looked delighted at her appreciation of his work.

"I am sorry I didn't come to see you first thing. You sat outside my room all that time."

"I had to make sure they were taking good care of you." He held her gaze.

"Thank you for caring."

Vincent said nothing for a long moment, his eyes studying her face. "I have a feeling that Mr. James has no idea what a treasure he has and will blow it. If he is that stupid, someday I'll make you dinner again." He smiled and the message he sent with those eyes, this morning the color of the deepest part of the ocean, was unmistakable. Next time, if there was a next time, there would be no, "I'm not ready," from Vincent.

Alice wanted to wrap her arms around him and… *Pull yourself together, Alice.* She couldn't just sit there looking at him. She returned his smile, nodded, and headed back to her office.

§

She stayed late in her office that evening, trying desperately to wear herself out. She answered every email and wrote twenty more pertaining to tomorrow's business. Alice finally closed her laptop after 8:00 p.m.. Once home she did forty minutes on the elliptical, downed a can of spaghetti and meatballs, listened to a new Jennifer Weiner novel on Audible for an hour and found it impossible to concentrate on the story, though Weiner was her favorite author. Still, she could not imagine sleeping. Brad had made another excuse this evening, but she knew he was busy. The men in her closet were never too busy.

She felt little need for male company of the hot and yummy variety this evening. None of the lovely men ever force themselves on her. She could almost always say no, though she never wanted to before.

Susan had another computer dating service date and thank goodness felt up to going alone.

Alice didn't want to be alone tonight. If she looked in the closet, and the jeans and t-shirt she'd worn the day of the attack were there, she could simply close the door, couldn't she? Slowly, Alice opened the door to her guest room closet a crack. A gown of cream-colored short nap velvet hung on the golden hanger. Pearls decorated the bodice, and the sleeves were of delicate lace. Once before, she had found something this beautiful in her closet. The sleeves of this gown had to be tied on, which meant the gown could be from the Renaissance exactly like the one she found once before. Tugging on the under shift, she remembered finding a man painting when last she's visited a similar time. It had been one of the few times she had merely enjoyed the details and atmosphere of the era and had not partaken of the Renaissance gentleman. That might be exactly what she needed tonight.

Alice hurried to pull on the gown and slip on the cream-colored shoes of soft leather. She tied the little cream satin ribbons that held on the lacey sleeves. Last time, a similarly gorgeous dress had made her feel like a princess; this time she merely wanted to go somewhere no one had beat her nearly to death.

Alice pulled open the balcony door and stood looking out a stained-glass window as she had before. This time, gloom filled the room. She smelled something burning. Through the window, she saw only darkness, and a torch burned in a sconce on the wall next to the window.

It was odd how her innate sense of time didn't work in

fantasy land. Last time she had smelled linseed oil and turpentine and heard the scratching of a paintbrush on canvas. This time she heard the tapping of metal on stone. She had seen a man painting a beautiful young woman standing in a sunbeam last time. She turned this time to see the same man standing with a chisel gently hammering chips from a block of white stone. He wore a large, flat brown velvet hat and a blue velvet coat with white stockings. On a raised wooden platform stood a young man. The young man stood tall, made of slender muscles with perfectly proportioned arms and legs. He wore nothing but a blank look and his head of dark curls bent downward with dark eyes looking only at the stone floor. Alice remembered that the young woman she had seen had seemed drugged, she had held so still. This lovely young man was similarly frozen.

The man working chipping away at the marble stopped his chiseling and turned to Alice. "Nice to see you again, Alice." His expression did not reveal any joy at her appearance.

Exactly like last time, she was shocked to hear a man from another time speak to her in perfect, unaccented, modern English, let alone know her name. "How do you know my name?" Alice took a cautious step backward and stopped with her back against the window.

"We are related, you and me. You may call me Michael."

"How exactly are we related?"

"It's difficult to explain, but be assured, the same blood runs in our veins and we share a gift." He pulled a small wooden stool from the corner. "Please sit. Last time you watched me paint. Sculpture is my true passion. I believe I was painting a nobleman's daughter before she went into a convent, most likely for the rest of her life. Such a waste. Her only crime was to be far too bright and beautiful." Michael picked up his chisel once more and continued to remove chips by gently tapping with a narrow hammer. The stone already had the basic shape of the man on the pedestal. The model lifted his head and a smile slowly spread across his face.

"Stai fermo, Angelo! Non ti gao per sorridere alle donne," roared Michael. The model's smile faded, and he resumed his position. Alice realized that he stood so still to assume a particular position for sculpting. With his head down, he managed to raise his eyes to look at her and she saw heat in them. The cream-colored gown's bodice was so tight, her breasts spilled up and over the top. By the look on his face, Angelo was a boob man. Most of these nightly fantasies ended in some lovely man or men rogering her royally. It did look as if Angelo might easily be up for such a possibility. This night, the thought of any strange man touching her made her shudder in the gloom of this stark room with stone walls and floors. Had those North Korean thugs taken her desire for sensual fantasies, too?

Alice sat on the stool and watched Michael until she could no longer be quiet. She remembered that last time he had yelled at her for interrupting him, but she couldn't stay quiet one minute more.

"What gift are you talking about?" She couldn't imagine any connection with this talented, gruff and mysterious man. Alice stood up and took a few steps closer to him.

When he turned to her, he was not angry, but smiled. His black eyes sparkled. With chestnut brown hair and a neat, trimmed beard, this time she found him handsome in a slightly creepy way.

"How did you come here to visit me?" He laid down his tools and crossed his arms.

"Who is to say I am actually here?"

"Isn't that for you to decide? There is a reason you travel. I am guessing you are lonely."

"Not exactly." It was none of this long-lost grandpa's business what she did when she put on the clothes and opened the balcony door.

"We who share the gift, all use it to find something we cannot get by day. We who travel by night." His eyes narrowed, and he stroked his beard.

"Who's to say we're not dreaming?"

"Absolutely no one is to say such a thing. But do dreams… satisfy?" He took her hand in his strong one and led her back to the stool. "Now be quiet a while. I have little time for your questions. I must finish tonight's work before…."

"You wake up?"

Michael gave Alice a long, puzzled look and when she thought he would say more, he turned back to the stone and the chips began to fly. The low wooden stool was not comfortable, but finally tired. Alice found her eyes getting heavy and closed them.

Chapter Thirty-Two

LOVE BITES

H er reflection in her closet's full-length mirror reassured her that tonight, Brad would be impressed. The little black dress she wore was revealing. With a deeply scooped neckline and full skirt slightly below her knee, it accentuated her strong suit, boobs and downplayed her generous derriere. The weight she had lost since the incident made this dress that had formerly been skintight, look elegant.

Searching her shoes, she decided the silver Nina kitten heels would be special enough for tonight. They shimmered softly, as if made of silver inlaid with ground diamonds. The delicate shoes wrapped her with little wisps of straps that made her feet appear to be wearing only jewelry—perfect.

Brad had made a reservation at one of the finest restaurants in all of St. Louis. Tony's was a spectacular eatery. The food was, of course, excellent, the décor elegant, but it was the servers, some of whom had worked there for decades, that made it beyond compare. They always made you feel like you were special because you were there.

Alice had seen little of Brad since she'd returned to work. He had texted her little things, both sweet and funny each day. She still felt connected to him in a way she had never felt. She knew he was under the gun because this was the time of the year hospitals, their main customers, signed contracts. He had a labor dispute with their manufacturing unit to handle, and the quarterly report would be due soon. Not to mention the cost overruns on both Excellosteo and Biocardia. She didn't envy him, or did she? Now that Biocardia was back on track, the fact that she wasn't at the helm when it went into production stung a little—or maybe a lot.

The Uber driver dropped her off in front of the restaurant. Brad had asked her to meet him there and parking in Clayton was challenging. She left her car at home, figuring he would give her a ride home or to his house, perhaps. She wasn't sure she was ready for Mr. James's brand of passion, but she missed his touch. The idea did make her smile as she sat reading the menu at an excellent table in an intimate corner. Alice felt a hand on her shoulder. She turned and Brad lightly brushed her lips with his.

"Sorry to keep you waiting, baby. You know how it is," he said, pulling the chair next to her out and sitting down. He always preferred to sit next to someone rather that across.

"Yes, I do."

"You look great." Brad motioned to the waiter. He looked tired and his jaw muscles were still work-day tight. "I will have a Truly Seltzer if you have it and please bring the lady a Tanqueray martini up with three olives." Brad told the server, an elegantly slender man in black who had introduced himself as Bruce. He bore a strong resemblance to Donald Sutherland. Not young hot Sutherland from M*A*S*H or Animal House, but how he looked in Hunger Games without the wild beard and sideburns.

"Tough day?" Alice asked.

"A lot going on…family stuff. My youngest is in the hospital." He pursed his lips like he always did when he had something to say that he'd rather not or was worried. "It's Hodgkin's disease."

Alice reached over and took his hand, strong and rough in hers. "Oh, my God. Is she alright?"

"Hope so. But her mother and I…" He looked almost embarrassed at the mention of his estranged wife. Alice remembered that he had told her she was in love with a woman and left him to be with her. She didn't think any divorce had become final.

"It's okay. I know Olivia is your children's mother. I'm not threatened."

"Yeah." He took a sip of the water the elegant young man in a tuxedo delivered. "The doctor said Jessica needs both her parents for this fight." Brad's lips disappeared into a tight line and his eye searched her face. "I have done some things I'm not proud of. But I am very proud of my children and have always done everything I could to help them grow up to be good human beings."

Alice felt her cheeks go hot and could hear the blood rush in her ears. Sleeping with her while still married was undoubtedly not something to be proud of. She had ended their first fling soon after discovering his marital status. Soon, maybe not immediately, but sleeping with married men was never her style.

Bruce set down their drinks and vanished with the expertise of someone who had been privy to thousands of serious conversations. She picked up her drink and took a sip for courage. "Your daughter is going to stay with you for a while, right?"

"Yeah."

"I can see how having her mother near would be good for her," said Alice, taking a big sip and chewing an olive.

"Olivia is staying in the guest room." Again, he paused to watch for a reaction. "The woman she was seeing left her, and she wanted to try to repair our marriage, but I told her about you and…"

"I get it. It would be better for your daughter to have both her parents there for her." Alice tried to look far more supportive than she felt as she ordered roast duck. Brad ordered a filet and chatted on about work details as she smiled and nodded, pushing her food around the plate. When Bruce had taken the plates, Alice summoned the courage to ask the question to which she had to have an answer.

"Do you still have feelings for Olivia?" Alice bravely met his eyes.

He looked surprised. "Some, of course. She's the mother of my children and we have a long history, but I love you." She saw the truth of his words in his eyes.

There, he'd said it. Brad had told her before that he cared for her. He had just told her that he loved her. Why did one little word feel so scary? She did not doubt his word. But she had to know, "If I wasn't in the picture, would you and Olivia get back together?" It took all her concentration to look directly into his dangerous blue eyes, but she did not look away.

Brad kept his eyes on hers and said nothing for an incredibly long time. A pair of hands set down the leather folder holding the check in front of Brad. Was Bruce clairvoyant? Did he know she did not want to hear him say the words his silence clearly spoke?

❧

Brad took her straight home to her apartment, as she had expected. They took the elevator and walked to her door in silence.

"I can come in, maybe stay a little…"

Alice reached up and put her fingers on his lips. "No. Go home to your family and… I love you, too."

He took her in his arms and gave her one of his luscious good-by kisses. First slipping his tongue gently between her lips and them softly sucking her upper and lower lip in turn before touching his forehead to hers.

"See you tomorrow," he said.

&

"And how does that make you feel?" Dr. Cindy asked Alice who sat on the doctor's velvet couch the next evening.

"He told me he loved me and I believed him, but..."

"Isn't that a good thing?" The doctor crossed her legs without wrinkling her black linen pants. Her red pullover exactly matched her elegant red suede heels.

Alice kept looking only at Dr. Cindy and said, "I think I might love him too."

A small smile crossed the doctor's lips, and she looked up from her yellow notepad.

"I know I love him enough to consider what's good for him as well as for me."

"Does this feel significant to you?"

"Yah think?" Alice laughed. "I'm not sure I've ever felt like this. Kind of sad to reach this age before it happens. He's my friend and my lover. I respect his talents in the bedroom and at work. He is...wonderful, and he loves me."

"How do you feel about the possibility of losing him? You two have a volatile history."

"Ooooh." She was quiet for a long moment. "I'm sure I'd be devastated, but I know I could love someone else, if Brad and I don't work out." Alice beamed at the doctor with this realization.

"Let's talk again about the strange artist in your last fantasy. Doesn't it seem he seems to bear evidence as the reality of your fantasies?"

"It was weird. None of my fantasies have ever repeated. He

was the only one that appeared twice and there was no sex either time. Only a weird guy who said we were related."

"Yet he didn't tell you how."

"No. He was all about his art and didn't want to be interrupted."

"Do you think maybe Dr. Hoffman might be able to help you answer more questions about your ability to manipulate time?" Dr. Cindy had put down her pad.

"Yeah. Hoffman is weird, but maybe. Michael, that was the artist's name, seemed so different, so real."

"We are almost out of time. How are you sleeping?" Dr.Cindy asked Alice.

"Fine." Her voice cracked with the lie.

"No flashbacks or nightmares?"

"Nope." Alice looked at the clock. "I think I got my money's worth today, huh? Same time next week?"

≷●

Alice sat calmly in Susan's pink cloud chair, sipping the wine she had been handed. "What an idiot!" said Susan, yelling from her kitchen the next evening. "He let her move back in to their house after she left him for someone else?" She set a bowl full of some chicken and vegetables that smelled way better than it looked down on her rough wood dining table. Alice left the cloud and sat down at the table in front of the bowl. Taking a chance, she dug in her spoon. It was delicious as always.

"I'm trying new recipes. The brown goo that looks a little like diarrhea is peanut sauce." Susan sat down across from Alice but held her spoon, waiting for her friend's reaction.

"I love it. Looks weird, but smells and tastes delicious. Yeah, his daughter is going through some serious medical issues." Alice kept eating, not looking up.

"Didn't he tell his wife about you?"

247

"Yes."

"Nothing to worry about, then." Susan took a bite. "He chose you."

"Yeah." Alice set down her spoon. "Except, the problem is… I might love him too."

"Tell me something I don't know. I knew he loved you when I saw him holding your hand and telling you business crap when you were in a coma. I knew you loved him when asked about him first, after nearly being murdered." Susan began to dish up the rest of the food in the crock pot into freezer bowls. "I thought you swore off love a long time ago?" She gave Alice a little side eye and began to pack bowls into the freezer. "One for your collection?" she said, holding a bowl toward Alice.

"Sure." Alice took the bowl. "I never believed in love before. Not for me, anyway. But last night at dinner… He told me about his daughter and the pain in his eyes…I could feel it almost as if it were my own." Alice took her empty bowl to the sink, rinsed it and put it in the dishwasher. "I don't want to talk about it anymore. Want to go get some Ted Drewes?"

"Okay, now I know you're in love. You never eat dessert and frozen custard has about a gazillion calories, but I'm in."

Chapter Thirty-Three

WHAT'S LOVE GOT TO DO WITH IT

The well-oiled machine that was Excellcardia, kept Alice busy for the next four days and rather than the odd work-related email, she had heard nothing from Brad. She thought it might be a good thing to leave him to handle his family turmoil without her getting in the way, and it gave her some breathing room to deal with this love thing. Alice was not good at being patient, but if you love someone, it was something you had to do she'd read somewhere. Both times she had opened the closet, she found only the jeans and t-shirt that she knew would take her right back to the lovely spring day and the human monsters behind that door. She spent most nights trying to sleep between bouts of reliving the terror.

This morning in her office, Alice had closed the door after feeding the kitties and heard the little tinkle of her office door's bell. Brad stood inside the door, smiling at her. His serious black suit, white shirt and purple tie combination made her smile.

"Good morning," said Brad with his eyes full of her.

Alice walked to her desk and sat down in her new leather chair. "It is," she said.

"Have something I think you will want to see." He placed the manilla folder he had brought in with him on her desk.

She picked it up. Opening it, she found the schedule for Biocardia's human trials. "Oh, my God. I thought this would never happen." She closed her eyes and held the folder against her chest.

"Yeah, it's finally happening. This incredible project wouldn't be without you. Gonna make this company a metric crapton of money. The Excellcardia board has no idea how valuable you are."

Alice got up from her desk and walked to him, and he wrapped his arms around her. "I can come over tonight—stay the night if you'd like," he said.

She wanted to sink into the comfort of his arms and to drown in his delicious kiss, but she knew what she had to do. Alice had not returned his embrace and now took a step back, pulling away. "You can't. Your family needs you. I won't take you away from them… I can't." Alice looked down at the lovely new carpet, not into his eyes.

"What exactly do you mean?" His voice held a tone she had never heard, almost desperate.

"I mean, it is over. It has to be. I won't take you from your family. Please don't make this any harder than it already is."

"You can't mean…" Brad said, sounding definitely desperate.

Alice looked directly into his eyes. "I mean exactly what I said. Go back to your family. We are finished." She held his gaze. He took a step back.

❧

She stood staring at him for a long moment until he turned and walked out the door. Alice dropped into her chair and sat staring, her eyes focusing on nothing. She had done the right thing. At some point in the future, if they'd tried to have a life together, he would resent her for taking him away. He had a long history with Olivia and his children, one of whom needed both her parents desperately right now and would for a while. She had done the right thing for Brad and for herself.

For some reason, this morning, sitting in her office alone, Alice thought of all the things she had lost in the past few months. She put her head in her hands and began to cry hard, making tiny lakes on her shiny black desk.

How could a baby she never knew and had no business having still leave a giant canyon in her heart? She sobbed. Her best little fur buddy for sixteen years had cancer, and she had held his little black paw as he left this life. Sleeping with him curled up behind her knees as she lay on her side might have made the nightmares a little easier to take, but he had cancer and was gone. Those horrible men had taken her ability to sleep and made her afraid of her closet once her greatest source of pleasure. Tears rained hard on the wood of her desk. Head of R and D was challenging. She had dreamed up a thrilling project in Excellosteo, but she was no longer CEO.

When pregnant, the reduced hours might have seemed attractive. CEOs work too late for baseball games or ballet recitals, at least the way Alice approached the job. Alice had doubted her own capability in the past, but now she knew that was a waste of effort. She was a CEO. Last, and perhaps worst of all, she had let a man who loved her go. The love she felt for him felt strong enough to do what was best for him. She could continue to cry until the finish peeled from her nice new desk, go home and go to bed, or act on the one thing still under her control.

Alice sat up and rummaged in her desk drawer for a tissue. Wiping her eyes, she opened her laptop and began to compose emails.

§.

Three hours later, she stood once again in Louise O'Neil's office. Louise wore a perfect white linen dress without a single wrinkle after hours of work. She felt certain Louise would have somehow managed to look elegant after recently being attacked by a pack of hyenas. Louise was a chic savant. Alice carefully explained her plan to Louise. Her head engineer began to take notes, nodding and asking questions when she needed. After nearly an hour, Louise summoned Mildred. Her assistant drifted into the room like an apparition in a pale gray striped dress, looking only at the floor.

"Mildred, we need you to help us stage a coup," said Louise.

The woman looked up. Her eyes went from Louise to Alice and back again, and she smiled. It was weak and fleeting, as if out of practice, but definitely a smile. Alice quickly explained what she needed. E-vites sent to board members, the conference room reserved, pastries and coffee ordered, all the things an administrative assistant would do. Her plan had to remain top secret and that wouldn't happen if Alice took these actions herself.

Ami Wen sat in a white leather chair in Alice's office holding her laptop at 8:00 p.m. that same night. "I've got the video nearly done. Ain't no dusty old Power Point neither. The micrographs of the osteoblasts growing on the matrix are absolute zero cool. Rosie is ready to show off her new knee. Who wouldn't be melted by those big ole golden retriever eyes? Even Pookie likes Rosie. The schedule for the human trials for Biocardia and Rosie will knock the granny panties and plaid boxers of off those crusty old boomers on the board."

"I hope we can keep this under wraps." Alice said as she paced. Good thing the dark hardwood of her office floor was impervious to ruts, though she had been careful not to pace on the beautiful Persian carpet.

"Pookie hasn't told a soul, Rosie ain't talkin' and you know

I can keep a secret. Everything you need for the presentation will be in your inbox by 8:00 a.m."

"Seven, please. I will need to check it over and print out hard copies. I doubt the board members will bring their laptops. I can connect the projection screen to my laptop, but I know them. They like to have papers in their hands." Alice stopped and walked over to Ami. "I am taking one hell of a risk."

"Yeah, but you were born for this." Amy beamed.

❧

The next morning, Alice held Rosie's leash and paced in the hall with the twelve-year-old golden retriever following behind wagging her tail, frisky as a puppy. Louise warmed up the board in the main conference room. By some miracle, this meeting seemed to have remained confidential. She wore her most spectacular work attire, her scarlet suit. The little peplum jacket and form-fitting skirt emphasized rather than disguised her feminine figure. She had chosen sensible black pumps with four-inch heels and only the teeniest rhinestone bows at the back. This board of directors needed to accept that the best CEO this company could possibly have was a woman.

Alice walked back out thirty minutes later with Rosie wagging her tail and trotting behind. She had presented both of the projects she was principally responsible for, reminded them of that fact and of their respective future profits, offered solutions to the current labor issues and suggested several cost-cutting measures to reduce the problem budget overruns. Brad had done a decent job for the past months with very little experience, but he was no Alice Hightower. She would never criticize Brad to the board. If the board had been dead set on replacing her after the theft of Biocardia by Dr. Petrus, he had been an expedient choice. Brad had been an adequate CEO, but he was a brilliant Vice President of Sales and the Board should recognize that fact, with a little nudge.

Now she had to wait. The board's president, Fred Hagan, emailed saying they would discuss the matter thoroughly and give her an answer within forty-eight hours. Alice closed her eyes as she sat at her desk and tried not to think of how Brad would react. She hadn't heard from him since she told him they were over three days ago. Undoubtedly, he was spending time with his daughter. She also doubted his ego would agree replacing him was the best thing for everyone. He would most likely resign and head up another company. It was a fact of business life that a male CEO might have a less difficult time finding a new position. His reputation had not been destroyed by Dr. Petrus's espionage. Brad had to know deep down, the best thing for his family would be for him to leave Excellcardia. Alice knew in her heart of hearts, staying away from him would be impossible. She would not tear apart his family after sacrificing so much to put it back together.

Chapter Thirty-Four

IT'S RAINING MEN

An exhausted Alice sat with her eyes closed on her white couch, clutching her purse that evening. It was Friday and she would not think of how she had spent so many other Friday nights with Brad. She had done the right thing, but once more her heart hurt. This time, she hadn't lost the man she loved; it had been her choice to give him up and a small part of her was proud. The rest of her ached with the thought of never seeing him again. Alice knew the company would be better off with her at the helm. The further away he was, the better for everyone. If the board turned her down, she would call Humpty Dumpty the headhunter and pray he could put her career back together again.

A tiny meow made her open her eyes and set down her purse. The little black ball of fluff looked up at her with round, emerald eyes.

"Hello. I have to figure out a name for you." The little black kitten that Ami had delivered to her office yesterday morning sat down and seemed to be waiting for something. Alice knew her food bowl was full.

The kitten meowed loudly, and after two bold attempts on stubby kitten legs, jumped onto her lap. Alice picked her up and felt her whole little body shaking in tiny popping purrs. "Oh, Ami was right about you. You are a sweetie." She held the kitten against her and kissed her fuzzy head. She had loved Otis's sleek, short fur, but the fact that this one had long fur to shed all over her immaculate apartment felt fine. She would never replace Otis. Right now, her recent wounds, both physical and emotional, felt a little less deep with this kitty in her lap.

Her phone made the little text beep and Alice tore herself from the bliss of kitten mommydom to have a look.

Hey, single gal. Let's paint ourselves up and go observe the male animal in the wild. Don't say no. I am about to knock on your door.

Setting the kitten on the floor and reminding her not to jump up—kitties had to learn—she opened the door to let Susan in before she knocked. A little furry black bullet of a kitten shot into the kitchen.

"Well, that one isn't very friendly," said Susan.

"She's only been here two days, and she is pretty little. Give her a break."

"Her? It's a girl." Susan walked in and shut the door behind her.

"I need a name. Remember when we used to do the duet of Unforgettable at Dr. Redbirds after two or five beers?"

"Yeah, you were a terrible Natalie, and I was a worse Nat King Cole."

"My favorite was 'I Will Always Love You,' by Dolly Pardon. Never did Dolly justice." Alice smiled down at the kitten. "Guys would buy us more beers to stop singing." She laughed at the college memory. "I think she looks like a Dolly after all. If I promise not to sing ever again, will you leave me alone tonight? I'm exhausted."

"Hells no." Susan twirled, displaying the slinky silver dress, short enough to show off her legs and still decently cover her panties. "I am dressed to kill and want to take you out for a night of fun and beverages."

"Where did you get those shoes?" Alice leaned over to get a closer look.

"Nieman Marcus, Frontenac." Susan beamed.

"No. You. Did. Not. You never spend that kind of money. Hello gorgeous," said Alice to the shoes. They were a metallic leather of rose gold four-inch platforms with a delicate chain encircling Susan's ankles.

"Yep. I thought I'd try and see what got you off so much about shoes."

"And?"

"They're not only children. Wait until you see the others I bought to keep them company." Susan giggled.

It felt so good to hear Susan laugh like the care-free college girls they had once been. Susan was right. She did need to go have some fun. "Let me change."

"What! That suit is to die for. Lose that high-necked blouse and unbutton some of those buttons."

Alice did as she was told.

"Yep. Perfect," said Susan, walking around to appraise her friend from all angles.

"Shows a lot of boobs." Alice buttoned up one more button.

"We aren't going to take them home. We will sip expensive drinks and watch them swarm around. We are professional women of quality."

"With killer legs and a decent quantity of cleavage." Alice laughed, and it felt wonderful.

As Alice and Susan stood laughing and waiting for their Uber in front of their building, Susan said, "Uh oh. You can cut this air with a knife."

"Hell, you can roll it up in a ball and pitch it across Busch Stadium. It's St. Louis in July. What do you expect?"

"My hair." Susan's normally soft brown waves had definitely increased in volume and now resembled a brown shrub. Alice giggled.

"Oh shut up. That smooth blonde crap on your head only gets smoother in this humidity," said Susan, running her fingers through her hair in a vain attempt to tame it.

"Foxy Brown Anderson. Afros are back, I heard. Seriously, it looks cute," said Alice with all the sincerity she could muster, and then she burst out laughing.

"Right. I am what I am." Susan laughed too.

"Gorgeous is what you are, big hair and all."

§

"Okay, here are tonight's rules," said Susan as they sat in the back of the Uber. "One, they can look, but no touching. Two, you can take their numbers, but do not give out yours. We are only window shopping tonight. Three, and most importantly, we come home together."

"Right," said Alice, surprised at the thrill she felt in this little game. "When did you get to be such an expert on single girl fun?"

"When I quit feeling sorry for myself. You should try it. I have had six terrible internet dates and am ready to relax and work up an appetite."

"Right." This time Alice laughed at the truth of Susan's words. None of these men were Brad or could ever compare. But a girl couldn't sit home forever and now the closet only brought her terror she needed to forget.

The Uber pulled in front of The Capital Grille in Clayton. "What? Not Bar Napoli?" said Alice. "I thought you said that's where the scene was now."

"We want quality, not quantity. Men come here with a colleague after work to share a drink. My assistant Julie told me. It's not a meat market. We are not meat. There will probably be suits." Susan leaned over and lifted her eyebrows.

"Oh my," said Alice.

There were exactly two seats open at the long granite bar. They took them. The number of pretty suits in the room made Alice shiver. They shone in greys, blacks and various shades of blue, like a rainbow of delicious, well-dressed masculinity. Around the bar, high round tables were filled with people laughing and drinking. Susan's assistant had been right; the majority of the drinkers were men.

"Whatcha drinking, ladies," said the pretty bartender. She had dark curly hair tied back loosely and her jet-black eyes sparkled. She gave them a dazzling smile that might have gone a long way to get larger tips out of lonely men, but was shared evenly with all her customers. Her name tag read Kacy.

"We are some thirsty bitches," said Susan.

"I'll have a Tanqueray martini up with three olives and my friend with the gorgeous legs will have a Hendricks and tonic, no fruit," said Alice.

"I'll get those," said a man's voice from behind them. When Alice turned to look at the man trying to pay for their drinks, she nearly fell off her bar stool. He was beautiful. His Italian suit, in a shade of soft gray with a faint windowpane pattern, impressed her. She longed to reach over and to touch it, but remembering the rules, she laughed.

"Now that's a lovely sound." The man stood a head taller than the other men standing around the bar. Alice swallowed. His head of shining silver hair was full and swept back, curling around his ears. The eyes that looked into hers were dark and unfathomable. Alice thought she detected an accent.

"I am Antony, and you are?"

"Alice."

"Susan," the ladies said simultaneously. Alice was now certain she heard an Italian accent. Antony told them he was a sales representative for a suit manufacturer in Rome. Alice's mouth fell open and Susan turned and struck up a conversation with a pleasant faced blond man to her left.

Two drinks, three hours and several interesting conversations later, Alice and Susan climbed into an Uber. "Whew. That was quite an evening," said Susan. "How many did you get?" Alice held up three business cards.

"Ha! I win. Five. You wasted too much time with that Italian guy."

"This isn't speed dating and I am happy for you. He works for the premiere suit maker in Italy. Promised to take me to their show room. And he was…"

"Whatever. He was pretty hot. But…"

"Beat this." Alice held up a pale blue card so Susan could read it.

"Shoe buyer at Nordstrom's. You win by a mile." Susan laughed.

❧

As Alice settled into her bed for the night, she heard the sound of tiny claws climbing up her sheets. Dolly wiggled in, and settled down under Alice's chin. The last thing Alice heard was the sound of purring as she fell into a deep sleep.

Chapter Thirty-Five

I WILL ALWAYS LOVE YOU

The next morning, as Alice cooked her breakfast and laughed at the memories of last night, she heard her phone tell her she had a text. Thinking it was Susan with some lunch plans, she was surprised to see a text from Sean. I need to see you. Urgent Eleven thirty, and an address in Kirkwood. That didn't take long. His big Chicago Real estate business must have gone bust. It was always some other person's fault. Usually the real fault was of a white powder he could never seem to resist for long. Alice had fallen asleep so happy and now this morning the old familiar cold grip of dread held her tight.

As she pulled on her jeans and a t-shirt, she ran over in her head how many times she had tried to rescue her brother. She had paid for him to go to rehab after an arrest, a car accident, and even picked him up once in the middle of a bloody fight. She had hoped this last time would help him. She knew that addiction was an illness, but a part of her had trouble accepting his relapses as anything but an attempt to get money and attention from her. She would do her best to be a good sister and help as best she could, one more time.

Parking in Kirkwood was never easy, and it took her fifteen

minutes in the rain to find a single spot two blocks from the address Sean had sent. The address Sean texted turned out to be a bar and sandwich shop. Not the kind of dark, creepy joint she had found him in, in the past. As soon as she opened the door, Sean got up from a seat at the counter and rushed to her.

"Glad you came. Wouldn't have blamed you if you didn't, but this time is different."

Isn't that what he always said? To Alice's surprise, Sean looked good. He was dressed in a nice pair of black jeans and a light blue sweater. His haircut looked fresh and his gray eyes clear. The look on his face was of concern, not desperation. She decided to say nothing and let him talk.

"I know you have gotten me out of some tight spots, but this is…" said Sean. He pointed to a stool at the counter. There sat a little girl. She looked about seven or eight and sat swinging her legs and scowling. Alice had seen that scowl ten thousand times as a child. The little girl's pale gray eyes glared, and she stuck out her lower lip as Sean always had when he hadn't gotten his way as a child.

"Her name is Amanda and evidently, she is my kid. Emilie, my girlfriend for about a minute, has a paternity test, and a court order and everything."

Alice looked at the child. She had hair the color of Sean's and her eyes were unmistakably the same as his. The girl's scowl grew darker under Alice's scrutiny and she crossed her arms.

"I am not any happier about this than you are, Daddy," said the little girl.

"Oh, lord, the Hightower rapier wit." Alice chuckled. "Nice to meet you, Amanda. I am your Aunt Alice," said Alice, bending over to look Amanda straight in the eyes. The sprinkling of freckles across her nose and stylish round horned rimmed glasses made her scowl a little less effective. Alice took a seat next to Amanda.

"My mom tells me yesterday that my father didn't die in

Afghanistan and that this guy is him. I am pretty sure he sucks or I would have met him before."

"That sort of surprise could suck, but I have known him all his life, and he only sucks a little."

"A little help here, Alice," said Sean. "I don't know a thing about little girls and could really use your advice."

"What do I know about kids?" Alice examined Amanda. She was pretty cute in her little blue checked dress, white tights and blue shoes with ribbon bows on the toes. The girl seemed whip-smart too. At least she didn't seem fooled by Sean.

"You used to be a little girl, I recall." Sean stood next to Alice as if he was trying to get as far away from the little girl as he could.

Amanda looked at the floor and her previous anger seemed replaced by sadness.

"Well, you may not be happy to have a new daddy, but I am very happy to have a brand-new niece."

"Those are cool shoes," said Amanda without looking up.

Alice had worn her favorite pair of cheetah print sandals Susan had brought her from Venice a couple of years ago. "You like shoes, Amanda?"

Amanda's scowl turned into a smile that lit up her entire face.

Alice and Sean took Amanda to lunch at the Dewey's Pizza across the street and then over to visit fuzzy little Dolly and Alice's shoe closet of joy. After trying on twenty pairs that didn't come close to fitting yet, Amanda admitted that at least her new auntie didn't suck. Alice helped Sean shop for a few things Amanda would need for her weekend visits and dropped them off at the airport to fly back to Chicago.

Sean would have custody every other weekend and Alice agreed to do all she could to help out. Chicago was a fun city and only a short flight away. Sean promised to come to St. Louis on weekends when Alice couldn't come to Chicago so it was all set. As Alice watched Sean and Amanda walk into the airport, she saw Amanda reach up to take her father's hand and she knew that having a niece would not suck at all.

***

Only eighty-seven emails in her inbox this morning. Alice sat faithfully answering them all when she heard the bell on her office door tinkle. There stood Brad in front of her desk, smiling and wearing shorts and a striped golf shirt.

"Is it casual Monday up on the top floor?" He looked so relaxed and handsome it hurt.

"I am dressed for the Arizona sunshine. That's where I'm heading. Handed in my resignation an hour ago."

"The board…"

"I knew immediately after the board meeting. Can't be a good leader without intel." He laughed the little laugh of his. The one that always made her want to hug him tight. She knew that would not be a good idea and stayed in her chair.

"The board hasn't made its decision yet," she said, closing her laptop.

"Yes, they have. I made it easy for them when I resigned."

Her blood rushed in her ears and a fist hit her in the middle of her chest. Two sets of emotions ripped through her simultaneously. She would be CEO of Excellcardia once more, but she would never see Brad again. How could he presume… and then she knew. Brad understood as well as she did what was best for everyone.

"Medco-Blanchard in Phoenix?" said Alice. The part of her that was happy for him smiled broadly.

"Yep. Their CEO and founder is finally retiring, and they thought I would be an excellent replacement."

"They are so right." She knew there was only one company in the country for which Brad James would not be the very best choice of CEO.

"You know I…"

"Yeah, I know. Me too." After standing there giving her his proud-of-her look for far too long, Brad turned and walked out the door. And Brad had done the right thing for her. He never would have gone back to being Vice President of Sales. Along with some pain, Alice felt pride. She had done the right thing and let Brad go. Maybe she wasn't the best CEO for any other company; she was far from perfect. But BioCardia and Excellosteo would make this company an industry leader in the near future and that was all because of her. Let the board take its time informing her. Now it was a forgone conclusion.

She would always care deeply for Brad—hell she loved him and probably always would. The company in Arizona was ten times the size of Excellcardia and probably came with a salary to match. Excellcardia was her company and she would soon be back at the helm.

❦

Alice sat on Dr. Cindy's couch that evening, anxious about the doctor's long silence in response to her confession. She had told the doctor that she wasn't getting over the trauma of that terrible afternoon. That the dreams and the sudden flashbacks were making her nights and even parts of her days…hell.

Finally Dr. Cindy looked up from her yellow legal pad and spoke softly. "I can't help you if you do not tell me the truth. I fire patients for this." Doctor Cindy merely looked at Alice with a look in her eyes that was cold as ice. Alice had not realized what a betrayal it was to lie to one's therapist. She didn't really think it was lying. She thought she would eventually get over the incident as time passed and she would stop reliving that day.

"I am sorry. I thought I could handle it on my own. I didn't want to relive it. I thought the dreams and the flashbacks would eventually go away."

"And have they?" Alice thought she heard anger in Cynthia Lester's voice.

"No." Alice's heart beat wildly. How could she lose one more thing? Dr. Cindy had been her rock and helped her understand and accept so much about herself. The silence in the blue room was so loud, the sound of her blood rushing in her ears nearly deafened her. Alice could hear herself swallow.

"There is a treatment called EMDR. Eye movement desensitizing and reprocessing. It works well to help with the obsessive thoughts of PTSD. Sort of helps them get unstuck." Dr. Lester's voice still held no emotion, nothing like the warmth and compassion Alice had always heard before.

Now you have done it, Alice, you idiot. She had gone and betrayed the one person who could help her keep everything together. She would lose the only person between her and her grip on reality. Alice's terror must have shown on her face.

"What are you so afraid of?"

Alice caught her breath, and the words came out without any thought. "That I will disintegrate. Fly into a million crazy little pieces that can never be put back together." There she had said it out loud.

"You will have to agree to be completely honest with me. The EMDR is intense and will require you to relive and discuss your attack. Can you do that?"

"Sure." A wave of relief passed over Alice. She would try anything Dr. Cindy recommended. She needed her life back and if this process could help, she had to do it.

"I do think we need to talk about your breakup with Brad."

"Okay." Alice felt more accepting of this decision each day. "I did what was best for him and his family and I'm okay with it."

"Do you think maybe you are okay with it because it is the best thing for you, too?"

Alice felt as if Dr. Cindy had hit her in the face with these words. The words stung more because they were true. Brad would never have stepped aside. She would never have gotten to be Excellcardia's CEO as long as he stayed. "Yeah, that's part of it. Makes me a little less proud, though."

"It is perfectly alright to do things for others that work out well for you. It is not so much selfishness as it is self-preservation, a good and healthy thing." Dr. Cindy put down her pad as if to emphasize what she had to say. "Loving yourself is vital to loving anyone else."

❧

The teeny black fur ball on her lap couldn't help but make her feel better as she sat on her couch in her apartment after her session with Dr. Cindy. She had nearly lost another therapist and had to admit, she was not the Mother Theresa of love affairs she thought she was when she ended things with Brad.

A knock on the door ended her kitty worship and self-pity. Looking at the screen of the door camera she had had installed after the attack, Alice saw the most beautiful man with eyes the color of chocolate smiling at her. Jonathan, who, when he learned the baby she had carried was not his, had disappeared like a puff of smoke.

She opened the door wide. She needed to hear what he had to say.

"Alice," said Jonathan with his arms spread wide and a puppy dog look on his handsome face.

"Mr. Salter," she replied, stepping back.

"I am certain I deserve that." He took a step toward her. Dolly, who had been sitting at her feet, hissed at him.

"She is little but protective." Alice bent over to pick up the kitten and hold her tight against her chest.

"I am not sure what to say, except I am sorry. I got scared. The thought of raising James's child was more than I could bear."

"But it was my child." She looked at him for a long moment and drew in a deep breath. "I had a miscarriage, by the way." She had backed toward the kitchen and sat down at the tall stool around her black granite table.

"I am so sorry for your loss." He sat on the couch, looking up at her. "Been giving some concerts in New York and Paris like you always thought I should. Even tried dating, but no use, I thought of you constantly. I miss you. I still love you."

"You left me when I needed you most. That's not love."

"Can't you give me another chance? I cancelled my concerts for the next six months so… You have to admit we were good together."

Alice looked at the beautiful man in his black suit and snow-white shirt and gleaming white silk tie. She saw his thick dark hair moussed perfectly in place, his lovely dark eyes imploring her. Alice could remember what it felt like for those talented hands to touch her, to please her. She felt a bit of nostalgia and nothing more.

"We were good together…once," she said. "I can't spend my life wondering and waiting for you to disappear."

"I see. Is it James? I assumed you and he would be together." His faced looked tight and hard.

Alice laughed. "We were, for a while. It turned out it was better for him…for both of us to be apart." She put the kitten down near her food bowl, walked to the door, and opened it. "I wish you the best, Jonathan. Your talent will take you far."

"Is there nothing I can say to get you to forgive me?" he said, now standing.

Alice knew she loved herself too much to be with someone she couldn't trust to love her, no matter what hardships came along. "Good luck, Jonathan. I wish you well." He walked out the door without another word.

Chapter Thirty-Six

THE TRUTH ABOUT LOVE

This had felt like a wonderful day, thought Alice as she rode the elevator to her apartment. All seven of her department meetings had gone well, and every single member of her team seemed happy to have her back in charge. She had spent her lunch hour with Dr. Cindy today and every day for the past two weeks. It wasn't easy reliving that horrible day over and over, but last night she had fallen asleep without one scene of those monsters hurting her. And not once today had any visions of terror randomly flashed in front of her eyes. She knew she wasn't cured, but she felt so much more whole, more Alice once again and not a prisoner of those memories. She was proud of herself for doing the hard work to get over the trauma.

Alice looked forward to flying to Chicago tomorrow morning. Having Sean and Amanda in her life had made her happier than she would ever have imagined. The little girl seemed smart and funny, and watching her brother struggle was beyond fun. Not to mention how much fun it was to be an auntie to such a child. She hoped Amanda would love the first addition of Alice's Adventures in Wonderland she'd bought for her as much as she had at her age.

Unlocking her door, she looked down at the little black flash running toward her. "How's my baby cat?" She bent down to pick up the purring kitten and held her close. "The best love of all, Dolly, is the love you give. Remember that."

After thirty minutes on her elliptical, and a quick change of shoes, Alice felt ready to meet Antony at Herbie's for a drink. She determined to have one drink, a couple of laughs and some lash batting, perhaps see if he was more than a pretty suit manufacturer's rep in a pretty suit.

A shiver went through her as she walked past the guest room. Could she just take a little peek inside that closet? It had been so long. Would the clothes still appear? Sliding the door open a couple of inches, she saw three hangers and a pair of shoes on the floor. The jeans and t-shirt she had found there so many nights were gone, replaced by deep blue brocade, black wool and silk. The shoes on the floor would have been adorable in any age. Alice closed the door and sat on the bed.

It would be nice to have a drink with a real man, but she wondered how long she should carry on the chit chat before telling him she had an early morning flight. After all, tonight she had another date. Inside her guest room closet were clothes that were Alice's ticket to

WONDERLAND.

❦

**Don't miss out on your next favorite book!
Join the Melange Books mailing list at**
www.melange-books.com/mail.html

THANK YOU FOR READING

❧

Did you enjoy this book?

We invite you to leave a review at your favorite book site, such as Goodreads, Amazon, Barnes & Noble, etc.

DID YOU KNOW THAT LEAVING A REVIEW…

- Helps other readers find books they may enjoy.
- Gives you a chance to let your voice be heard.
- Gives authors recognition for their hard work.
- Doesn't have to be long. A sentence or two about why you liked the book will do.

ABOUT THE AUTHOR

As a little girl, Melissa Rea would fall asleep whispering stories to herself in the dark. She got in to trouble in elementary school for embellishing when the truth just seemed too mundane. She grew up and the stories became just daydreams and she pursued a sensible career. Melissa filled her spare time with the wondrous worlds of Bram Stoker, Mary Shelly, Robert Heinlein, Philippa Gregory, Stephen King, Dean Coontz, Jackie Collins, Jennifer Weiner, Sarah Dunant and any and all authors who caught her fancy. And still, the stories in her head were there, now influenced by the delicious words of others. One day, the stories could no longer be contained, and she began to write novels. *Conjuring Casanova* was published in 2016 and was a Recommended Idie Book by Kirkus Review. It won first place in the Beverly Hills International Book Awards for Romantic Comedy, a first place in ReadersViews Reviewers Choice Awards for Romance and was a finalist in Forward Reviews Book of the Year in the Romance category. She lives in St. Louis where she has a solo dental practice and lives with her husband and rescue cats.

f facebook.com/melissareaauthor

ALSO BY MELISSA REA

Nights of Alice Series

Rabbithole

Pool of Tears

૪ે.

Novels with Melange Books

Maestro